ONE

❀

SUMMER

❀

IN

❀

BETWEEN

Books by Melissa Mather

ONE SUMMER IN BETWEEN

ROUGH ROAD HOME

ONE

SUMMER

❦

IN

❦

BETWEEN

❦

by Melissa Mather

HARPER & ROW, PUBLISHERS

NEW YORK, EVANSTON, AND LONDON

LIBRARY OF CONGRESS CATALOG CARD NUMBER: 66–20751

K-R

TO MY SISTER

Mary

ONE

❀

SUMMER

❀

IN

❀

BETWEEN

I

❀

East Barnstead, Vermont
June 7th

I am feeling a million miles from home.

I am not, of course, homesick. It's simply that this is a very peculiar part of the country and I haven't had time to get used to it yet.

I am wearing my coat as I write this, and I have my blanket tucked around my legs. Wait until Aunt Lydia hears they had a frost day before yesterday—"touch of frost" was what they called it—and they would have lost their tomato plants if they hadn't covered them up! I asked the children if they didn't think it is cold for the month of June, and they said, "Cold? It's not cold! Look— it's seventy-four in the sun!" This was at three o'clock in the after- noon, the hottest time of day. And then the sun took its own sweet time about setting; it hung around in the sky until long after supper, but just the same, I had to go and get my coat.

I suppose my blood will thicken up. I imagine it takes two or three months, though, and by that time I'll be heading home.

At the moment I am sitting on my bed, or rather my cot, and I have some cushions at my back so that I can use my bed as a sofa, because there is no chair. My bed is against the inside wall of a small room that is going to be the library, I am told. This wall, the one I am leaning against, has some kind of wallboard nailed to the other side, and I daresay I am not likely to fall through. The wall to the hall also has wallboard, but there is no door which can be closed, only a folding screen hiding the doorway. The other two walls, the outside walls, are shiny silver where the insulation shows, and the effect of this is strangely charming.

Unfortunately the windows haven't any shades or any curtains, and they stare at me with blank black eyes. There's nothing out there, just fields which belong to the Daleys, and beyond the woods there are hills on which nobody lives. Mrs. Daley explained that no one here uses window shades because there's nobody to look in. "Don't worry," she said, "there's nobody out there," and I think she meant this to be reassuring.

However, I'm not sure how much actual privacy I'll have. I haven't any reason to think the children would poke around in my things, but I do seem to fascinate them—they gaze at me wide-eyed when they think I'm not looking—and they might be tempted. Perhaps I ought to take Mr. Carr up on his offer to file our notes for us.

He tucked this suggestion into his farewell speech to the class, sandwiched between all sorts of zestful advice: "You students who expect to get extra credit next fall for this summer's research, be sure you tackle the project with an open mind. Whatever your experiences, traumatic or trivial, enter them into your journal frankly and without self-censorship. Enjoy your summer, enjoy your adventures," etc., etc. He declared he envied us, and wished he were coming with us. This by way of peroration, after he had urged us to keep in touch, not to hesitate to ask for advice, and to feel free to mail him our notes if at any time we should have reason to fear they might "fall into the hands of our employer, or other social contacts, if any." I remember I found this suggestion bleakly depressing. I sat there idly sketching Mr. Carr's profile and wondering what a summer entirely without "social contacts" would be like, and if I would feel unusually dislocated, several hundred miles north of my native habitat. Alone, not in a comfortable flock, but flying solo, like one of those nearly extinct birds no one is supposed to shoot at.

Because, of course, we all would have to scatter. It wouldn't do to invade the North en masse. Singly, we would be so much better exposed, so much more vulnerable to accurate impressions. And then Mr. Hobart Gamaliel Carr can pool these impressions in the hope that at the very least he will in due time come up with a Ph.D., if not with a definitive statement about the North.

I can't think of anything more inhibiting than the idea that my instructor in sociology is peering over my shoulder as I write "frankly and without self-censorship" about my daily life. That settles it. I'll not mail these notes away to anybody in Jacob's Ladder Teachers College, South Carolina. I'll keep them right here, safe at hand, deep in darkest Vermont. Later on, I can do some prudent editing.

I confess I do not like all that land stretching as far as I can see (during the daylight) and not a house in sight, and now there is just all that emptiness out there, no lights anywhere, just blackness humped beneath the sky. These white people moved out here to get away from people, and they seem to think it is a great blessing, no neighbors. Naturally they wouldn't understand how I feel, even if I troubled to tell them. But I wish there were people out there, even white people would be better than nobody.

However, I have a lamp, and a radio, which is Maureen's, the eleven-year-old. She lent it to me after supper, saying maybe I wouldn't be so lonesome all by myself if I had a radio to play me some music. It took me a few moments to realize she didn't mean I was all by myself here in Vermont, she meant I was all by myself in this room. I am the only one on this farm who has a room to myself (himself? grammar?).

At least I am not alone in the house. No sooner had I arrived this morning than the two girls, Maureen and her sister Mary, who is about five, I think, moved into the room overhead, which is finished and already had the beds set up. I understand the bigger boys, who are between the girls in age, will be moving into their room in a few days, but the little boys, Timmy, three, and the baby, will stay in the old house until this house is more nearly finished. Of course Mr. and Mrs. Daley are in the old house, too.

Everybody was waiting very impatiently for me to get here so that some of the children could move out of the old house "before it smashed on our heads," as Maureen put it. They seem to consider themselves very crowded down there. But everybody can't move yet, because only the upstairs here is finished. The upstairs has a toilet room complete with door, so *that's* taken care of, but the downstairs bath (the parents' room will be downstairs) still has no walls. The hall and living room and dining room and bath are all open to each other, it's like looking through an old corn patch, all those wooden supports showing.

So for baths we all have to go to the old house. And for meals, too—there's no kitchen up here yet.

Mr. Carr said to get ourselves jobs with typical families, but I really couldn't say if this is a typical family for this region or not. The six children seems to be a trifle above average in number, but not much. Mrs. Daley is somewhere between thirty-five and forty, neither thin nor fat, and not very well groomed. She was wearing blue jeans and a sweater when she met me this morning, and she wore the same outfit right through dinner and the evening. Judging by the paintings which are hanging from nails in those wooden uprights where the living room will be, I presume she is a frustrated artist, which doesn't make her much different from most housewives her age. If it isn't art, it's writing, or acting, or even singing, that they "gave up when they married." It gives me a laugh to read what a great sacrifice educated white women make when they marry—now somebody is going to support them all their lives, isn't it a shame?

Mr. Daley is a farmer who has to "work out" (as the phrase is up here) in order to support his farm and his family. He farms early in the morning, in the evening, and on weekends. The rest of the time he works out, that is, he leaves his farm and drives to another, second, full-time job or business. Farmers who do make a living from farming alone look down on farmers who also work out: information courtesy of Maureen, who helped me do the supper dishes and then trailed me to my room, where she spent the evening sitting cross-legged on my rug (which I think is actually a bathmat) and talking. I believe she talks when she inhales as well as when she exhales.

"We could live on what Daddy makes on this farm," she said, "but that wouldn't leave anything extra for books—my parents are always buying books, it's some kind of an addiction, Daddy says. My God, he says, why do we have to buy a book in order to read it? Aren't there libraries any more? I see you brought some of your own," she observed approvingly as I emptied my suitcase of the ten paperbacks I hope to absorb this summer, thus getting the jump on next term's required reading. "Though I must say that's rather like ice to Alaska," she rattled on without a pause. "And then there's college for us children, and all that, so Daddy restores old houses for summer people. You can make lots and lots of money this way. I don't mean by *cheating*," she said, although I hadn't suggested any such thing. "I mean summer people do not pinch pennies. Maybe they don't have to, or maybe they don't know how. Anyway, they will pay a man cabinetmaker's wages to make a warped window to match all the other warped windows. It's ridiculous, really."

I inquired who or what are summer people.

"They're people who don't really live here. They don't come until practically June and they leave before the weather gets cold. They can't take it. And they can't make a living here, either. They have to go where there's more money floating around loose."

"Where's that?" I said.

"Anywhere else in the U.S."

"What gave you that idea?" I said.

"My father says so. He says there's *less* money floating around loose in Vermont than anywhere in the United States."

I said that did not surprise me, because no doubt it was frozen solid. How cold does it get in winter? I asked, and she said, worse than Alaska. She said they close the schools when it gets thirty below, and I said, "Do you mean thirty below *zero?*"

She said, yes, of course, what did I think? And she said, "But that's happened only twice since I started going to school. One of those times it was actually forty-eight below, and the *New York Times* had a news story that it was forty-five below in Anchorage, Alaska, which they called 'the coldest spot in the United States,' and they never mentioned Taftsville, Vermont, where it was officially forty-eight below. And my mother," she said, "was real disgusted, and said that just went to show that the *New York Times* had a *provincial* outlook."

She brought out this statement with a certain éclat, but I couldn't think of any pertinent comment, and went on unpacking. So she went on talking. "My mother says you, Harriet Brown, are an intellectual aristocrat."

"A what?" I said.

"An intellectual aristocrat," she repeated. "You know what an aristocrat is, don't you? It's a person who gives everything he's got for whatever is important to him. Aren't you earning money for college? Mother says you are. She says that's why you're working this summer, so you'll have money for college, and that proves you're an intellectual aristocrat. Now my *father* is an architectural aristocrat, she says, because he gives his whole *life* to propping up old houses, and he says *she* is an agricultural aristocrat, and I guess she is, anyway, she's the one who is crazy about the farm. She doesn't do the dirty work, understand, she just enjoys the unfenced feeling—"

"And what kind of an aristocrat are you, Maureen?" I asked.

She recognized this tactic for what it was, and shrugged. "I dunno," she said. After a moment, unabashed, she went on. "My sister Mary is an amorous aristocrat—she loves birds, crickets, snakes, everything—I've even seen her sobbing over a mouse in a trap. Is it all right if I gossip about my sister? I mean, you don't think gossip is a sin, or anything, do you? I'm interested in people. They *fascinate* me."

She propped her chin on her hand and stared at me.

"I'll be here tomorrow," I said, and she gave me a saucy smile, said good night, and left me alone.

I can't keep my eyes open. So here endeth my first day's report.

June 8th

I had better tell about my trip North before it's blotted out by the sheer energetic frenzy of my life here.

To begin with, I wasn't sure how this job would work out. It seemed to me there was something just a little too kindly-kindly about the arrangements we were making. I'd have a room to myself, Mrs. Daley wrote, and I wouldn't have to work too hard, and she'd see I got to church. Lord, I wondered if I was going to find a Southern *laydee* living in Vermont, expecting me to drip molasses when I talk and wipe my hands on my apron as a sign I "know my place."

Of course, I could put up with that attitude—God knows I've managed to put up with it before, it's a kind of occupational hazard—but would it be helpful for my research? If the Northern attitude toward the Negro is, after all, the same as the Southern attitude toward the Negro, where would this get me? Well, then I decided this would get me to a conclusion, anyway, a very interesting conclusion. And in any case I'd have my report, and with luck it would be a valuable contribution to the pool of information Mr. Carr was after.

So I accepted her terms of twenty-five dollars a week, room, board, and bus fare, and when a letter came with a long streamer of bus tickets attached to each other, Abbot's Level to Washington, Washington to New York, New York to Springfield, Mass., etc., at first I thought, now doesn't she trust me? If she sent the money, did she think I'd just keep it and never turn up? And then I saw there was a five-dollar bill in the letter, so I proceeded to read the letter—intelligent of me!—and she said the travel agent wasn't sure when the bus left Abbot's Level, but it was the one that reached Washington by 6 P.M., and perhaps I could find out its time of departure. I would have to change in Washington, she said, and in New York, but after that it was straight through to Windsor, Vermont, where I would arrive at eleven o'clock in the morning. She would meet me there, she said, but if for any reason she was delayed, and when I got off the bus she wasn't there, I was not to get upset or worried, I was to go and sit on the hotel porch, which was right by where the bus stopped.

Right then I knew this summer was going to be a gold mine for me. My paper would just about write itself. What would happen if I went and sat on that porch? Would it really be *really* all right? Or would the whites stop talking and act ill at ease, as if they didn't know whether to tell me to leave, or to ignore me, or what? Or would they actually tell me to leave? Everybody says it's no different in the North than in the South, it's just as prejudiced. All right, supposing nobody made any nasty cracks and nobody told me to leave and nobody called the police or anything—still it would be worth a couple of paragraphs just to find out what it's like to walk up where there's empty chairs and sit down in one and nobody mind.

It certainly is going to be interesting, I thought, and read on. The five dollars is for food, she said. I'm to go in and get a good meal, in Washington, and in New York, and in Springfield, Mass. I'm to keep up my strength and my spirits. And if the money isn't enough, she'd make it up. But she thought it ought to be about right.

Well, that's five dollars to the good, I thought. Aunt Lydia was fixing enough food for the trip for at least two of me, fried chicken and potato salad and chocolate cake. And Aunt Lydia and all my cousins came down to the bus stop and saw me off, and so I left, feeling a combination of instant homesickness and buoyant excitement.

The further North I came, the more peculiar I felt.

When I first set out, all around me were decent dark faces, familiar, reassuring. All the way to Baltimore it was the same. We changed buses at Richmond, bypassing Washington—in spite of what my lineup of tickets said I was to do—but still it was like at home, the Negroes going to the rear as long as there were any seats there. In Baltimore the balance began to change. Some Negroes got on and sat up front, and white people had to walk past them to the seats available farther back. They got off in Philadelphia. It interested me that where there are more whites, the Negroes act more like white people—that is, they sit wherever they please— whereas at home, where there are far more Negroes, we don't. It's odd, when you stop to think about it.

Then we were in New York. The bus terminal was about the size of a monstrous factory, as populated as a large town, and I don't think there were more than a hundred other Negroes there, that I could see, anyway. Maybe they were there, out of sight, working somewhere, but if so, I didn't see them. There certainly weren't any Negroes working as redcaps, *nobody* was working as a redcap. I had nearly three-quarters of an hour to wait, and I wanted to see as much as I could, and I was glad I owned no more than I did own, or my arms would have been pulled from their sockets. I rode up and down the moving stairways, and looked in the shop windows—the terminal has all kinds of shops in it, camera and luggage and clothing and candy and a bakery and of course newspaper stands and coffee shops—and it didn't matter that it was the middle of the night and I couldn't go see the city itself. I was seeing a small city right there. And here and there I saw Negroes working as salesgirls or waitresses, and there would be white salesgirls or waitresses working right along with them, and white and Negro customers going in and out, having coffee at a counter, together, I mean sitting side by side, and I wished the Governor could have been there, because these white people stayed as white as ever, didn't turn black or brown or break out with dark blotches like a pinto horse, or anything, although there they sat, drinking coffee at the same counters. Bless his poor segregated heart, I thought, it would reassure the Gov to see that the white race's whiteness isn't anywhere near as fragile or as easily destroyed as one might think, listening to him yammer his hysterical fear of whites being adjacent to, or in juxtaposition with, Negroes.

Of course, there is some of this side-by-side sitting in the South, in some of the big cities. But the remarkable part to me was that everybody in New York took it so for granted. Nobody seemed to be noticing it was happening, except me. Everybody seemed to be invisible to everybody else, whites to whites, blacks to blacks, whites to blacks and blacks to whites. It's a wonder as they walk around they don't crash into each other. New Yorkers must have some kind of radar, like bats. Because they do *not* look at each other.

But I didn't go in and get any coffee. I don't quite know why I didn't, but I didn't.

All right, I *do* know why I didn't, but I don't care to write it down.

Then I got on the bus for Springfield, Mass., and I ate my second box lunch and went to sleep, and when I woke, it was broad daylight and we were pulling into Springfield. I looked out, and there wasn't a Negro in sight. There wasn't another Negro on the bus, either. They must have got off during the night.

Everybody went into the station to use the rest rooms, etc., and these seemed always to have been divided only by sex. I couldn't see any evidence of a converted "colored" or "white only" sign anywhere. Had this been from absence of prejudice or simply a strong sense of economy? It would hardly have paid to install one just for me!

But I did drink a cup of coffee at the lunch counter. I ordered it, I was served in my turn, I paid for it, and I was invisible. I mean, I was just another cup-of-coffee-that's-ten-cents-pay-now-please. The waitress was grumpy, but she was grumpy with everybody. No discrimination.

I enjoyed my coffee in Springfield, Mass.

Then we left Springfield, and headed even more North, and I was the sole representative of my race on the bus, in the fields, on the streets, anywhere. And this was another first for me: I had never before in my life been surrounded completely by whites, been the only Negro within shouting distance, or even, as the miles flew by, within driving distance. And I knew that when we pulled into Windsor, if there wasn't anybody there to meet me, I was not going to go and sit on the hotel porch, I was going to stand smack in my tracks until I either took root or was rescued. (Harriet Brown, Southern-style chicken.) My nerves were on edge, and I had to force myself to appear at ease, and not sit bolt upright with my feet together and my elbows clamped to my sides.

And then we were there, and the driver swung down first, and then a couple of boys, and then I got off, and the driver took me by the elbow to help me down. I was so startled I thought I would stumble, but I managed not to. Then he helped another woman down, saying, "Watch your step, now," and the white woman said, "Thank you," and I was annoyed that I hadn't shown good manners, too. When he opened the hatch at the side of the bus and took out my suitcases and set them on the sidewalk, I said, "Thank you," as calmly as I could, and I was proud of my tongue that it didn't automatically add, "Sir." My blood was still racing with shock, a curious response to so casual a touch by a white man, I thought, and one worth pondering over when I had more time.

The bus drove off, and I felt as conspicuous as the flag on the post office. For one thing, people passing me were looking at me. Not friendly, not unfriendly, but I knew I was no longer invisible. I felt that most of them could probably have described me in court if they had to, because they looked at me as if they really saw me standing there. And then they were all so *white*. I had never seen such white-looking white folks. I thought at first it was because that's all there was, only whites passing, that the total seemed such a whiteness. And then I realized that these white people were really very pale. Of course they weren't *white*—only clowns are white and that's paint—but they looked bleached, like asparagus when you first scrape the soil away. I thought maybe they were scared of the sun. Nobody was wearing a sunback dress or even had bare arms showing. And then the sun passed behind a cloud and I shivered, and it struck me that I must be near the Arctic Circle. This certainly wasn't summer!

Then the Daleys drove up in their station wagon—it's a not very new Chevy, pretty rusty, too—and Mrs. Daley hopped out and came around to where I was standing and she said, "You must be Harriet Brown—how do you do?" And she thrust out her hand, and I had to shake it.

And I thought, I've lived nineteen years and never had a white person touch me on purpose but not mad, and here in the space of fifteen minutes it's happened twice.

"I'm sorry I'm late," she was saying, "but everybody wanted to come and meet you, and it took us a long time to find shoes and things." She certainly did look hurried, her shirt was kind of rumpled where it showed under her cardigan, and her lipstick looked chewed. White women ought to take time with their lipstick, it's so conspicuous.

Maureen was in the front seat, holding the baby. The middle seat was bursting with children, two of whom spilled out onto the sidewalk after my suitcases. "That's Robert and that's Richard," said Maureen. "Robert's in fourth, Richard's in second grade. That's Mary, she's only five and she doesn't go to school. And Timmy—*smile,* Timmy—he's three, and this is John Anthony, he can't talk yet but he can walk. Mary, get in the back and make room for Harriet Brown. You too, Timmy."

They were all staring at me as if I had a purple face.

I got in, and we set out, and Mrs. Daley asked me if I had a pleasant trip, and I said, "Yes, ma'am."

She pays my wages, I'll give her a ma'am. That's fair enough.

She asked me if I had had enough to eat on the way, and I said, "Yes, ma'am," and she asked me if I was tired, and I said, "No, ma'am," and I could see her looking at me in the mirror.

"Harriet," she said, "I want to make it clear to you, and I want

: 12 :

these children to have it clear in their heads, that you are here to help *me,* I am the only overworked member of this group, and these children are not to sweet-talk you into doing their chores for them."

I said, "Yes, ma'am," before I realized she was really talking to her children, not to me. The boy Richard let out a kind of whoop and he said, "Yeah, sure, sure, Roger, okay, I get it," and Mrs. Daley said, "Yes, *Mother,*" and they all said, "Yes, Mother," but it didn't seem to me they were being especially polite. I've heard that Northern children haven't any manners.

"Stop staring," said Maureen. "It's rude. You, Richard—stop, *staring.*"

"That will be enough, Maureen," said Mrs. Daley.

"Well, he was staring," said Maureen.

"I was *not,*" said Richard.

"Perhaps they've never seen one of my race before," I said.

"Not close up," said Maureen, "but I have. We used to live in the South, years ago when I was very little, but I have a most unusual memory and I can clearly remember things back to when I was three or even younger. I'm not like Robert, who cannot remember where he put his shoes last night—"

"You have a most unusual tongue, too," said Robert. "It's hitched in the middle and waggles at both ends."

"That will be *enough,*" said Mrs. Daley.

And she started acting like a guide and pointing out the sights, and I looked around and everywhere I looked it was simply country, rough, hilly, lots of trees, houses scattered every quarter mile or so, here and there a handsome brick house, but mostly the houses were wood and needed paint. The further we drove, the poorer the houses, and now and then they weren't more than tar-paper shacks. I certainly was surprised. I had been given to understand that all the people who live in the country who are that poor live in the rural South.

She knew the names of every family. "That's the So-and-Sos'," she would say (I can't remember the names). "He's a writer and she paints." And then, after a little, "That's the So-and-Sos', they have Holsteins, almost sixty head." And so on.

And then we drove along a very narrow dirt road, and through some woods, and up a valley, and through more woods, and everything very wild-looking. And then we headed up another hill, the car groaning and shifting gears, and then we turned in a lane, and Mary, the five-year-old, whirled around and sang out, "Here we are!" as if to say, this is Heaven!

The house was right near the road, and it certainly didn't look like much. The roof sagged, with that hammock-swing look that means trouble soon if not sooner, come rain, and the paint was peeling off the clapboard.

"This is our old house," said Maureen, "and now that you're here I'm moving out! Because you're living in the new house, Harriet, and I'm moving in with you!"

And that's how I found out I am working for a two-house family, as Mrs. D. puts it.

June 9th

The trouble with writing a book (which is what I appear to be doing) is your body wears out before your mind does. There I was, right in the middle of an important scene—my first impressions of my employers' home, and so on—when, due to the hour, which was very late, and the air, which is full of a kind of powerful purity, my eyes refused to stay open. Not being very good at writing with my eyes shut, I went to bed.

So, to go back to my entry yesterday into the "old house":

Immediately I could see why they are building a new one. Not only the roof sags, but the floors, too.

"It's the underpinnings," Robert told me. "There aren't any. I mean, they've rotted. Don't jump up and down, Harriet. You might go through to the cellar."

I promised I would not jump up and down.

"There's nothing holding you up but the linoleum, no kidding," said Richard.

"But don't get the idea we're poor," said Maureen, "just because the wallpaper is peeling off in the living room and it leaks upstairs and down when it rains and the front door won't open because the eaves have sagged—"

"Because Daddy is building us a new house!" said Mary, in that same tone of look-the-pearly-gates-are-opening.

"And someday we'll all go marching in," said Mrs. Daley. "Meanwhile, let's eat."

It turned out I was to eat in the kitchen.

"But why?" Maureen demanded. "Why isn't Harriet eating with us?"

"There isn't room," said Robert. "There isn't even room for John Anthony."

"We could *make* room," Maureen said. "We always do, when there's company."

"Why don't you shut up?" Robert suggested.

"That will do," said Mrs. Daley. She looked embarrassed, but I was not about to help her out with any tactful comments. I am the hired help here.

After lunch Maureen came into the kitchen. "Wouldn't you like to eat with us?" she whispered. "You must be lonely out here."

"Not at all," I said. "I can read while I'm eating. It wouldn't be polite to read if I were not by myself."

"Mother and Daddy read all the time at meals," she said. "They say it's the only chance they get."

"I like it by myself," I said. I didn't explain further—why should I? I don't owe anybody any explanations for my feelings.

I am willing to work for white folks, but I certainly don't want to eat with them.

When the dishes were done, I was given the grand tour. The children took me to see the chickens, where I discovered that Northern chicken houses smell the same as Southern, and the pigs, who were very cute, being about seven weeks old, and the cows, which I immediately did not like. They all came to the pasture fence and stared at me, chewing and chewing as they stared, and the lack of expression on their faces and the incessant movement of their jaws reminded me of that sheriff who arrested us that time, only his cud had been chewing tobacco.

"That's Pansy, over there," said Richard. "She's so dumb she doesn't know how to use the water bowl."

"She can't help it," said Mary.

"She's dumb just the same," said Richard.

"What's a water bowl?" I said. It sounded vaguely as if the cow wasn't housebroken, or something.

"It's what they drink out of in the barn," said Richard. "Are you from the *city,* Harriet? The cow has to shove on the lever so the water will come in, and Pansy can't grasp this simple fact. She bellows and bellows—"

"And that's Fern, the creamy one," said Maureen. "She has a great sense of humor. She shoves the lever and lets the water pour all over the floor!"

"And Daddy bellows," said Robert.

"Daddy has a radio in the barn," Mary said. "The cows just love music!"

"They don't like the Beatles as much as they do Frank Sinatra," Maureen said. "Did you ever hear of Frank Sinatra? I guess the cows are very conservative."

"How do you know what they like?" I said.

"By how much milk they give. They give more milk when Frankie sings. Or Bing." She ducked under the barbed wire. "This is Peony, and this is Daffodil, we call her Daffy, and here is Violet, she had her first calf in the woods, that's why we call her Violet— shy, get it? Fern is her daughter, born among the ferns, you see. And that's Forsythia, her name has nothing to do with her disposition which is terrible, she hates the milking machine and stomps on it if you don't look out—"

"Come on, Harriet, come see my ducks," said Robert, and

opened the gate and obviously expected me to follow him right into that pasture and walk right past those cows.

"Some other time," I said. "Maybe. I'm sure I have duties I should be attending to."

"You don't like the great outdoors, do you?" said Maureen.

"I can take it or leave it," I said.

I could see I had lost caste. They looked at me soberly and I clearly got the impression they were minding their manners. I've been here only two days but already I know this: Northerners—Vermonters, anyway—when they don't say anything, are being polite, or as polite as they know how to be. The smooth phrase is not their talent. Just to keep still and not say what they're thinking, this is the most you can ask.

School is already over for the year, and that is why the children were available to meet me when I arrived. Yesterday, Thursday, was the eighth-grade graduation, and today there were class picnics. Not wanting to write until sunup, I didn't tell about the graduation in last night's entry.

Naturally Maureen wanted to see the ceremonies, and Mrs. D. said she herself didn't have time, would I mind very much taking her? I drove, didn't I?

I said I would be glad to take Maureen, and I did drive, that is, I knew how, but I didn't have a license. Impasse. Maureen suggested going with the Drakes, they were taking their pickup truck, she was sure, and there would be all kinds of room. We would only have to walk half a mile to where the Drakes' road joined ours. So Mrs. D. phoned, and it was arranged.

Then of course I wondered what to wear. I have a couple of uniforms furnished me, which is okay with me because I really don't have anything suitable to wear on the job here, and I would hate to wear the clothes I'm saving for college, and get them all worn out. But does one wear a uniform to an eighth-grade graduation? And I decided one does, if one is going only because one is the hired help.

When I appeared at the proper time, ready to leave, Mrs. Daley

: 17 :

shot me a startled glance and said, "Harriet, would you mind wearing one of your own dresses? I would prefer it. You would be much too conspicuous in that uniform in our village."

Now will you figure that one out, please?

I decided Mrs. Daley was afflicted by a species of reverse snobbery. I was the maid, but nobody was to know. Or at any rate the fact was to be soft-pedaled. Very well, I'd play along.

The graduation was funnier than an old movie on TV. They played a kind of funeral march for the children to come in by, and in they came, one by one, every single child looking as if he thought he was headed for his execution. They even carried their heads thrust forward at an angle convenient for the axe.

Up on the platform they marched, and, with some stumbling and shuffling, found their places. We all rose and saluted the flag, prayers were said, and then the more talented, or less ungifted—however you want to put it—displayed their talents and gifts. One girl spoke the oration of Mark Antony over the body of Caesar. A boy—the shortest child on the platform—took five minutes to describe the rise of Communism and to analyze what steps we should take to combat it. Several groups presumably sang. I was in no difficulty so far. I sat wooden-faced, and I observed, and I was observed. Maureen kept whispering to me who was related to whom, which performer was the older brother or sister of which of her classmates. I nodded to show I had registered the information, and I was just beginning to understand that this whole ceremony, so absurd and yet in its own way so sentimental and indeed charming, was a kind of tribal rite, a marking by the community of the achievements of the next generation, and no doubt one of the means by which the community keeps control over the behavior of the young (approval expressed for scholastic standing, etc.), when a music stand was brought out, and a boy came out with a trumpet.

He fussed with his music on the stand and he put his instrument to his mouth and he began.

Oh, dear Lord! I shut my eyes and prayed. Give me strength, make me deaf, but dear God! don't let me give way to hysteria. Harriet Brown, *control* yourself. You start rolling in the aisles and you'll offend everybody here; they'll think you're some kind of emotional Mau Mau and just to get even they'll vote the straight White Supremacy ticket. Pretend it isn't happening—pretend you're deaf, you can't hear that split note, that flat blat. Stop shaking, Harriet Brown, stop breathing, but don't—you—laugh.

And I didn't.

I might write Mr. Carr and suggest he pass along a warning to the rest of the class. It won't help the public image of Jacob's Ladder if all over the North this summer his students are giving way to uncontrollable mirth when exposed to certain local ceremonies. Nor would his own standing with the college be unaffected, were a large percentage of us in Sociology III (Pressures of Emotional Prejudices on Environment) to be among the missing, come September, having been flung into the clink by outraged Northern natives. He really ought to be grateful for the warning. Or would he prefer that we go ahead and find out if "disturbing the peace" is as elastic a term in the North as it is in the South? I could ask.

It seems to me he'd have to answer such a letter. But do I have the nerve to write it? Maybe he'll think it's nothing but a pitifully transparent bid for attention. Oh, come on, Harriet, *carpe diem*. Didn't Mr. Carr say to keep in touch?

The ceremonies which stimulated the above line of reasoning were now safely concluded, and we wove our way past groups of people taking snapshots of children who stood blinking in the bright sunlight and clutching their diplomas with shy pride. Maureen skipped over to a stout, grey-haired woman in a housedress made of silk, and she said, "Mrs. Platt, this is Harriet Brown, she's from South Carolina and she's going to be a junior in college and she's helping my mother this summer because she's earning her own way!" Maureen then whirled toward me and said, "Mrs. Platt was my teacher this year and I was hoping I'd flunk so I'd have her again!"

The woman smiled nicely enough and I was afraid she might offer me her hand, but she didn't.

"How do you do, Miss Brown," she said.

"How do you do," I said faintly. *Miss Brown,* from a white woman: chalk up another first.

"I hope you enjoy your summer," she went on. "Is this your first visit to Vermont?"

"I've never been north of Richmond before," I said, and I thought all this conversation lacked was the clatter of teacups. The atmosphere was noticeably social.

"You're acquiring an unshakable habit, you'll find," she said. "Once exposed, forever smitten. It's dangerous to come to Vermont—afterwards, you're never really happy anywhere else. At least, that was my case."

There's nothing profound or unusual about this exchange of remarks. I record it because I am being very thorough, as instructed, and because it was the first casual conversation I ever had with a white person whom I met casually.

But it gave me something to think about as we clung to the sides of the Drakes' pickup truck and rattled over the dusty roads towards home.

I wondered where she came from, Maureen's teacher, and why she had felt obliged to be so cordial to me. Was it because I am a Negro that she singled me out? Was her apparent graciousness a kind of condescension to my color? Or do I analyze everything too much?

And there I had stood, dreading that she'd offer me her hand, either in greeting or in parting, after I thought I was getting used to casual contacts with whites. After all, I'd managed not to faint when Mrs. Daley shook hands with me the day I came. Why am I so acutely conscious of the lack of color in white people's hands? I mean, especially in their hands? I don't see how we'll ever take our physical differences for granted, be able to ignore these differences, simply not be aware of them, as Mr. Carr keeps saying some day we will. Judging by myself, he couldn't be more wrong.

I watched the billows of dust pluming behind us, and I thought maybe that's all I'm doing now, making a mighty fuss over the passage of one small idea across my dusty brain.

Mrs. Daley wanted to know how everything went.

"Oh, simply splendid!" said Maureen. "Mother, Jimmy Hancock has really improved with his trumpet!"

"I'm relieved to hear it," she said, and caught my eye. "Were you impressed, Harriet?"

"He can still improve," I said, and I went up to the new house to get into my uniform again, and I sat on my bed and laughed until I cried.

Jimmy Hancock is not an acoustics aristocrat, that's for sure.

One other item for today: I have my ticket home. Mrs. Daley handed me an envelope with the reverse route, Windsor, Vt., to Springfield, Mass., Springfield to New York, etc., inside. "Oh, by the way, you look after this, Harriet," she said. "I've been known to lose things. If you have it, you'll know where it is."

I wonder. Was she really afraid she might lose it? Or did she too want to make a kind gesture, one carefully chosen to go with her role of Northern White Liberal? "Harriet, honey chile, hold your ticket snug in your hand and you won't feel so far from home"—well, why not, when it wouldn't cost her anything?

June 10th

There may possibly be days when there isn't anything to record —hard as it is to imagine such a day—but this day wasn't one of them.

Right after breakfast, when I was washing up the milking pails and Mr. Daley had left for the village on the tractor—it needed something done to give it more pep, and he was hoping to start haying, he said, the rains had certainly brought the grass along— and the baby was reasonably contented in his pen on the lawn outside the kitchen window, and Timmy was standing on a chair between me and the sink, "helping" with the pans, and Maureen and her mother had gone to the new house to put a few more square yards of paint on the north side, and Robert and Richard were playing catch over by the pasture fence—in other words, it was a bright morning and everybody happy—when all of a sudden Richard came racing into the house and he was calling out, "Come quick! Robert's lying on the grass and he says his leg's broken!"

I snatched Timmy off the chair and, lugging him with me, I ran outside. There was Robert on the ground, and he wasn't crying or screaming or anything, he was just staring at his leg.

"Get your mother," I said, because I had glanced at the leg, and I felt sick.

It looked as if somebody had swung a meat hook at his muscle. There was a great gaping hole torn open and you could see the muscle fibers in layers like a drawing in an anatomy book, only not so neat. And blood was pouring out, and it was too red, and too much of it, and all I could manage to do was to say, "Don't move, Robert. Don't move."

"I'm not moving," he said. And he was breathing kind of fast.

Mrs. Daley and Maureen came running down the hill, and when Mrs. D. saw Robert she said, "Oh, my goodness! Oh, what did you do that for?" And she sounded very angry.

She crouched down by him and her fingers slid along the bone. "Go get those gauze pads, Maureen, they're in the medicine chest," she said, suddenly calm as you please. "I don't think it's broken," she said to Robert, and he looked a little less scared. Then she cupped her hand over that terrible hole and began shoving the flesh back in place. "Harriet, there's an old sheet on the shelves in the workroom. Bring it here and we'll tear off a couple of strips."

Well, she fashioned a rough bandage over that leg, moving it not at all, and then she got a board, and tied it to that. And as she worked, she said to Robert, "And what were you doing, may I ask?"

"I was just trying to catch the ball," he said. "I hit my leg on the fence."

"The *fence?*" she said. "How could you do that to yourself on the fence?"

"By the gate," he said. "I whammed into the fence, and at first

I didn't know I did anything, I was running away and I looked down and saw my leg . . ."

I had gone over to the gate, and I saw where he'd hit. There was the end of a bolt sticking out about an inch and a half, and some pink scraps clung to it.

When Mrs. D. came over and looked, too, she turned a queer color for a moment. "Well, Harriet," she said, "this is a typical start for the summer." She sounded mad again. "Last summer Mary fell out of an apple tree and broke her shoulder, and the summer before that, Richard jumped on a hay fork and drove it through his foot. This family just does not believe in vacations."

She started for the house. "I'll call the doctor and tell him we're on our way," she said. *"Damnation."*

We left Maureen home with the younger children, and I sat on the edge of the middle seat so as to keep Robert from rolling off—we had him propped crosswise—and we took him to the doctor, who seemed to know his business, or at any rate behaved as if he thought the situation was not out of control, because he told Mrs. D. to go sit down somewhere, he'd sew Robert up. And he told me to go stay with Mrs. Daley, and I did, and we sat in the waiting room and stared at magazines. After about half an hour the doctor came in and said to Mrs. Daley, "Kate, it isn't as bad as I thought. None of the main nerves are cut, and he ought to have full use of his leg and foot. There may be some numbness but even that may wear off after a few months."

She said, "That's good."

"I'm going to repair it now and I'll put on a cast that'll hold his leg still. I don't want him moving the muscles and pulling loose the healing flesh—"

"No," she said.

"Have you any shopping to do? It'll be an hour or so."

"Thank you," she said.

So we sat and stared at magazines some more and then we sat and stared at people, who were restive, I suppose wondering what was keeping the doctor.

"This will certainly mess up his training program," Mrs. Daley said at last. "He's been training for the 1972 Olympics. Running the 5000 meters."

"I saw him yesterday," I said.

"He times himself with an alarm clock," she said, and she looked out of the window, and her face had that pinched look as if she'd like to bawl, but couldn't, because it was too public and she was too old.

So put this down: white parents grieve for their children the same as Negro parents. I know this probably is not a new discovery, but I hadn't thought about it before, particularly.

It was nearly noon when we collected Robert from the emergency room, and there he was, perched in a wheelchair and carrying a set of crutches like a lance.

"I have to stay in bed *two weeks!*" he announced, as if such a thing were scarcely possible.

"Good," said Mrs. D. briskly. "For once I'll know just where you are."

And so we took Robert home. It was decided that the best thing to do was to move him to the new house right away, because the boys' bedroom is right next to the upstairs lavatory, and in the old house the only bathroom is downstairs. Meals would have to be carted up the hill on a tray, which certainly would be a bother for somebody, and I could guess who, but it was better than bedpans.

So we made a number of trips up the hill with mattresses and springs and bedding—naturally Richard insisted on moving, too, thus doubling the freightage—and Maureen helped carry Robert upstairs, boasting of her muscles. "I can lick every boy in the fifth grade," she said, "and all but two in the sixth." She is skinny, but she is tough. I think she's almost stronger than her mother.

"We would wait for Mr. Daley, Harriet," said Mrs. D. when she caught her breath, "if we simply couldn't possibly do this ourselves. But I hate to take five minutes of his time right now, he's so rushed."

"I was going to do the baling this year," Robert said, and scrunched his eyes shut and a couple of tears slid out.

It was the first he had cried since he got hurt.

When Mr. D. came back over the hill about two o'clock, the tractor roaring with a better noise, even I could tell, he was greeted with the news of Robert in a cast, and he jumped down from the tractor and said, "Oh, for the love of Gawd!" in an angry tone, and ran up the hill toward the new house.

Later he took the tractor into the barnyard and then I heard it leaving again, and Maureen came in to report that Daddy was starting to mow. "Pray it doesn't rain, Harriet," she said.

"Who is going to help your father hay?" I inquired.

"We are," she said, as if the question surprised her. "Mother and Richard and I. Mary is too little, and you're too busy, with Timmy and the baby and all."

It sounded like pretty heavy work for a woman and two children, and I said so.

"Oh, *no,* Harriet! It's good for us," Maureen assured me. "It makes muscles! Richard and I will stack—you know, pile the bales on the truck—and Daddy tosses the bales to us. Daddy does the mowing, but Mother rakes and bales. That's what Robert was hoping to do this year. It isn't hard, Mother says, you just have to watch what you're doing. Daddy switches all the parts on the tractor, takes off the rake, puts on the mower, all that stuff, because Mother can't do that, although I bet she could learn. Mother drives the truck when we pick up the bales, and Daddy unloads at the barn and we stack them there, too. The only trouble is, if anything goes wrong, and Daddy isn't here, we have to wait until he gets home, and that louses everything up!"

This needed clarifying. Somehow I had got the idea that Mr. Daley would be taking time off for haying, but no.

"Not now!" Maureen said. "Daddy couldn't take a vacation now—all the summer people are coming back. Now is when he really cleans up—you know, rakes it in—"

"Makes money," I said, to make it perfectly clear I am *au courant* with the idiom.

"That's what I said. And it's tough the haying has to be done now, too, but you can't argue with the calendar, Daddy says."

"Seems to me he could use a man," I said.

"Sure he could, but the three of us are just as good. Anyway, you can't find a man to hire these days, Harriet. Daddy says they all want too much money, and then they wreck the machinery or burn the barn down or something, so it doesn't pay no matter how you look at it." She grinned. "That's why we have you, Harriet, don't you see? So you can help Mother and then Mother can help Daddy. Like the Mad Hatter's tea party—get it?"

I nodded. "Everybody shift over one place." This looked like a good chance to clear up something that had been puzzling me, so I said, "You mean you usually have a girl to help every summer? I'm not just an experiment in Civil Living, or anything like that?"

"Oh, no. Mother always gets a college girl to help her—she says it takes real brains to do the housework here. And each of you is supposed to be an Enriching Experience," Maureen rattled on, "for us children, she means, so she tries to have variety. This year she wanted a foreign student because they are a Most Enriching Experience, but I guess they were in short supply—anyway, Daddy said be satisfied to See America First. We've had some mighty rare specimens, though—is that what you meant by 'experiment'? Last year we had a genius from Bennington who spoke German to the cows, she danced barefoot in the orchard at moonrise, and the year before we had a soprano from Juilliard who used to sit on the barn roof and practice her scales—it was marvelous, they echoed six times!" She gave me her high-beam-headlight look. "You can imagine we could hardly *wait* to meet you!"

"Sorry I'm a disappointment," I said.

"Oh, you're not a disappointment at all, Harriet!" and she skipped out of the kitchen before I could ask her to be more specific.

When we were getting supper, and I was fixing a tray for Robert, I said to Mrs. Daley, more or less to take her mind off her troubles, "Maybe I should have told you sooner, ma'am, but the fact is, I have a jail record."

"Really? You surprise me," she said, calm as could be. "What on earth did you do?"

"I disturbed the peace," I said.

She looked at me and laughed. *"You* did? Honestly?"

"Yes, ma'am," I said. "I sang 'God Bless America' in front of the city hall."

"Solo?" said Maureen. "And they arrested you? Oh, come on, Harriet, sing something—"

"You hush," said Mrs. D. "What were you doing, Harriet? Protesting some local custom?"

"We wanted to eat at the lunch counter in the five-and-dime," I said. "Jacob's Ladder students helped start the sit-ins, and it wasn't anything new, of course, for students to be arrested. But it was *my* first time—this was nearly two years ago—and what happened was, we were chased away from the store, and so we went and sang in front of the city hall. That was about eleven o'clock in the morning. There were maybe thirty of us, nine of us were girls. The sheriff and some of his friends took us off to jail and there we stayed until ten o'clock that night."

"Were you scared?" said Maureen.

"Yes, I was," I said. "We all were. So we sang and cracked jokes and so forth. And we got hungry. But about four in the afternoon the NAACP lawyers got there, and they brought us sandwiches and Cokes, and about ten o'clock they came back with papers which made the sheriff release us. They had put up our bail."

"And all you were doing was eating?" Maureen said.

"No, we weren't eating," I said. "We wanted to eat—"

"You mean you were hungry and they wouldn't let you eat?" Maureen demanded.

"We weren't really hungry," I said. "It was the principle of the thing. They wouldn't serve us just because we were Negroes. There was a sign that said, 'White only'—"

Maureen whirled on her mother. "You see!" she said. "Harriet ought to eat with us—I knew it!"

Hired help or no, I thought maybe I could explain to her better than anybody else, since it was my feelings that were at issue. "Look, Maureen," I said, "I am *not* company, I am *working* here.

If I were working in a store, I would not expect to eat with the manager. In fact, I would rather not. Look—do you want to eat with your teachers in school?"

It was an unfortunate comparison.

"Okay, I get you," Maureen said. "I don't *want* to, but I *have* to. There's one at every table, and boy, does it wreck our fun! They even make us chew!"

June 11th

Today is Sunday, and my letters won't go out until tomorrow, Monday. I put them in the mailbox at the end of the lane, and there they'll stay until the mailman picks them up around eleven-thirty in the morning. I didn't even have to stamp them, just put nickels with them and the mailman will stamp them for me. Mrs. Daley says she does the same with packages, except she doesn't have to leave any money. The mailman takes them to town and weighs them, and the next day he leaves a little envelope with the postage needed marked on it. Sending off their mail by this method is the only way in which country people have it easier than city people, that I have noticed so far, that is.

We observed the Sabbath by thanking God it wasn't raining, so that the hay would dry that was already cut, and so Mr. Daley could cut some more hay in the morning, and in the afternoon he could ted up the hay he cut yesterday, this in hopes that tomorrow the rest of us can rake it and bale it. The children were weeding the peas and beans, and Richard was lugging to Robert vast amounts of material designed to divert the mind. It seemed obvious to me that the family did not include churchgoing in their plans for the day.

But, it turned out, Mrs. Daley did, at least for me.

"Harriet," she said, coming up from the cellar with a chunk of solid-frozen meat she expected to be able to eat by noon, "what church do you go to?"

I said, "Church of Zion."

"Oh," she said. "I don't believe there's one nearby."

"I don't suppose there is," I said.

"Is that something like the Baptist church?"

I said it wasn't exactly.

"The children and their father go to the Catholic church," she said, "when they go. I imagine the Church of Zion is more like the Baptist than the Catholic?"

I said I imagined it was.

"But don't worry, ma'am," I said, "it's all right if I don't get to church."

I meant I wouldn't go to Hell or anything, but I didn't say so in so many words. I've noticed anything you say to Catholics, they can get mad, no matter what you meant.

"No, that wouldn't be right, Harriet," she said. "We agreed you could get to church. I go to the Episcopal church but that might seem almost as strange to you as the Catholic. There's a Protestant church in the village that is a combined church of some sort—I mean it isn't formal or anything. *I* don't cross myself but that's only because I wasn't taught to as a child, but some people do, in my church." She hesitated. "Perhaps you might like the church in the village. I could leave you there on my way."

Did she think for one minute I was going to march into a White church by myself?

"I wouldn't want you to drive out of your way," I said.

"Does your church have an altar?"

I said yes, it did.

"The village church does not," she said. "So that settles it. You might as well come with me. You're going to feel strange anyway, you might as well feel strange sitting in the pew next to me."

I said, "I don't have a hat."

She looked at me for a long moment. "Harriet," she said, "if you don't want to go to church, say so. Nobody's going to hold it against you. It's your business. But if you don't want to go just because you don't have a hat, I'll *lend* you a hat."

"I have a scarf," I said stiffly.

"For heaven's sake, Harriet, do as you like," said Mrs. Daley. "You don't have to wear anything on your head if you don't want to."

I got the distinct impression Mrs. Daley didn't think God would care one way or the other if I were to go to church completely bald. On the other hand, did I want Mrs. Daley's God to have to tolerate me? I'd accepted gifts of clothing from my employers in the South all my life—they were considered practically fringe benefits to which I was entitled—why did I resent a similar offer from a Northern woman? Or did she really mean she was lending me her hat which she expected me to return? You *lend* your possessions only to an equal.

"Mrs. Daley," I said cautiously, "I'd be proud to accept the offer of your hat."

So she brought out a little white lid which she said was really too young for her anyway, but she thought it would be becoming to me. Just don't overdo it, I thought, don't say too much, I'm going to wear your hat, don't spoil it.

I perched it on top of my head, and I had to admit I liked the way it looked.

We set out. The road ran through the woods, and over a mountain, and down a steep hill, and through a valley with those hills on either side, and everything was speckled and dappled with sunlight. And the way seemed short to me, because I was nervous. I didn't think Mrs. Daley was terribly stupid, or anything, but I did think she had no doubt been kind of sheltered all her life, so she was naïve, and probably had no idea of what might happen.

What if they wouldn't let me in? Supposing some fine gentleman stood smack in my way and wouldn't step aside? What would Mrs. Daley do—ask me to give her the pitch and start singing "We Shall Overcome"? If she did, would we both be arrested?

Well, supposing nobody stopped us and we walked right in, ought I to take a pew by myself? What if there wasn't an empty one, and people already there got up and shifted places so as not to have to share a seat with me—what would Mrs. Daley do then?

In any case it was going to be interesting, I thought. I just hoped it wasn't going to be *too* interesting.

I said, "I hope I won't get arrested."

"Why would you be arrested?"

"For disturbing the peace," I said.

"You mean when you sing?"

"Yes, then," I said.

"Just don't burst out with 'God Bless America' when the rest of us are on the 'Te Deum,' " she said, and laughed. "This is an adventure, isn't it?"

"Yes, ma'am," I said.

Maybe she does know what she's doing, I thought. Or maybe she's trying to prove something to herself. I shrugged. The state of Mrs. Daley's soul was her problem, not mine.

We were almost late. It was a pretty town, with trees and lawns and houses all neat and prosperous-looking. The church was stone, with colored glass windows. Mrs. Daley hurried up the stone steps, with me right on her heels. I could hear an organ. As we went in, a man handed Mrs. Daley a piece of paper like a program, and wished her good morning in a low, proper voice, and then he handed me a piece of paper and I said nothing, I wasn't going to open my mouth, and I followed Mrs. Daley into church. She sort of dipped her knee towards the front of the church, I suppose towards the altar, and slid into the pew, and I slid into the pew after her. I did not dip my knee.

Nobody paid any attention.

Just then a door up near the front opened and the music changed and swung into "Hail Thee, Festival Day" and in came the choir, and I was astounded to see that the man carrying the Cross was a Negro. And there were four little Negro boys walking before the minister. They were wearing robes and they were very,

: 32 :

very black, and it wasn't just because of the white robes they were wearing, or the fact that everybody else in the choir was white. They looked as if they'd just flown in from the Congo, and hadn't acquired a drop of white blood on the way.

And then I noticed that among the people standing in the church there were several young men, Negroes, and with them a group of Negro boys. No wonder there'd been no fuss at the door —this church was already integrated. I wished Mrs. Daley had thought to mention it, because then I wouldn't have worried so.

It was a very pleasant service, though full of lots of kneelings and standings and kneelings and standings, and sudden singings out of answers to something the minister had just said. But the music wasn't much. The organ was very nice, but the singing of the choir was an agony to listen to, and nobody in the congregation seemed to have the courage to sing above a squeak. So I didn't sing.

When it was over, and we were walking out, the minister was at the door to say good morning to everybody, and so we were walking out slowly. A number of people said good morning to Mrs. Daley, and asked after her children. And then, seeing that I was with her, they looked directly at me and they said, "Good morning," to me. And I swear that if you'd been blind and only heard their voices and not been able to see me at all, you'd never have known they were saying good morning to somebody not their own race. There wasn't a hint that I could hear that they were just being polite for the sake of Mrs. Daley.

And I said, "Good morning," in a clear voice right back.

And then we reached the minister, and Mrs. Daley said, "Father Tillington, this is Harriet Brown, who is with us this summer."

"How do you do, Miss Brown," he said, taking my hand and holding it, in that cordial way ministers have of slowing down the escape of members of the congregation. "I hope you will be with us every Sunday."

The thought zipped through my mind that maybe he was putting on a demonstration: a minister is under orders to love all

: 33 :

God's creatures, however unworthy, and look, he can even smile fraternally while shaking the hand of a Black Brother, or, as in this case, Sister.

I withdrew my hand. "I hope to be," I said.

"Splendid. Then perhaps we'll see you, too, Kate."

"Every rainy Sunday, anyway, Father," she said with a smile, and we went on down the steps and got in the car and headed for home.

"We'll go the long way," said Mrs. D. "I have to pick up the Sunday paper in the village."

We drove along.

"Well, Harriet," said Mrs. Daley, "how do you feel? Do you feel you've been to church?" Before I could answer, she went on, "I mean, when I go to a Catholic or a lumped-together Protestant—you know, a strange church—I don't feel I've *been*."

"Oh, yes, I feel I've been," I said.

"Good for you. You are more adaptable than I am."

"Because your friends said good morning to me," I said. I was watching her face out of the corner of my eye. "That was the first time in my life that any white person ever said good morning to me, without any . . . provocation."

I could see she was startled, and I was pleased.

"When I walk along the street at home," I said, "and I pass by some white person I know, maybe even have worked for, they don't speak to me. They act as if I'm not there."

Mrs. Daley didn't say anything.

"Even," I said, "if I say good morning to them." This was a lie, because I don't say good morning to a white person. They don't see me, okay, I don't see them.

"You know, Harriet, that's really very rude. It's very ill-bred." She spoke in a tight voice, and I saw she was embarrassed because her race, so "culturally superior," could have such bad manners.

"As a matter of fact, Harriet," she went on, "I find it just a little hard to believe. I haven't been South for some years, I admit, and I know many things have changed, but I always thought Southerners make a point of speaking to the Negroes they know personally."

"That's just it, Mrs. Daley, times have changed," I said. I filed the information that Mrs. D. maybe knew more about the South than I realized, in which case I'd better watch myself. I enjoy stretching the truth in order to make a point, but I surely won't accomplish much if I stretch it so far it snaps back in my face. "It's true white folks used to speak to 'their' Negroes, as they put it," I went on, "but they'd say, 'Good morning, Auntie,' or 'How are you, Sarah?' or 'Come here, boy,' like that, and we won't answer any more, it's part of our fight for our rights, it has to be 'Mrs.' or 'Mr.' or 'Miss' or else! And where I live, anyway, the white folks won't speak to us like that—correctly, you know—they can't bring themselves to do it, I guess. So they act like they never saw us before, and they don't say anything, unless, of course, they're look- ing to start something."

Mrs. Daley said, "What if you answered the same way? Let them see how it feels to be spoken to so familiarly? A Mr. Thomas Jones, for instance, says, 'Good morning, Harriet,' to you. You could reply, 'Good morning, Tom.' "

Good grief, I thought, Mrs. Daley doesn't know *anything* about the South.

"Or say a Miss Ottilia James insists on calling you Hattie," Mrs. Daley went on, "you could say, 'Hello, Tillie.' "

It was scary just to listen to her. I changed the subject.

"Who were all those little black boys?" I asked. "Those little boys who were taking part, and there were some more in the audience."

"I don't know," she said. "Every summer there they are, like migrating birds. There's a camp a few miles north of town. Those young men are counselors there, I believe, but what kind of camp it is I do not know."

"Maybe it's run by your church," I suggested.

"I don't think so. We've never been asked for donations that I know of. It's odd, now that I think of it, that I've never bothered to ask." She gave a little laugh. "Aren't they sweet, those acolytes? I just love the shape of their heads."

I thought that one over. "They looked like little imps to me," I said. "Did you see that one on the left kick the one next to him? When they were supposed to start down the steps—"

"Now, Harriet, don't exaggerate. That was no more than a nudge." She shot me a glance. "Why didn't you sing? I was hoping to hear you sing."

"Those were new hymns to me," I said.

"Hmm. You just didn't want to show everybody up."

"No, honestly, I didn't know the music," I said.

She didn't say any more. We picked up the *New York Times* and it was enormous. It would take a month to read it. It's ridiculous, really.

Then we got home and I went up to change my clothes, and Maureen came flying up the hill.

"Well, Harriet, how was it?" she demanded.

"*Very* nice," I said. "Can't you see the change in me? Now I am a lady. Next week I'm going to wear gloves, and everybody will think I was born here."

"We had *some* excitement while you were gone," she said. "The pigs got out, and the mower broke down. Boy! You missed it!"

"Better luck next time," I said.

Robert was hollering from upstairs. I went up to see what was the matter.

"Have you any change?" he said. "You know—money. Nickels, dimes, quarters, pennies. Let me see your money, Harriet. I won't swipe any, honest. Look, I'm collecting—look at this, look how much these coins are worth."

He was thrusting some kind of a paperback at me.

I told him I had to get the dinner, but I'd be back.

"Be back in a flash with the cash," he said.

"Aren't you in the mood for some food?" I said.

"Harriet's a poet and boy! does she know it!" he crowed.

I gave a controlled, regal wave of my hand to acknowledge this praise, and hurried to the old house.

Dinner went smoothly, the meat having thawed and cooked by itself, the potatoes and vegetables ready at the same time, courtesy of Maureen, so nobody had to wait for food, which was just as well. Mr. Daley had fixed the mower, but it had put him behind schedule, and the entire family was walking quietly and being very polite to each other, in order to reinforce Daddy's self-control.

I put the baby down for his nap in his parents' bedroom (old house) and I tucked Timmy into his crib in the room he inherited from Richard and Robert, over the living room (old house), and then I went up to see if Robert (new house) could get rich with my money. It turned out that my money is practically worthless.

"It's too new, Harriet," he said. "It's just worth its face value and that's all. See—1957, 1960, that's a Philadelphia—don't you have any old money stashed away anywhere?"

"Money doesn't stay by me long enough to get old," I told him.

"A 1916 D dime would be worth seventy-five dollars," he said. "Think what you could do with that money!"

"Just so long as my dimes are worth ten cents," I said, "I'm happy."

"Here comes Harriet in her mule-drawn chariot," he said absently, counting some common one-cent pennies.

I retorted, "If I had a choice, I'd drive a Rolls-Royce."

"Hurray for Harriet! She's got such a brain she can hardly carry it!" he shouted, and whooped with delight.

"That," I said, "does not scan."

"Free verse," he said with a grin.

I said, "Free verse is rarely terse."

"From bed to verse," he replied, and fell back among the pillows, stunned, as I told him, by his own *ver*satility.

: 37 :

Monday, June 12th

Last night, the night of June 11th, the eve of June 12th, there
was a *killing frost.*

(Sound the tocsin. Ring the bell. Vermont in June is cold as
Hell.)

I was still writing my notes of the events of yesterday and I was
wrapped in a blanket and had my coat on, but no gloves or mittens
—they would have been awkward—when I became aware of a
commotion outside. I could see lights in the vegetable patch, lights
moving around, and I could hear voices, a kind of chorus of hollering and lamenting and exclaiming over fate. Nobody called me,
but I went out anyway to see what was amiss.

Everybody was working desperately, right down to Mary age
five. They were lugging newspapers and bushel baskets and large
flowerpots and even metal wastebaskets, anything they could lay
their hands on. "Cover the tomato plants first," said Mr. Daley,
and we set baskets over the tomatoes—only fourteen inches high
and here it's nearly the middle of June!—and then we put tents of
newspaper along the rows of corn (four inches high) and an-
chored the edges with stones, which the garden has plenty of, God
knows. We spread newspaper over the cucumber vines (barely two
feet long) and over the melon and squash hills. And then we ran
out of materials.

"Never mind the damned beans, we can replant," said Mr. D.

"We always have too many beans, Daddy," Maureen said
soothingly.

"Harriet, let's fix some cocoa," said Mrs. Daley, watching her
husband as if he were a nervous horse. We all headed for the old
house. I could see my breath steaming as we went in past the
lighted doorway.

"I wish somebody would tell me why the devil I cut the hay,"
said Mr. Daley bitterly, "since we don't have facilities to quick-
freeze it."

Richard reported with gloomy relish, "Daddy, it's twenty-nine already! Do you suppose the pipes in the new house will freeze?"

"My Gawd!" said Mr. Daley.

"Be quiet, children, you'll wake Timmy," said Mrs. Daley, casting another anxious glance at her husband. She was washing her hands at the sink, like any field hand.

I had the cocoa hot, and as I filled the cups I tried to keep my teeth from chattering. Mrs. Daley fetched a bottle of rum from somewhere and added a couple of glop-glops to Mr. Daley's cup. Funny how the laws of physics affect humans inversely: hot rum and cocoa cooled him right down.

"Maybe we better drop our other projects and move the furnace," he said. "I don't think the pipes will freeze, but Harriet might. She's a tropical flower."

Maureen went upstairs to the storeroom and brought down her electric blanket.

"I only use it in the winter," she said graciously, thrusting it at me.

I was really touched, otherwise I would not have mentioned what was on my mind. "What about the car—is there any chance it might freeze?"

"We never take the antifreeze out," Mr. Daley said. "It's so hard to predict just which week we'll have summer."

Richard, Maureen, Mary and I went up to the new house. The stars were sharp and bright and everything was very still, the trees not moving, no bird making a noise. I could smell trouble. And in the morning the grass was white with frost. I had seen it before, I knew what it was: it was death, death to every young and growing thing. The color of death is not black, it is white.

Mrs. Daley was already getting breakfast. "I couldn't sleep," she said. "It's twenty-six outside. *Twenty-six!* Damnation!"

I said, "Is everything killed?"

"I'm not even going to look until the air has warmed up," she said. "Then I'll go uncover things and see what's left. The peas and carrots and cabbages and lettuce will probably be all right, anyway."

I fixed a tray for Robert, and took it up to the new house. Already the frost was vanishing under the risen sun. Only the shadows were still white. It looked strange, as if the world were suddenly seen in negative.

Robert told me he believes this is the beginning of another ice age.

"I'll not argue," I said.

"How fast is it coming?" Richard wanted to know. Richard needs a haircut, so he looks worried all the time—his hair stands up at the back of his head, reminding me of a portable radio—but this remark of Robert's really shook him.

"It should get here in about ten thousand years," said Robert.

"Last year we had a frost on the seventeenth of June," Richard said. "The squash vines looked like seaweed."

"Black and slimy," Robert said, digging happily into his cereal.

"Did you have to buy your food?" I said.

"Buy food—of course not! We replanted. But lots of things didn't have time to ripen. The corn was terrible, we didn't have enough to freeze any, and we had to pick all the tomatoes green. They tasted like store-bought. Mother said she didn't know why she bothered with a garden. She kept hollering damnation! and saying she wouldn't have one this year."

"But she didn't keep her word," Richard said. "This year's is bigger than last year's, and *we* have to weed it."

"*You* do," said Robert, "if I may say *ha*."

Richard said, "Louse!" and looked for something to use as a weapon. He picked up a sweatshirt (dirty).

"Never hit a one-legged man," I said. "It's bad luck."

But I wonder why anyone in this latitude does bother with a vegetable garden. The summer is simply too short to make it worthwhile. Nobody ever plants more than one crop of anything except possibly peas and lettuce, Mrs. D. says, and usually the second peas aren't worth much. And you can't grow sweet potatoes, or okra, or peanuts, or eggplant, or even decent melons—imagine eating a watermelon no bigger than a grapefruit!

At nine-thirty Mrs. Daley went out to the garden and started lifting baskets off tomatoes. I went out to help.

"I think they're all right," she said. "We were lucky. Look—you can see where the cold hit."

There was a streak down the center of the garden, of top leaves shriveled or drooping, and blackened, as if burnt, not frosted. Yet underneath these damaged leaves the plants looked healthy enough.

"Isn't it strange how the cold flows downhill like a river?" she said. We continued to uncover. "Squash okay. Cukes—oh, darn, these vines weren't all the way under! Oh, damnation! I forgot the pepper plants!"

I joined her at the foot of the slope. She was mourning a row of has-beens: ugly, misshapen leaves hanging limp around the foot-high stalks.

"I raised them from seed," she grieved. "I planted them in March, and coddled them, and nursed them. Never again!"

I preserved a sympathetic silence.

By noon the air was pleasantly warm. By three in the afternoon it was eighty-eight in the sun.

This way lies madness.

Tuesday, June 13th

Today I have been here one week. Seven days done, served, like seven days of a sentence. And so far I am satisfied with me. I have remembered all Mr. Carr's admonitions. I have minded my manners. I have indeed been the Noble Negro, never permitting an unsaintly thought to peep through a crack in my saintly exterior. "At all times let your behavior bear witness to the justice of our cause!" he cried, pacing back and forth on the platform, his eyes flashing, his voice ringing like a clarion. "Remember, whites think in stereotypes. If one of you steals, all Negroes are thieves! If one of you pulls some stupid, boneheaded stunt, all Negroes are dolts!

You are ambassadors of Afro-America! Be diligent and upright, mannerly and noble," et cetera. Well, that's me all right. But I'm not saying how long I can keep it up. It's a strain, maintaining this pose of perfection. And I'm not sure I *should*. I mean, is it right to feed the whites a lot of illusions about us? Or am I just getting awfully tired of walking around with what Mr. Carr seems to feel is the whole future of our people balanced on my halo? I mean, what if it slips?

I think I'll write Mr. Carr and ask if it's okay for me to take a day off, during which I can whine and complain and look messy and act lazy, like whites, when they feel that way, and not worry that by being human I'm sabotaging our struggle. One day of rest out of seven, like God. That's reasonable.

However, I am learning many things. I have learned that a tedder is a machine which is hitched to the rear of a tractor, where it behaves in the manner of a colt, kicking up the hay which is drying too much on the topside and not enough underneath. Definition courtesy of Maureen. Yesterday afternoon Maureen herself rode on the tractor and tedded the hay, while I washed the clothes and hung them on the line and got them in, and I looked after Timmy and John Anthony and started the supper, and Mary and Richard weeded, and Mrs. Daley dashed into town after groceries, more paint for the house, and a dozen pepper plants.

This morning Maureen went out and tedded Sunday's cutting (yesterday it was Saturday's cutting she was tedding). Then at noon Mr. Daley drove in like mad, took off tedder, put on rake, and drove out again. Mrs. Daley then went out on the tractor and raked Saturday's hay into long ribbons called windrows, and Maureen took a handrake and evened the corners, while I took care of Timmy and John Anthony and put sunburn lotion on Mary and did some ironing and started the supper. Richard was weeding. At five o'clock Mr. D. came driving in like mad, and he took off the rake and hitched on the baler, and went over the hill with the baler clattering behind the tractor, and everybody but Mr. Daley ate, and I took a tray to Robert, who wasn't saying *ha!* or anything like it, but was feeling sorry for himself. And then Mrs. Daley went to finish baling while Mr. Daley ate, and then he got out the hay truck and we all piled on, including John Anthony, and we rode over the hill and there in the field down by the woods were neat blops of greenish-beige, cubes of hay, and Mrs. D. had nearly finished baling, the baler chewing up the last few curling rows, depositing a bale behind it every now and then.

My job was to keep Timmy and John Anthony out of the way and safe, so we sat down in some ferns by the hedgerow and watched. Mary rode on top of the cab of the truck, drumming her heels and crowing. Richard was on the platform of the truck, and he was stacking, and Mrs. Daley was driving. Maureen was helping haul the bales over to within throwing distance, and Mr. Daley was hauling two at a time, and tossing them up to Richard. And over this whole scene of violent activity the peaceful evening light was glowing, and although it was cool, it was pleasant. There weren't even any mosquitoes.

And I thought, all they have to do to avoid all this is to buy their milk at the store. And I bet it would be cheaper.

Maureen tells me that today is a sample day in haying season. You just repeat today over and over, except some days you add mowing to everything else, and other days you "really hurry" because it looks like rain, and still other days it does rain, when you grieve, because the rain is taking all the nutrition out of the hay, and poor Pansy and Fern and Daffodil and Peony and Forsythia are not going to be happy about the taste of their hay next winter. The point is, you do this day after day until, maybe two weeks later, maybe three weeks, depending on the weather, the "first cutting" is in.

"And then in August we do it again," she said, "but it's worse, then, because the beans and everything are ripe and Mother is going mad trying to can and freeze and pickle and preserve a couple of million meals. Mother enjoys the haying in June, she says, but in August, she's tired."

My, my. I find it very hard, almost impossible, to feel sorry for them. Because they don't *have* to work like this. What ails them? Why don't they sell those fool cows and take it easy? For that matter, why do they live way out here at the end of nowhere? What are they running away from? And all the time pinning medals on themselves because of how hard they work.

My father didn't think there's any virtue in slaving like the very devil, but then, he really knew what hard work was. I remember setting his supper before him when he was too tired to eat, and I had to coax him.

Work you can quit whenever you've a mind to? That's nothing but child's play.

Sometimes these Daleys make *me* tired.

June 14th

Today was a red-letter day, all right: I got a letter from Hobart Gamaliel Carr. I would put a happy exclamation point after this statement, because any letter from Mr. Carr is better than none, except for two things: I have to admit I fished for this letter, he merely rose to my bait; and it's not really a letter at all, it's a sermon.

Why do I feel so superior to whites? Just because a bunch of schoolchildren didn't show the polish of professionals, must I preen myself that I'm Negro and they're White and aren't they mediocre? For goodness' sake, Miss Brown, says he, bear in mind how much you resent the whites' assumption of superiority, how furious it makes you that they think us an inferior race not fit to associate with them. Where is it going to get us if we Negroes, seeking equality, strive to achieve equality of faults as well?

Now just a minute, Mr. Carr! I say there's nothing wrong with thinking you're superior when you *are* superior. What I can't stand is for someone to think they're superior when they aren't. I don't say the white race is inferior to us, physically or mentally—that would be unintelligent of me, and prejudiced, too—I just say it's not superior. Culturally, I mean.

For one thing, white people are often filthy. You have only to sit near them in hot weather to notice it. And when they are poor, or even not so poor, they keep their houses in a shocking state. They don't wash up their dishes. They don't pick up their dirty clothes. I can name you half a dozen women—friends of Aunt Lydia's—who clean by the day in white folks' houses, and they all can tell you stories that would disgust a cat. As for slums, the only reason that nobody talks about white slums up here is because they're scattered in bits and pieces all over the countryside. If somebody were to gather up and put in one place some of the dooryards I've seen right here in Vermont, you'd have a slum that for trash, filth, rats, etc., would have Harlem beat by a mile. Right outside the village there's a place where the yard is just one huge, knocked-over trash can: papers blowing, cans and bottles everywhere, old boards tangled up with furniture they got sick and tired of and heaved out of the house, and now there's a sofa, its guts spilling out and rotting. The whole place looks as if they'd been bombed, or something. It's a mighty good thing whites are living there, because if they were Negroes, Mr. Carr, they'd set the Cause back another century.

And they—whites—don't look after each other, either. Think of the old people's homes packed and jammed with somebody's parents. Sure, it takes money to put your parents in such a place, and not many Negroes have that kind of money, but just the same, those places are full of white folks that nobody had enough *love* to take care of. Even if I have a million dollars some day, I'm not going to see Aunt Lydia in one. If she gets soft in the head and has to be looked after like a baby, I'm going to be the one to do it. She raised me, I'll take care of her.

You know the real trouble with whites? They don't know how to love. They have a terrible time enjoying themselves because they don't love *life*. Watch them dance sometime. God knows where they keep the beat. Listen to them sing. They don't *sing*, open up their throats and let it pour out, no, they just worry how they sound to somebody else. They don't love anybody or anything—not God, not being alive, not each other, not even themselves. Do you think anybody capable of loving himself could plot and plan and put a bomb where it would blow up little children? He *hated* himself. That's why he had to destroy somebody. He was a damn filthy white coward who hated his own guts and you tell me my problem is to forget what I've been learning ever since I've been born and you are *so* right, Mr. Carr.

That's my problem all right!

I don't want white people to touch me. I don't want to have to grieve over their griefs and I don't want to have to laugh when they're happy. And they needn't cry for me, either, or clap when I do well. I just want them to leave me—*me,* Harriet Brown—alone!

So now you have a sermon, too. Equal rights, Mr. Carr. Equal rights!

June 16th, Friday

Yesterday I had my first day off, and I didn't do much of anything except loll around in a lounge chair and read. I didn't feel like writing my daily report. Now and then I did do a bit of brooding about my impassioned reply to Mr. Carr's letter. I don't exactly regret anything I said but just the same I can't help wondering why the sight of pen and paper always goes to my head, dissolving my inhibitions. Maybe I want to be a writer. I wonder. I know it's unwise to put myself down on paper, yet there I go, baring my innermost feelings, things which if we were face to face I'd not say, not in words right out like that. And not just to Mr. Carr, but to everybody I care about—Josie, Aunt Lydia, everybody. When I'm with them I talk nonsense, froth, soap bubbles, but when I write them I act as if nobody is actually going to read what I'm writing, it's just between me and myself. And there I go, making a permanent record of the shriveled-up state of my soul.

Today it was raining and further introspection was out of the question. Mrs. D. said she would whiz into town and do her grocery shopping, since nobody could do anything about the hay. Naturally all the children wanted to go, and Mrs. D. said she couldn't manage unless I went, too, and so we all set out about nine o'clock, Maureen holding John Anthony and I holding Timmy. Mrs. D. said it is of "paramount importance" when driving with children that they each have a window to look out of. "Fresh air and a good view of the world," she said. "Remember that, Harriet, if you would avoid car sickness in the young."

"I have to get Robert some coin folders," Richard said. "Can I have my allowance, Mother? You owe me for three weeks."

"May I," she said.

"May I have mine and Robert's, too?"

Mrs. Daley muttered to herself.

"That's seventy-five cents for me and fifty for Robert," he went on. "Robert says you owe him for only two weeks."

"Owe, owe," she said. "I hate that word in connection with an allowance. Confound it, say you have it coming, but spare my feelings. Don't say I *owe* it. The only person I owe money to is Harriet—by the way, Harriet, how do you want to be paid?"

I wasn't sure what she meant. "Ma'am?" I said, that useful phrase when you're feeling your way.

"Do you want me to pay you every week, or all at once at the end of the summer?"

"Every week, please," I said, thinking what if there just doesn't happen to be any money at the end of the summer? My, my, what a shame!

"Check or cash?"

"Cash, please," I said.

"Checks are safer," said Maureen.

"Not everybody will cash checks," I said.

"Only government checks," Mrs. Daley said. "You know why you have no trouble cashing them? Because if you've stolen them or forged the signature or something, the FBI takes over, so the banks don't worry."

"I'll bet sometimes the banks hope you *have* stolen them," said Richard, "just so they can call the FBI. Wouldn't you like to call the FBI, Harriet?"

"My God, no," I said. If I were a Catholic I'd have crossed myself.

Richard started making urgent dialing noises.

"Hush," said Mrs. D. "Harriet, you stay in the car with Timmy and John Anthony. Maureen, you go with Richard to the dime store—"

"I don't need anybody with me," said Richard.

"You will do as you are told," said Mrs. Daley, "and without any discussion, for once. I'm going to the bank first, then I'll give you your money, Harriet, and when Maureen gets back, you can do any errands you may have."

That was the procedure. Mrs. D. returned shortly, and handed me an envelope with the bank's address printed on it, in which there had been slipped, modestly, two tens and a five. She then vanished on her grocery rounds, and after a while clerks began arriving with cartons of food. Finally Maureen and Richard returned, dripping, and I slipped out and scooted into the drugstore. I didn't need much, but I remembered I was nearly out of Silky-Strate, for one thing.

I wasn't the least bit worried about being waited on, because I figured storekeepers are the same North as South, happy to take your money. And right away a neat woman with a good figure came over and asked if she could help me.

"A jar of Silky-Strate, please," I said.

She looked as if she didn't understand. "What?" she said.

"Silky-Strate," I said.

"I'm not sure we have any," she said. "Just a moment while I ask." She went to the back of the store and spoke to a man in a tan cotton jacket. I was beginning to feel conspicuous, so I drifted towards the rear of the store, too.

"How do you spell it?" she said, turning to me.

"S-t-r-a-t-e," I said.

"We don't carry it," said the man. "What is it? Maybe we have something similar."

"It's hair straightener," I said.

You know how sometimes when you say something, just at that moment a silence has fallen so your voice rings out? Well, just as I spoke, one of those silences had fallen. Everybody in the store turned and stared at me, and at my head, and I felt wretchedly embarrassed, as if I had shouted out that I wanted some kind of birth-control stuff, or a cure for VD, or something.

"I'm sorry," said the man, "we don't carry any in stock. There's another drugstore next to the bank—maybe they have some."

"Thank you," I said stiffly. I started to leave. The woman followed me.

"We have all sorts of hair sprays, lacquers and so forth," she said. "Or brilliantine—you couldn't use anything like that?"

"I'm afraid not," I said. I wished she'd leave me alone.

"Try in Hanover, or Rutland," she said. "The shops there carry a much wider selection than we have any call for. The colleges, you know."

I thanked her and I hurried out to the car. Everybody was waiting for me.

"Did you find what you wanted?" Mrs. D. asked.

"No, ma'am," I said before I thought. "But it isn't important," I added hastily.

"We have plenty of time," she said.

"No, that's all right," I said.

"What did you want, Harriet?" said Maureen. "I bet I can find it for you."

Oh, the heck with it, I thought. "I wanted some hair straightener," I said clearly. "I don't think they carry it here."

"Hair *straightener?*" said Maureen. "Are you crazy? My goodness, Harriet, I've been living for years and *years* on the crusts of bread because when I was very young and impressionable I was told that if I ate my bread crusts some day my hair would be a mass of beautiful ringlets—"

"Instead of a mess," said Richard.

"Shut up," Maureen advised her brother. "*Yours* is so straight it

: 50 :

grows at right angles to your head. You look as if you're sending messages short-wave."

"Hush," said Mrs. Daley. She was backing cautiously out of the parking space. When she had shifted into forward, and we were moving safely out of town, she went on, "I have to go to Hanover next week, Harriet. I'll get you some there. Write down the name for me."

"I still think you are nuts," Maureen said with that frankness I do not find charming. "I'd give *anything* if my hair was curly!"

"Were curly," I said.

"I didn't say 'hairs,'" she said.

"I'm reminding you to use the subjunctive," I said, looking at her sleek, shiny, satiny stream of straight hair. "Contrary to fact."

"But *why* do you want to have straight hair?" Maureen persisted.

"It's the contrariness of human nature," said Mrs. Daley lightly, as if she were luring Maureen back down from a thin limb and hoped no one would notice her maneuver. "Harriet's hair is curly, so she wants it straight. Yours is straight, so you want it curly."

"And my skin is white as a fish's belly," said Maureen, "and every summer I can hardly *wait* to get a good tan!"

Silence.

Maureen turned around and caught my eye. She grinned. "Please pass the peroxide," she said.

We all burst out laughing. I don't know what the Daleys were laughing at—perhaps they were embarrassed—but I was delighted that Maureen would notice how absurd it is for whites to want more pigmentation, when they reject those who are born that way.

"In Vermont," Richard said, " 'suntanners' is a dirty word."

"It's all a matter of status," said Mrs. Daley. "There are places where a suntan in February means you are affluent enough for a winter vacation—"

"Or maybe you have a sunlamp," said Richard.

"That implies the time to use it," said Mrs. Daley. "Here in

Vermont people with leisure to tan their skins winter or summer are called 'suntanners' by the natives, because a suntan obviously implies its possessor is a worthless character who does not labor three hundred and sixty-five days a year. Not only does such a fellow do more loafing than he's entitled to, but he does it in such down-country ways, lolling on a beach, or even just stretching out in a pair of gaudy shorts on his terrace. He is, in other words, an outsider, a newcomer, a fellow likely to vote something in Town Meeting that might raise the taxes."

"Like a library for the school!" Maureen shifted John Anthony onto her other arm and turned around the other way. "Harriet, boy, are you lucky you're not going to be teaching here! We didn't get a library in our school until this year—imagine! It's in the basement—they had to divide off a section from where we eat our hot lunch—and listen to this! Mother was at a parents' meeting and one of the fathers, he was puffing on a cigarette, he looked through the glass door of the library at the shelves of books and he said to this friend of his who was standing there also puffing on a cigarette—the air was getting thicker and thicker, you could hardly breathe—he said, 'Look at all them God-damned books!' That's what he *said*," Maureen said, directing this last at Richard.

"I didn't say anything," Richard said.

"Well, don't think *I'm* swearing," Maureen said. "Then this father said, 'And they're putting another God-damned library in the school to the north of town. And in five years, they'll want some other God-damned thing, you'll see. Where's the money coming from, that's what I say.' And then he looked around and said, 'Where's an ash tray? Not a damned ash tray in the place.' And Mother said, sweet as honey, 'Why, they're only in the first grade. After we bought the books, we didn't have money enough for ash trays for *everybody*.'"

"And with that, Harriet, I tarred my name for good," said Mrs. Daley. "I've lived here nearly twenty years, but I'll bet I'm cussed as a suntanner from now on!"

"But Mother, you do get a suntan every summer," said Mary in a worried voice.

"Mine is an honorable tan," said Mrs. D. "It's very uneven. I get it standing on my head in the vegetable patch."

So now I know that strangers are mistrusted and resented in the North the same as in the South, and new ideas are unpopular all over. At least if they're thought up by somebody not born there. And maybe even then.

There is something so sinister about a new idea, you know. *Sinister*. Sneaking in from the *left*.

Do you suppose that's why so many new ideas are suspect, and thought to be Communist-inspired?

June 17th

Today was a normal Saturday here. Timmy came close to killing himself.

It happened like this: I thought I might get to cleaning the oven while John Anthony and Timmy took their naps. But what with one thing and another—the rain still raining and therefore ruining Mr. Daley's Saturday (he had planned to finish up one field and get another mowed, but he couldn't even ted up the hay he planned to bale, let alone bale it)—the rain, and the mud tracked in, and the wet clothes (Richard and Maureen helped their father string the wires for the peas and put up the tomato stakes)—well, I did not get around to cleaning the oven and I had the jar out ready. And I was getting supper, and was working at the sink peeling potatoes, so my back was to the room, when I heard Timmy start to cry.

I turned around and oh Lord! There he was standing on a chair by the counter and he was holding the jar of oven cleaner in one hand and the top in the other and tears were rolling down his face and his mouth was in an O like a fish mask.

"Don't swallow," I said, a sopping-wet towel appearing in my hand without my knowing how it got there. I wiped his lips. "Stick out your tongue." I didn't see anything on there but I wiped it anyway. "Don't swallow, Timmy," and I had him under my arm

: 53 :

and at the sink and I was filling a glass and I said, "Swish this around and spit it out."

His mother stood in the doorway.

"Now let's wash again," I said, relieved that he had stopped crying and was doing just as he was told.

"What is it? What did he get into?"

"Lye," I said.

"We don't have any lye," Mrs. Daley said.

"Oven cleaner," I said. "I left it there on the counter."

She was looking Timmy over very carefully. "I don't think he got any in his mouth," she said. "There are a couple of little burns on his lips—let's wash you again, Timmy—but inside he seems all right."

"I just tasted it," Timmy said, when he could talk, and he burst into tears.

"Now stop crying," his mother said. "Nobody's mad at you." She hugged him and kissed him. "Thank goodness you were right here, Harriet."

I was screwing the top on the jar. A fat lot of good I did being here, I thought. Not ten feet away, and that child ate poison.

"I should have warned you about Timmy," she said. "Once he drank half a bottle of ink—"

"All children get into things," I said stiffly. "I left that jar there, and I blame myself." I wished she wouldn't be so confoundedly decent about it, all graciousness—as if all I'd done was to spill the milk.

"I'm thankful you were so quick and so calm," she said.

Oh, sure, the big hero, I thought. Harriet Brown, genius. And I knew I was being childish, but I wished she'd cuss me out, because then I wouldn't be so mad at myself but could even be mad at her for being unreasonable, because Heaven knows I wasn't loafing! And then I felt resentful that she should be so very clever she didn't cuss me out, thus leaving all my guilt feelings unrelieved. And now that I figured some reason to be mad at somebody else, I felt better.

This morning was wet and shining, the rain over and the sun up very early, and everything sopping and sparkling and bright. Nothing would be ready in the fields before noon at least, and probably not then, so Mrs. D. put a roast in the oven and left instructions with Maureen how to proceed, and she and I set off alone for church. I had not thought to provide myself with any gloves, but I felt like a lady just the same. It restores the self-esteem not to work on Sunday morning. The Lord knew what He was doing, all right, when He said to rest on His day.

We were late. The choir was already filing into its stalls up in front when we came in. There were people in the pew where we sat last week, so we had to sit on the other side, way up front. Being that near the choir, and therefore being surrounded by more noise during the hymns, and also not feeling so strange because this wasn't my first time, I did some singing, too, and enjoyed myself. I noticed Mrs. Daley was also singing away. I could barely hear her, but she seemed to have a fairly good voice for a white woman. It was thin, no body, but at least she was on key and she didn't drag. The choir was inclined to be just behind the beat, so when the service was over and they were walking out, using the aisle that crossed just in front of us, I thought I'd help them, encourage them even, and I enjoyed myself some more.

On the way out, Mrs. Daley and I were at the tag end of the line shaking hands with the minister. When it was my turn, he said, "Harriet Brown! *You* are going to save our choir! You will sing in the choir, won't you? My dear child, we need you! I'm counting on you. Rehearsals at seven-thirty on Thursday evenings. Don't say no—you can't refuse! Make a joyful noise unto the Lord, you know!"

What could I say?

"Kate!" said the minister, dropping my hand and seizing Mrs. Daley's. "You will bring her to choir practice, won't you? Just an hour, you know. And on Sundays be here at ten-thirty. Now don't say you're too busy, Kate. You know you can find the time."

Mrs. Daley looked at me. "Would you like to sing in the choir, Harriet?"

I said I would like to.

"Very well, I'll bring my mending," she said, in anything but a hearty tone.

I said doubtfully, "I'm afraid I would be imposing on you, Mrs. Daley." I didn't want her blaming me if she got further behind in her work.

"No, Harriet," she said, "I would never feel right about it if you gave up the choir because of me. Besides, here in Vermont it so often seems that what looks at first glance to be difficult or downright impossible, in the end turns out to have been very, very important. So don't worry about the time it takes to ferry you back and forth. It will all prove to be most worthwhile, you'll see."

And that's how it happens that this entry is being written by a member of the choir of St. Michael's-in-the-Fields.

I'm glad I didn't buy any gloves. It would have been a waste of money. Choir robes are provided.

June 21st, Wednesday

This is the longest day of the year.

It certainly was!

The sun came up at five-oh-four Daylight Saving Time, and it hasn't set yet (it's nearly nine o'clock). And from morning until evening we were haying, haying, haying, and I was helping, too, because it simply had to get done. Mr. Daley actually took the day off from work, and was here all the time to help. That meant some brisk phoning after breakfast to caution two or three summer-people families not to look for him. And we brought in 489 bales, which is about 300 too many for one day, Mr. Daley said. And I am exhausted, Mrs. Daley is exhausted, Mr. Daley is exhausted, everybody is exhausted except Maureen, who is Above Exhaustion, she told me.

What I did, I helped drag bales to the truck, and I helped stack bales in the barn. Mary did not ride on the truck cab, she took care of Timmy, and John Anthony was in his playpen in the ferns. We ate when we could, snatching sandwiches and pitchers of lemonade and pitchers of milk, and hardly even sitting down to eat.

But the hay is safely in, and if it rains tomorrow, who cares? Richard keeps count of the bales, he says we have a total of 769 now, or fifteen and a half tons, enough for more than seven cows (Jerseys). There is one more field to cut, from which Mr. Daley hopes to get about 300 bales. And this will give him enough hay for the cows he has, and the calves he expects to have, to carry them through the winter. So the hay they cut in August—the rowen, it is called—they can sell. Or maybe save, against a drought next year.

"If gambling is a sin, Harriet," said Mr. D., "then all farmers are sinners."

"Life is a gamble," I told him, "and we are all sinners."

"Do they preach hell-fire in your church, Harriet," he said, "the way they do in mine?"

"What do you know about what they preach in your church?" said Mrs. Daley. "You never go."

"That's because I'm counting on your prayers, Kate," he said, "to keep me out of trouble."

I had a feeling he was teasing but she wasn't.

"Oh, yes, we hear about hell-fire right along," I said. "Reverend Douglass really loves to elaborate on it—you can practically hear the crackle of flames."

"Well, Harriet, you are now singing in the choir of a church that debunks Hell," said Mr. Daley. "I am informed that the Episcopalians claim Hell, the whole concept of Hell, is the result of a bit of shoddy scholarship on the part of some scribes."

"Hell," said Mrs. Daley, her face pink, "was actually the city dump, Harriet. It was the place outside Jerusalem where the trash was burned, hence 'eternal fires' and so on."

"Kate, what are you doing?" said Mr. D. "Harriet is a good

Christian girl and you're trying to tell her she isn't going to burn forever. What kind of talk is this? She'll think you're a heathen."

"Tom, you are impossible," said Mrs. Daley, and she was laughing.

We went back to throwing bales around. Each bale weighs about fifty pounds, so after a while we were just walking around like pieces of machinery ourselves, our eyes glazed. And I got to thinking that if Reverend Douglass ever were to hear there isn't any Hell, not only would he be terribly disappointed, but also he'd be somewhat at a loss for something to preach about.

"That would leave him only Heaven," I said, the next time we were all pouring lemonade into us. "He'd have nothing for contrast."

"He'd still have hell on earth," said Mr. Daley. "Considering where you live, that should give him plenty of scope."

Richard's hair almost crackled. *"Where* does Harriet live?" he demanded. "Daddy—where does she *live?"*

"Well, it's hot there," I said, "but that probably isn't what your father meant."

"Hell here on earth, Richard," said Mrs. Daley, "means a denial of God, not knowing Him, not loving Him, and therefore not obeying Him."

Mr. Daley was looking in the sandwiches to see which had the raw onions. (I have seen him peel and eat a raw onion as if it were an apple, this at 10 P.M. and Mrs. Daley giving him a funny look.) "Don't you ever get the feeling that your concept of the God of Love is too tame?" he remarked. "Let's revive the Devil, Harriet, that ought to spark things up a bit. Let's disguise him as a ranting segregationist—"

Wow, I thought to myself. Reverend Douglass, you're back in business.

"A bomb-thrower?" I said.

"Now, Harriet, don't underestimate the Devil," said Mr. Daley. "He doesn't throw the bomb into the church, he doesn't unleash the dogs on the crowd, he doesn't even jeer at the children going into the integrated kindergarten. *Hell* no, Harriet. He doesn't do the *work*. He's the fellow who whispers in their ear that they're better, better than the blacks, who fans their pride. There's your eternal flames of Hell, Kate, my dear. Pride burning away, corroding and scarring, purifying nothing."

He swirled the ice cubes around in his glass and said, "End of oration. What did you kids put in this lemonade, anyway?"

"Nothing," said Maureen. "Honest, Daddy, I wouldn't dream of spiking a working man's lemonade with liquor!"

"I should live to see the day," said Mrs. Daley, "when an Irishman needs an excuse for a speech." She was smiling at her husband and her eyes were soft. "I like your mind," she said. "I always have."

"I know, that's why you married me," said Mr. Daley. "Because of my brilliant mind, keen, profound, illuminating, yet rational withal." He stood up and hauled her to her feet. "Back to work, woman. God knows you didn't marry me for my money."

"With all what, Daddy?" said Richard. "Rational with all what?"

"Oh, Lord," his father groaned. He rubbed Richard on the head. "Befuddling my own son. I should be ashamed. And I am. I suffer from lack of sophrosyne, Richard; you'll just have to put up with it."

"What's soff-roz-in-ee?"

"Knowing when enough's enough," his father said.

That *no one* has on this farm. Not even the sun! It did finally set, and the dusk is fading. But it's ridiculous—it's nearly eleven o'clock!

June 22nd

Today was my day off, and I began it by writing another letter to Mr. Hobart G. Carr, who has not, as yet, replied to my blast-off of last week, an unfortunate circumstance, because I was in fine fettle mentally right after breakfast and probably could have zipped off some brilliant and incisive replies to whatever rebuttal he makes. However, I took advantage of the excellent mutual communications the various parts of my brain were having, and I drew up a report on my observations (so far) of the attitudes toward the Negro of natives of this particular Northern state—Caucasian natives, that is, and all Am. Indians will kindly not gnash their teeth.

It is my impression, Mr. Carr, said I, that the attitude of the Northern whites is more or less neutral. Of course, from what I've seen of Vermont so far, there simply aren't enough of us in this area to arouse any of the Southern white's "stay back—don't crowd us" attitude. I suspect that if the white people where I am now treat our race with normal Christian decency (whatever *that* is!) it may be merely a matter of Virtue Untempted Is Virtue Untried. It is far too soon, I said, to give them any credit for their civilized behavior. Let's wait and see what happens when the Negroes, too, are affluent enough to want summer places in the country, or camps to send their children to while they gad about Europe.

And all this I embellished with what wit I was able. It is a joy to write to a man whose brain is not something that has to be treated with condescension. It is so boring to talk to stupid men; they resent female brains and you have to pretend all the time that you don't have any, otherwise you alienate them and they don't pay your way into the movies or buy you a dinner. Women have to be so two-faced to get along in this world, unless they are fantastically lucky and are corresponding (face to face or merely by letter) with a man with a brain that functions. No matter how much I disagree with Hobart Gamaliel Carr when he is expounding on the morality and wisdom of Non-Violence (in class I used to sit there, silent and furious, and say to myself, oh *do* shut up, Mr. Hit-Me-Again-Harder-Harder!), I can't help feeling fascinated by his mind. Sometimes when he was lecturing it was like a whirlpool sucking me under.

Naturally I didn't let any hint of this creep into my letter, because none of this is any of Mr. Carr's business. I'm not angling for a meal or a movie, just a meeting of the minds. I wanted to end on an impersonal note which at the same time he really ought to answer (Harriet Brown, Machiavelli!), so I asked him to explain Mr. Daley, to interpret him, as it were, as an atypical white male. Mr. Daley obviously has a good education, and he is really gifted in architectural design, judging by the folder in the new house living room. (This folder is full of his drawings, very exact, to scale, and crisply clean, of doorways and the edges of roofs and so on.) So what is he doing shoveling manure? I don't get it.

After mailing H.G.C.'s letter, I thought I'd spend the rest of the morning entertaining Robert. We have all been so busy, he has been left alone a lot of the time. I found him in good spirits, his leg propped on a pillow as required by the doctor, his bed covered with a drift of papers, and enough books on the floor to cheer a future teacher like me.

"Give me a man who reads," I said.

"God, Harriet!" he said. "This stuff is fantastic! Listen to this— it's one of Richard's lessons—listen: 'Ted hasn't any feet. Betty hasn't any face. Bob has no hands. May hasn't any nose.' " He crowed with delight. "*What* an essay! God! There's more—listen: 'Tom hasn't any eyes. Bill hasn't any ears. Sally hasn't any mouth. Dick hasn't any feet.' Oh, I *love* it!"

"What on earth?" I said, and I took the paper. At the top was printed laboriously: RICHARD DALEY, NOV. 10, CONTRACTIONS.

"Here's some more," Robert said. "This is dated May fifth. It's called 'My Classmates,' only he spelled it with one *s* and no *e*— 'Clasmats'—God! Listen, it's *great:* 'My clasmats are very inturest- ing. One of my clasmats smokes a sigar and can drive a tractor.' Remember, Harriet, when he wrote this Richard was in the second grade! 'Another of my clasmats brings sardin sandwiges for his lunch. And sometimes he brings crunched potato chip sandwiges. Finaly I have a clasmat a girl who is home sick because her brother walked in his sleep and jumped up and down on her stomik.' He did, too, Harriet, I know the guy—"

"School is not dull for Richard, I gather," I said.

"Oh, he loves school. His teacher played marbles with the kids at recess, played for keeps, but he's a lousy player so they were always winning their marbles back."

"Back?" I said.

"Yeah, if a marble falls on the floor during school time, the teacher takes it. That's how he gets his to play with."

I told him this struck me as an unconventional approach to pedagogy, but not one to be condemned. I then said his mother was going into Hanover that afternoon, and wished to know if he had any errands.

"Within reason, she specified," I said.

"Some kind of magazine on coin collecting, anything she can find. And Harriet, ask her to hang onto her change. You know, pay with a dollar bill."

I nodded. "Feed the till with a dollar bill," I said, agreeably.

The mail came, and in it was a snappy word of cheer from H. G. Carr that made me glad I'd written him my witty missive of the morning. Next time I get to lamenting, quoth Carr with tongue conspicuously in cheek, that I never have a really relaxing day off, when I can let down my hair lest I let down the Cause, I'm not to envy God that He could rest on the seventh day—I'm to remind myself that even He didn't rest until He got the job done.

Oh, funny.

Mrs. D. left for town after lunch and I refused an invitation to go along. I thanked her but I had some letters to write, I said. So in the afternoon I sat in the lounge chair and wrote to several of my *clasmats*. Maureen came up to me, plopped herself on the grass, and remarked that that chair was her father's. "Mother had us children give it to him for Father's Day two years ago," she said. "She bought it and had us put our names on the card."

"Maybe I ought not to sit in it?"

"Why not? *He* never does. I think he sat in it for five minutes, to test it, when he got it. He hasn't had time since."

"He ought to take time," I said.

"My father gets nervous doing nothing," Maureen said.

I wonder if it's the climate. Nobody sits still up here. I never see old folks rocking on the porch, or sitting on a bench anywhere. Maybe everybody keeps on the move all the time so they won't freeze. So far, not once has the day been warm enough for me to enjoy loafing. The sun is warm, but there's always a breeze down my neck. I use my sweater for a windbreak.

"Your father is a very unusual man," I said.

"Mother says there's nobody like him, just nobody at all," Maureen said. "Sometimes when she says it, it's because she loves him—you mustn't think she doesn't, just because she gets mad at him—and sometimes, of course, she is mad when she says it and she means the opposite. Do you understand what I mean?"

"Certainly," I said. "You could hardly be more clear. But what I meant was, it seems to me this is a strange part of the world for your father to choose to live in, with his abilities and education and all."

"Harriet, sometimes I just don't understand you. Where *else* would Daddy want to live? The United States is the best country in the world to live in, isn't it? And Vermont is the best state, and this is the best hill in Vermont, and Daddy is building us the best house on this hill." She rolled over on her stomach and propped her chin in her hands. "That's what Daddy says, and I am a dutiful daughter and I believe him. Mother, of course, tells it differently. She says Daddy really does like the human race, no matter what he claims. She says it's just that he doesn't like the individual members of the human race that he comes across. Except for us, of course."

"I don't know," I said doubtfully, "it seems to me he's a friendly man."

"Only when he chooses to be," Maureen said. "Vermont is full of people, Mother says, who moved here just so they could hold the human race at arm's length."

"That I can well understand," I said. "Arm's length is minimum. Personally I prefer a ten-foot pole."

"Why stop at ten feet?" she said.

"Good grief, I can't afford one made-to-order," I said. "Poles for not touching things come in ten-foot lengths, don't you know anything?"

She grinned. "I think I'll call you Ann Throw-pee," she said. I stared. *"Miss* Ann Throw-pee, if I must be formal," she explained. "What's the matter—did I say something I shouldn't? That's a joke of Daddy's."

"I'm relieved," I said. "Most eleven-year-olds don't make up jokes like that."

"Oh, is it naughty?"

"No, it is not naughty," I said. "It's Greek—I think."

"You don't want me to make up jokes in Greek?"

I didn't know whether to be exasperated or amused. "Not right now," I said, "because at the moment I am off duty."

Maureen rolled over on her back and stared up at the branches overhead, while I finished my letter to Josie and started one to Aunt Lydia. Maureen's lips moved now and then, and finally I said, "What's the matter?"

"I have thunk up a poem," she said. "It's for you. It's your theme song. Want to hear it?"

"Certainly," I said.

"You have to say 'please' to poets," she said.

"Please," I said.

"It's called 'Day Off,' " she said. "It goes like this:

> Don't pester me with puns
> Or dazzle me with wit—
> I poke you with my ten-foot pole
> And wish that you would flit.

What do you think of it?"

"Not very flattering," I said, "but perceptive."

"If I don't say anything may I stay here?"

"Certainly," I said, and she didn't say anything, and I finished my letter to Aunt Lydia and started one to a *clasmat* working in

Connecticut. And Mrs. Daley came back from Hanover with a coin book for Robert and an expression of regret for me.

"No Silky-Strate anywhere, Harriet," she said. "Everybody wanted to sell me brilliantine. I said no, it wouldn't do. They offered to put in a special order, but it would take four to six weeks, they said."

I said it wasn't important, please to forget it. I said I could put a postscript on Aunt Lydia's letter, she wouldn't mind to send me some.

After supper, a very early supper, Mrs. Daley took me to choir practice. It was in a room to the rear of the church, the Sunday-school room, I suppose. On a table there was set up the Cross and candles, the way they are on the altar in the church itself. There was a piano in one corner of the room, and small chairs in a circle in another, and the rest of the room was filled with folding chairs, the kind that are hitched together in twos and threes. The members of the choir—four men, three women, and five young girls about fifteen years old—had provided themselves with hymnals from a stack on a bookshelf near the door. I took one, and sat down near the choir, and Mrs. Daley sat apart from us, and worked on her mending, like a duenna.

The rehearsal went all right, in general. The leader of the choir seemed to know his music. He was a little man with straight flat hair and bright brown eyes, and he made no speech of welcome beyond, "Hi, glad to have you," and then he started right in on the anthem for next Sunday. We worked on that for about half the time, and the rest on the processional and a couple of responses he wasn't satisfied with.

The leader did ask me as he was passing out the music for the anthem if I could read music and I said I could. He also asked what I sang, and I said alto, first alto usually, and everybody kind of laughed, and one of the young girls said, "Hurray for our side!" It turned out she had been the only alto in the choir until I came. So we sat together.

We worked on phrases, and so forth, and then we started to

sing it through, and suddenly the choir leader stopped and we waited and he said to me, "Miss Brown, have you ever done any choral work before?" I said I had. He said, "Well, then, you know it is important to keep everything in balance. Please don't sing out as if you are singing solo. Hold your voice to the level of the rest of the choir, please."

I didn't say anything, but I thought, good grief, I *am* holding it in.

When the rehearsal was over, he thanked us abruptly, grabbed his music, said he'd see us at ten-thirty Sunday and everybody be on time for once, and he left.

The other alto told me he lived miles away, up in Royalton or somewhere. She then started introducing the rest of the choir, but I don't remember any of the names, I'm afraid I wasn't listening. I was looking at the various members and thinking what they looked like, each so different, assorted, like an old-time *Saturday Evening Post* cover.

One of the basses, a white-haired man with the profile of an eagle, said very courteously, "I do hope you enjoy singing with us, Miss Brown. As much as you are allowed to sing, of course." He appeared to be thinking of a joke, and he began to chuckle. "The altos now outnumber the sopranos by two to seven," he said.

June 23rd

Today I received Mr. Carr's letter, and this time I don't get a sermon—no, nothing so adult. This time I get a scolding. Naughty Harriet, don't you know you're not non-violent? Naughty naughty.

Well, not in those precise words, but that was the idea.

Damn and blast. I cannot imagine why he thinks I am not completely aware that I am *not* non-violent. I know very well I am not non-violent! How can I be? I try very hard, but I do not love my enemies. All right, so I don't try very hard. But I don't love them, and that's a fact.

Why should I? They don't love each other, do they? I thought I pointed that out to him.

And I do wish he wouldn't give me that bit about love-is-not-love-if-it-has-to-be-earned. I know God loves us and we don't deserve it, et cetera, but why shouldn't He? Parents love their children and they don't deserve it, either. And also I am not God, I am only Harriet Brown, born nineteen years ago in the White Man's South. I Know My Place, thank yo' kindly, suh, but I'm not going to live there. And I don't think it makes very much difference how I feel, how *non*-non-violent I am inside, as long as I *act* nonviolent.

As far as I am concerned, that goes for everybody. I don't care a hoot whether or not they want me in the front of the bus, I just want to sit down wherever there's a seat.

Parenthetical thought: What about you, Mr. Carr? I mean, what are you, a teacher or a preacher? Or is it impossible to be one without the other?

June 24th

Today was Robert's second try at having a summer vacation. We took him in to have the cast removed, and the wound inspected, and it appeared that everything is healing nicely. At any rate, the cast came off according to schedule, and a long, wound-around bandage went on, and Robert received permission to move about as long as he didn't use his leg. He will be on crutches for three or four weeks, depending on his speed of healing.

I went along on this expedition because today is Saturday and therefore Mr. Daley is mowing. Maureen can keep an eye on John Anthony in his playpen, but Timmy is something else again, especially when there is machinery busy. So Timmy went along, and Richard, and Mary, and Mrs. D. would need someone to supervise them while she and Robert saw the doctor, and so I got to ride into town.

Afterwards everybody had to go to the snack bar and have ice cream cones. It was to be a real celebration. While we were sitting there and I was mopping Timmy's front and Richard was warning Mary of the inevitable consequences if she bit off the bottom of her cone (he was right, of course), Mrs. Daley wanted to know if there was anything I had in mind to get, now that I was in town. I spoke out and said yes, I had been thinking I'd like to do some crocheting, I'd make her a doily if she liked. "One of those full ones, all ruching," I said. "You keep adding and adding more and more and it gets fuller and fuller until it stands up in a kind of wreath—have you ever seen one?" She said she had not. "My Aunt Lydia showed me how," I said. "They're very pretty."

Mrs. Daley said she'd love to have something that I had made, and that she'd be glad to get the crochet thread if I'd do all the crocheting, and I was relieved when she mentioned buying the thread herself because it takes a large amount, maybe more than five dollars' worth, and five dollars to spend on the Daleys I do not have.

So I went to the dime store and bought, with her money, four big balls of thread, enough to get well started. And then we headed for home, everybody feeling very merry and well satisfied with our existence at that moment.

We came the short way, over the mountain and along the brook, and then sharp over a rickety bridge and up the ridge road. We were all caterwauling like lonesome coyotes, "I Want to Hold Your Ha-a-a-a-and," Timmy pretending he had a guitar, everybody very gay, when we went over a rise in the road and there, smack dab in front of the car, not thirty feet away, were two little pigs.

Mrs. Daley slammed on the brakes. The little pigs kept trotting towards us, for all the world like two children sent on an errand, side by side and very businesslike.

"Those are our pigs!" Mrs. Daley gasped, and she leaped out of the car. "Heavens! That's next winter's pork! Harriet—don't let them get away!"

I had got out on the other side, and Richard was piling out, and Mary, and the pigs took fright and dashed up the bank and scampered through some young pines, and Richard and I were right after them.

I could hear Mary commence to wail, and Mrs. Daley urging her to hush, and then Richard and I had crashed through the pines and out into the open. There were the pigs at the other side of the clearing, heading for the woods, which were thick and dark with hemlocks close together. We raced on and I was getting winded and then we were thrusting ourselves into the woods, and the branches low down were all dead and scratchy and it was impossible to look ahead, you had to have your arms across your face. My dress caught on a broken branch and Richard was yipping as his bare arms met a defensework of dead branches. And we stopped.

"Listen!" I said. We could hear scamperings further on. "Come on!" I said, and tore myself loose, and off we went again, scrunched over low, now, and crawling under the worst of the thickets of branches. I had no idea how I was going to latch onto those pigs if I should catch up with them. I was simply blindly racing after "next winter's pork."

Now we were scrambling up the mountain, it was getting steeper and steeper, and every time we stopped, we could hear something racing on ahead. Richard was sobbing for breath and my chest hurt. On we drove ourselves, until we burst out of the trees and there we were in a kind of clearing. It was half grown over with berry bushes, with vicious thorns and canes intertwined, all loaded with white blossoms and very pretty (if your eyes weren't pounding with blood in your eyeballs) and humming with bees, as we could hear after we stopped rasping and gasping in our throats.

"Enough," I gasped. "I can't go on."

"We can *never* get them out of here," Richard said. "This is Boulder Hill blackberry patch, and nobody can get in. We just pick around the edges. They could stay in there forever."

"What's beyond it?" I said. "Maybe those pigs went straight on through."

"Let's go back," he urged. "There's *nothing* over the hill, just scenery. And beyond that is Massachusetts, and beyond that is the Atlantic Ocean. It's *hopeless.*"

I asked him if he knew the way back, and he said he did. We made our way painfully down, down, down, and then we could hear voices, and we were in the clearing and then through the pines, and there was the car.

"Harriet! My goodness!" said Mrs. Daley. "Richard! You're a wreck!"

We were, too. Our clothes were snagged and my legs and arms and Richard's arms—the lucky boy was wearing jeans—were crisscrossed with scratches, and one of my sandals had a broken strap.

"They got away," said Richard.

"No kidding," Robert said.

"Shut up," Richard said.

So in anything but a jolly mood we drove the rest of the way home.

Just as we pulled into the lane, Mr. Daley came up from the field on the tractor, the mower bar hitched high, giving it a jaunty, triumphant look.

Mrs. Daley leaped out and said, "Tom! Our pigs are loose! They got away! We couldn't catch them, they're loose on Boulder Hill!"

"You don't say." He looked at Richard and me. "Were you two the search party?"

"Tom! For heaven's sake don't just *sit* there, those pigs will get clean away!"

Mr. Daley dismounted calmly, and walked toward the pigpen. Mrs. Daley, simmering like a teakettle, trotted after him. "I'm not chasing any pigs I'm not positive are my own," said Mr. Daley, and he looked in the pigpen. "Well, ours aren't in here, anyway," he said.

"Is that a fact, now?" said Mrs. Daley, dripping ice. "Why don't we gamble a few minutes of our time, then, on the off chance that the two pigs loose in the neighborhood just might possibly be *our* pigs that are not in their pigpen?"

"Kate, don't always be so emotional," said Mr. Daley. "Richard, get a couple of grain sacks while I get a bucket of mash. Who's coming on the Great Pig Pursuit?"

It turned out we all were, including Maureen and John Anthony. We all piled into the car, practically in layers, Mr. Daley driving, Mrs. Daley sitting next to him but not speaking. I unwound a bit of twine from one sack and tied my sandal securely. Just beyond where we had met our errant porkers, Mr. Daley turned into an opening in the hedgerow and set the brake.

Everybody, with a few exceptions, got out.

"Fan out," said Mr. Daley. "Don't make any more racket than you have to. If you hear the pigs, stand still, don't charge after them, just call me and I'll come and catch them."

That I would like to see, I thought. Who does he think he is, Jesse Owens?

We spread out and started cautiously forward. I hadn't got halfway across the first clearing when Maureen sang out, from somewhere in the hemlocks on my right, "Here they are, Daddy! Here they are!"

Mr. Daley cut across the clearing, still lugging the pail of mash, and when he neared the edge of the woods he called to Maureen, softly, to come on out, and she did, on a crouch.

Mr. Daley went to the edge of the woods and began making noises. *Slurp slurp slurp slurp* he went, for all the world like a hungry pig with its nose in a well-filled trough. *Slurp slurp slurp* . . . We could hear something bounding around in the shadows. *Slurp slurp slurp slurp smack smack smack* . . . and out came a little pig.

"Take the pail, Maureen," said Mr. D. softly, as the little pig came forward, sniffing, grunting, poking here and there . . . *slurp smack yumyum* . . . Oh, there's the pail! And he put his nose into the mash, and snatch! Mr. Daley grabbed at him—almost missed—caught his two hind legs—what a shrieking and squealing! What a wriggling and squirming! It was so exciting, Maureen and I were clapping our hands and dancing about as if we were demented.

"Hang on, Daddy! Hang on!" cried Maureen.

The little pig's forelegs were going like parts of a machine, and forward he went, like a wheelbarrow, his rear legs hoisted high, the pig and Mr. Daley flying over the ground towards the car, Mr. Daley kind of bent over, naturally, and with an intent look of concentration on his face.

"Kate, get a sack!" he gasped, his face maroon with exertion. He and Pig One made a couple of turns around the car at triple speed while Mrs. Daley snatched a sack and held it open. Mr. Daley then aimed the front end of Pig One towards the sack, and Mrs. Daley and I eased it over him, like a huge sock going on a frantic foot, and "Got him!" cried Mr. Daley, tying the end of the sack with a self-knot.

The sack began to leap and gyrate about. It shrieked and squealed without ceasing.

Mr. Daley and I heaved that animated sack into the rear of the station wagon, and Robert was to guard it with his crutch—make sure, that is, that the sack didn't spiral itself right out again and away to freedom. John Anthony and Timmy retreated into the front seat, from which point of safety they stared with round and horrified eyes at the shrilling sack.

The rest of us went back to try to locate Pig Two.

We had no luck at all. Our tactics had been faulty. We never should have left the rest of the mash unguarded. The pail was now empty, and a well-satisfied little pig refused to be lured into sight, no matter how we grunted, no matter how we snuffled and snorted.

At last the hunt was called off and we drove home. After all, we hadn't had any lunch. As Robert said plaintively, what would be the point in worrying about next winter's food if we let ourselves starve now?

The pigpen was inspected and the escape route, a kind of shallow ditch burrowed under the bottom board of the fence, was closed up with a rock, and Pig One was released into his yard, where he trotted about lonesomely, snuffling to himself about the hopelessness of it all.

During lunch I could hear a good deal of gloomy talk about how there was now approximately thirty-five dollars' worth of pork loose on Boulder Hill, if it still *was* on the hill, and hadn't headed south to cross the state line, or north towards Canada. This was spiced with a few comments from Mrs. Daley about how essential it is not to dilly-dally around when facing an emergency: the first few minutes are worth hours later, she said pointedly, whether you're fighting a fire or just trying to recapture a couple of pigs.

"What a woman to harbor a grudge!" said Mr. Daley. "Just because I didn't fly into hysteria at the news our pigs were out—"

"You were insulting, actually," said Mrs. Daley. "You were obviously sneering at my intelligence—"

"Kate, my God, must you be so conventional?" Mr. Daley said. "Just like all beautiful women, you constantly crave praise for your brain!"

"Some day your timing will be thirty seconds off," said Mrs. Daley, "and no matter how you sweet-talk me, I'll *stay* mad."

"I'm so glad you don't go in for clandestine quarreling," Maureen said. "This way we don't miss anything."

I thought to myself this wasn't much of a quarrel, but if it was the best they could do, I'd have to make the most of it. I realized I was enjoying hearing them quarrel—if that's what they were doing—because I guess I haven't had much experience where there's a whole family, woman and man, I mean. I remember my father, of course, although I didn't know him very long, and then he was such a long time dying, and you couldn't really call any of it normal, or following a normal pattern, as they say in Sociology. Which of my friends had a father, I mean a real father, not just a man who begot her? Nobody. I couldn't think of anybody. A man who went off in the morning to his work, and came home proud of himself and with money in his pockets, and his wife glad to see him and his kids hopping around, waiting to hug him, the way the Daley children do when their father comes home. I couldn't think of anybody who had this kind of family, that I knew. So I find myself sucking on the edges of the Daley family life. I'm not proud of this, but I can't seem to help it.

Well, after the lunch dishes were done, and Timmy and John Anthony had retired for their naps, and Robert was settled on his bed, his leg up on a couple of pillows and his coin collection comfortably at hand, Maureen and Richard and I volunteered to go back and look for Pig Two. Maybe he was getting hungry by now, said Richard, it doesn't take very long for pigs to get hungry. Maureen said she knew of a good hiding place or two on that hill. The only reason I volunteered to go along was because three are better than two at cornering anything, and thirty-five dollars is a lot of money.

Mr. Daley intended to go on with his haying, and Mrs. Daley said she could manage to keep busy without searching for swine which didn't need to get loose in the first place. However, they gave us their blessing, and a bucket of mash, and a sack, and a bag with three oranges and some cookies to sustain us.

I was now wearing sneakers, borrowed blue jeans, and a long-sleeved pullover, and the children were similarly armored. "No point in shedding any more blood," said Maureen crisply.

It was about two o'clock when we set out, and it was six-thirty when we returned, and not once did we see hide nor hair of Pig Two. We wove back and forth along the base of Boulder Hill, we climbed once to the top and admired New York State to the west and Massachusetts to the south and what Maureen swore was the Presidential Range off to the northeast, although I don't think this is possible. We made our painful way around the berry patch but heard nothing porcine therein. We explored two cellar holes now overgrown with poplars, and I gazed, awe-struck, at hundreds of yards of stone walls disappearing into the bushes and trees which are claiming what once were open fields, or so Maureen says.

"Who used to live up here?" I demanded, because there wasn't any road that I could see, nor ever had been.

"People who raised sheep," she said. "This all used to be pastureland a hundred years ago. They dragged all those rocks off the fields, and you know what they did with a lot of the trees they cut down? Just burnt them. They had so much wood they just *burnt* it!"

"It's funny to think of them doing that," I said. "You always hear that Yankees are thrifty."

"Well, that's what they did," Maureen said. "Golly, I ought to know. We spend one whole year in school studying Vermont history. We have to make notebooks by the yard. You want to know anything about Ethan Allen and his Green Mountain Boys, just ask me. I'm a walking encyclopedia."

"Okay, tell me this," I said. "How come, with a billion rocks in Vermont, anybody named this hill Boulder Hill, as if a boulder was anything unusual?"

"It's nothing to do with rocks," Maureen said. "Somebody by that name lived up here once. The boys went off to the Civil War and got killed, and the old folks moved away because they couldn't manage by themselves."

"Maybe they lived right here," said Richard.

We were sitting on the stone doorstep in front of one of the cellar holes, and we were eating our rations of cookies and fruit. From where we sat you could see the foundation of what must have been the barn, rocks set against the hillside in an L. Everywhere were ferns and little evergreens and bushes, and above us towered maple trees and birches. It was very quiet. You could hear birds now and then, and a wind stirring, but there wasn't any sound of people, not anywhere, not even a car or a tractor, or anything. It was kind of uncanny.

"It must have seemed very far away, that war," I said.

"That's what I thought, Harriet, when we were talking about it in school. I should think it's one thing to fight if it's right in your dooryard, you know, or down in the village. But it was awfully far away." She was hugging her knees with her skinny arms, and her face looked solemn and rather sad. "All those hundreds of miles and then to get killed. I hate the idea of it. And everybody waiting at home and you don't come back."

"Why did they go then?" Richard demanded. "Did they get drafted?"

"Drafted? *Vermonters*—for the *Civil War?*" Maureen looked shocked. "Are you crazy? Because they hated slavery, that's why! Vermonters can't stand the idea of anything but freedom—they never could! That's why they came here in the first place!" She grinned. "It's contagious—look at the way our pigs act!"

"And the cows, if you don't watch out," Richard said. "They're always bustin' loose."

Maureen was back in the Civil War. "More men went from Vermont than from any other Northern state, Harriet," she said proudly. "In proportion, I mean. You know who held the line against Pickett? Vermonters—the Second Brigade, it was, under General Stannard."

"I never heard of him," I said. "And what did they care, anyway? I mean, it's one thing to want freedom for yourself, but why did they care about black people hundreds of miles away? It's hard to believe that was why they fought. Are you sure it wasn't something about money—you know, the tariff, the wool coming in from Australia and ruining their businesses here, something like that?"

Maureen looked at me, and then looked away. She didn't say anything. I began to feel self-conscious, as if I had been pretty crude. After all, she was just a child, I ought not to run down her people that way—how could she defend them? She simply had been repeating what she had learned in school.

"Well, I don't care why they went, Maureen," I said. "They *did* go, and that's the important thing."

"No, that's *not* the important thing." Maureen looked stormy. "Didn't anyone ever tell you it makes a difference *why* you do anything? Right across the street from Mother's church there's a house where they used to hide runaway slaves. It was a station in the Underground Railroad—didn't you ever hear of that? Those slaves didn't have any money and nobody was paying those people to help those slaves get to Canada." She jumped up. "You can't tell *me* they did it for money!"

To my astonishment she was close to tears.

I scrambled to my feet. "Maureen, you have convinced me," I said. "You must forgive me for being so cynical. Remember, I learned my history in the South, and the way the history books tell it back home would make you so mad you'd be spitting nails."

"Yes, I know, the South got licked and that makes them bitter," she said. "I just wish *you* felt differently, that's all."

"Me?" I said. We were going single file along some kind of a track, Maureen ahead of me, Richard behind. "I'm not bitter the South lost—I'm delighted."

"No, I mean the way you feel about white people," she said, her back very straight. She turned and looked at me. "You never can give them any credit for anything."

"Why do you say that?" I said. I was interested to note that she put "white people" in the third person.

"Oh, just a feeling I have," she said. "Even when they're on your side, you wonder what they're hoping to get out of you."

We went down through a beech woods and across another poplar-dappled pasture, and all the time not saying anything. She was right about the way I felt, so what was there to say? What was so wonderful about Vermonters being against slavery, for that matter, because with their climate they couldn't have kept Africans alive anyway, could they? And even with two hundred years to get used to the cold, how many American black men had chosen to settle in Vermont?

We startled a doe and two fawns, and sent them bounding away through the underbrush. Something about these wild creatures, something about the way they looked at me before they fled, looked at me and through me as if I were transparent, every line of their body taut with extraordinarily sensitive perception, quivering to receive the slightest sound or sight or hint of danger, made me think of Maureen, the way she glanced at me sometimes, as if she too were trying to see right through me, to see what lay within me, was I safe or was I a danger to her. Was she kin to these creatures of the woods? Where did she get it, this perception that had made her recognize my feelings towards white people, how I

: 77 :

mistrust their motives? I watched her walking on ahead of me, delicately, lightly stepping, and I tried to think what I had said or done in her hearing which might lead her to say what she did. And I couldn't think of anything.

We saw lots of birds, but we saw nothing and heard nothing of our runaway. And we were getting hungry ourselves, and tired—at least I was tired, tired and strangely depressed—and so we set out for the farm.

June 25th

Today I sang in the choir. There isn't anything more to tell about it than this simple fact. There were no complications, no reverberations, no fireworks. I simply put on my robe and I walked in and out without anything going wrong. And I sang, keeping my voice to the proper level of volume, and I enjoyed myself, and that's that.

In the afternoon some mild haying was being done by the rest of the family, but I wasn't needed to help. Nobody organized a pig search. It seems the loss of Pig Two has been accepted as final, although all the way to and from church Mrs. Daley and I kept a sharp lookout, just in case that escapee had had enough of freedom. Needless to say, no pig did we see.

June 26th

This morning was Monday (okay, all day was Monday—this is the sort of repartee one develops when surrounded by immature minds) and Mrs. Daley and I finished the washing early. This gave us the rest of the day to catch up on the weeding. Or try to.

One can't use a hoe here, at least I can't. Too many stones! It's easier to stoop over and pluck the weeds out with my fingers. That's what we were doing, about three in the afternoon when the sun was strong and the air was warm, and if the ground had only been red instead of bleached brown, and if there hadn't been twenty rocks per lineal yard of bean row (and if the beans had been ready for picking instead of not even blossoming yet), I could have thought myself in Aunt Lydia's back yard, because I wasn't cold, I was actually comfortable.

Except that Mrs. Daley wouldn't have been there working along with me, nor anybody remotely like Mrs. Daley.

I think much of the time she is lonesome; anyway, she talks a lot. Today she was talking about the land.

"It's a funny thing," she said, "how people draw their strength from different things. Some people have to live near the sea. Others have to have the mountains. Take my father, for example. He was born and raised in South Dakota, that southeast part where the land is as flat as a pancake—step out of your farmhouse and in every direction the land stretches out of sight with scarcely a ripple—it's *level,* and that's that. And from horizon to horizon there's a great sweep of sky. My father went away when he was twenty, went off to the state university, and then to his work, and never lived there again. But years later, when he was going into New York by train every day—you know the Jersey meadows?"

"I saw them from the bus," I said.

"Well, every day he would pretend, as the train snaked across those marshes with their tall waving grass, he would pretend he was crossing the prairies. He would dream he was home."

I called to mind those meadows as I had seen them that night. It hadn't been dark, not really dark, neon lights everywhere and the horizon a ring of cities casting their glow, a sullen orange smear, over the blackness. The meadows had been crisscrossed by highways, riddled with sulky dirty ditches where trash floated in oily water, and the grasses were tangled with papers glowing, and the sky a muck of smoke from the fires of a dozen city dumps.

"Very sad," I said.

"Now I'm happiest when I'm growing something," she said. "My grandfather was a farmer, and his father before him. My name was Brown before I married—same as yours. My people came from Scotland. Brown is a common name there."

I said, "My people did not come from Scotland."

"I imagine you, Harriet, are really happy only where it is good and hot."

I thought that over. Happy . . . I suppose she meant comfortable in spirit? I didn't think climate should have anything to do with whether or not one was *happy*. If the temperature of the air or the levelness or up-and-downness of the horizon really decided whether or not one was happy, wasn't this a kind of self-indulgence? A kind of dramatizing of how difficult you, dear sensitive creature that you are, find it to be happy?

I didn't tell her any of this. I just said, "Ma'am, it can get too hot even for me to be happy, believe it or not. Picking tobacco, for instance."

She didn't reply to this, and I began to feel ashamed of myself; the fact that I was in a prickly mood was certainly no excuse to be rude. So I said, "Mrs. Daley, you better do something about your back. You're going to get a burn."

When she bent over, her shorts and her topper, a kind of halter, would part company at the waist, and the strip of skin exposed there had been a sickly white but now was turning red.

She straightened, and tugged her halter down. "Darn it, it won't stay put," she said.

I took off my apron. "Tie this over you," I said. "You could get a terrible burn."

I went on working, and as I weeded, I was conscious of the color of her legs, which had considerable tan by now, and they were a kind of khaki color, or maple-candy color, or the color of a camel-hair coat, whereas my arms, which I was also staring at, they being right in front of my face as I worked, were such a dark brown they almost had an overlay of blue—or was that the sun? It must be strange to look down at your body and not see brown skin.

"Harriet, don't you ever get a sunburn?"

"Me?" I said, surprised. "No, ma'am, that's one worry I do not have."

"Supposing you were on the beach, and you fell asleep, and slept two or three hours. You mean you wouldn't burn even then?"

"No, I wouldn't," I said. "I might have a headache from the sun, and if I lay there long enough I could get a sunstroke. But I wouldn't burn, not to blister, anyway." I straightened, to ease my back. "Although I can't imagine why I would be lying on the beach," I went on. "I'm not much for swimming, and I've got all the suntan I need."

Mrs. Daley laughed, and bent over and went on weeding. And I wondered what on earth had prompted me—some kind of latent Uncle-Tomism?—that I should kick my heels and crack a joke to make the white folks laugh. I could see the perspiration running down into her eyes and now and then dripping off the tip of her nose, and I thought, everybody to his own environment, but it isn't *that* hot. And I knew what I'd been thinking, if I'd been thinking consciously at all: I'd been thinking that she looked tired and had a lot to do before night and I didn't have to go slamming the door on the topics of conversation she dragged up. My God, I'd been thinking she can't help it if she was born white. Since she didn't choose—and even if she would have so chosen, given the chance—I didn't have to hold it against her, did I?

As I went on weeding, I thought over what I had just been thinking, and I was shocked at myself. Not to blame somebody for being born white—is this progress? Am I climbing out of what Hobart G. Carr calls "our mental ghetto"? No doubt *he* would say I am "developing empathy through exposure to an alien culture." That sounds lovely, dear Mr. Carr, I would say, but what I think has actually happened to me is that my standards are crumbling, I'm going soft. If I don't watch myself, I'll be just another namby-pamby ol'-black-mammy-minded *nothing*.

June 27th

We are eating radishes and green onions and the thinnings from the lettuce rows, and everybody acts as if summer is now officially here. I still wear my sweater until ten in the morning, but after all, until it's over sixty, a sweater is proper. *Enough* about the weather and the climate—but no wonder people talk about little else up here, the weather has all the fascination of horse races and besides, it contributes to status. The worse the weather, the higher the status of the one who survives it. So in a perverse way people are glad when their personal piece of earth is coldest, or has the latest frost, or deepest snow, or longest dry spell. You'd think here was this wretched piece of land and God looked around for a real hero to wrench a living out of it.

June 28th

There was a deer in the strawberry patch last night, and we are poking shiny pieces of aluminum foil onto branches and ramming these in the rows, and laying dirty socks on the ground here and there, hoping to fool the deer that there are people about. There was some discussion of whose socks would be the dirtiest, and it was decided that Richard's would be, as he often loses them under his bed, where they ripen.

Mrs. Daley was sorting books today. She is sifting through the contents of many cardboard boxes, hoping, she says, to find a few volumes she can weed out. "Two copies of *Wind in the Willows*—now how did that happen?"

"The usual way, Mother," Maureen said. "You gave me one for my birthday, and Robert one for Christmas."

Mrs. Daley was muttering something to herself, something about an aberration of the brain, and I thought about Aunt Lydia and I was suddenly angry that anybody would have two copies of anything, would have the money to spend so thoughtlessly, not having to plot and scrimp and maneuver, and I said, trying to pass it off carelessly, "My aunt could use it, as a matter of fact." And then I added, as if it didn't matter really, "But I don't suppose you want to give away a *given* book."

"You can have my copy, Harriet," Maureen said. "Mother won't mind."

"Mother will be happy to have the evidence removed," said Mrs. Daley. "How many children does your aunt have?"

"It's not just for my cousins," I said. "She runs a kind of school, my aunt does, but she's not an organized charity or anything, so I guess you couldn't deduct this from your taxes."

"Good Lord," said Mrs. Daley, "I'd have to have a computer for a brain." She started going over a box she had already sorted. "Maybe there's something else. How old are her pupils?"

I said, "No special age. This is a school for children who can't go to the regular school. Maybe they're retarded or they're spastics or maybe they've had rheumatic fever or broken a bone and it doesn't heal. My aunt got to worrying about all those children and so she started a little class and more and more children came. She can use just any kind of book because there's such a mixture and of course their parents can't pay her very much."

"Doesn't she get any tax support?" Mrs. Daley said. "What on earth does she use for money?"

"Whatever they can give her," I explained. "Whenever they have anything, they bring it, whatever it is—fifty cents, or a sack of potatoes, a side of bacon, maybe a dress handed along to them from an employer. There aren't any public funds for special schools, not that we heard of, anyway. Besides, Aunt Lydia wouldn't qualify. She never went to high school herself, and when I was little she even had me helping teach. I'd read the Bible to the class and I'd chalk the words on the wall of our house—the school was on our porch—and everybody would memorize. We really used the books we had: not only the Bible, but old telephone books—Reverend Douglass collects old phone books from the businesses in town—and newspapers—"

"Whatever did you do with old phone books?" Maureen asked.

"The yellow pages," I said, "the ads. They're all arranged alphabetically, and that's helpful, and there are often pictures along with the ads, and that makes it easier for anybody trying to learn the idea of reading." I felt suddenly like a guide taking tourists through a slum, and I said, almost irritably, "And magazines— Granny McNair gathered old issues for us from the white families she worked for—"

"Your Aunt Lydia sounds like a wonderful woman," said Mrs. Daley.

"Well, she's left her mark on Abbot's Level," I said. "She gets so mad when she finds some poor little lame-brain hidden away somewhere. She says, 'What do you think this is, the seventeenth century?' And then she tries to get them to send that child to her school. By now everybody knows it's *not* the seventeenth century, although not everybody in town knows what century it *is*."

Mrs. Daley wanted to know if I am going to teach retarded children.

"Not me; no, ma'am," I said. "I don't have that kind of soul."

And I don't. I really can't bear to be around any of God's failures or mistakes. I can't take it in stride, to see their wobbly heads and sweet vacant smiles and whole wasted lives. I'm angry all the time I'm around Aunt Lydia's children. I hide it, but I'm mad clear through.

When I get to Heaven, if I ever do, I'm going to walk right up to Whoever has all the answers up there and I'm going to say, "Okay, let's hear Your explanation."

And it had better be good.

June 29th

Today was my day off, and I spent the time right after breakfast up in Robert's room, beating him at Canfield, beating him at dominoes, beating him at checkers.

"Do you think I could learn to play chess?" he said.

"How should I know?" I said. "I don't know how to play chess myself."

"How about poker?"

"What I know about poker I am not teaching you, child," I said. "Your mother didn't hire me to teach you to gamble."

"Why do you always keep yammering about being the hired girl?" he said. "Are you afraid somebody will take you for a member of the family?"

"Psychological warfare," I said, "and it doesn't work," and I jumped his king.

"Mind over matter," he retorted, and darned if he didn't jump two of my men.

"I don't mind and you don't matter," I said, as one of my men reached his king row.

"Gee, Harriet, don't dredge up those oldies. Originality is everything, especially when you're trying to pass the insults."

"Make sure that it's new when I'm rude to you?" I said.

He paused, his hand hovering over a checker. "If your bark is worse than your bite, make sure each crunch is a brand-new delight!" he said triumphantly.

"Too long," I said. "If your bark is worse than your bite, don't be trite."

"Too short," he said.

"Okay, Shakespeare," I said, "it's your turn."

"What are you doing this afternoon?" he said. "Are you going back to Boulder Hill looking for Pig Two?" Before I had a chance to say I do not search for pigs in my free time, he crowed in triumph, "Back to the hill with the swill!"

I groaned. "Please!" I said. I stood up to leave. "By now the grass ought to be dry," I said. "Today I am privileged to learn to run the power mower."

"Keep your feet out of it," he said.

"*You* are advising *me* to look out?"

"Everybody gets a good idea once in a while," he said. "I'm not ashamed of it. Why should I apologize?"

I whacked at his pillows and my needlework magazine slid to the floor, a piece of paper skidding out.

"How did that get here?" I said.

Robert's face was pink. "That's a project of Richard's—we just borrowed your magazine, Harriet. We meant to sneak it back to you—"

I said, "If you want something, ask for it." I picked up the paper and glanced at it.

"That's a letter Richard wants mailed," Robert said hastily. "He hasn't an envelope—"

"Well, I have," I said. "I'll take care of it." What I wanted to do, I wanted to copy the letter. Here it is, exactly as Richard wrote it:

> Superior Sales, Co., Dept. 284
> 195 peoria St.
>
> Dear sirs,   June 28
> I have a nickel that is
> 1941 dated. Yov said on the
> back of my freinds workbasket
> (mag) that yov would pay 6,000.00
> for a nickel before 1945.
> Please lookinto.
>
>   Jitterly,
>   Richard Daley
>
>
> Richard Daley
> R.F.D. 1
> East Barnstead, Vermont
>
> P.S. We have the coin
> in our posessun.

I include this as evidence of why I want to teach. And who. All the "jitterly" children—delicious! I love love love them all!

And then my delight was tainted by doubt. Where had the children found my needlework booklet? I could have sworn I left it on my bed. I decided they must have been in my room. Next thing, they'd be poking around in my things.

Well, let them, I thought. I don't have much to interest anybody but myself—except my journal, of course. Or Mr. Carr's letters. I hated to think of anybody looking at or handling his letters. Not that there is anything in them. But they're *mine*.

Then there was my money. Up to now I've been keeping my slowly accumulating five- and ten-dollar bills wrapped in a hand-kerchief and tucked under my mattress. I realized this was the most obvious hiding place possible, an absolutely amateurish choice. Aunt Lydia says it may be a sin to steal, but it's also a sin to tempt the poor, and the Daley children must feel poor because they keep scheming to make money. I decided I'd better find a real hiding place for my pay.

After some thought, I rolled my money inside an empty baking powder can, screwed the top on securely (against mice, I suppose), and, working a bit of the shiny insulation loose, I slid the can behind it, onto a cross-brace in the wall. My few letters and my journal, a soft-covered spiral notebook, I tucked into the inner cover of my pillow, zipped it shut, replaced the pillowcase, and smoothed the pillow. Now, I thought, everything ought to be perfectly safe from casual trespassers.

Unless, of course, someone were to sit on the pillow, or lean on it. Even then there wouldn't be any real damage done, except possibly to my bus ticket, which I've been using as a marker in my journal. Mindful of all those warnings "not good if detached," I retrieved the ticket, and after some further thought I put it in an envelope and taped this to the underside of the radio Maureen lent me. I've often done this way at home, to keep my treasures safe from Aunt Lydia's pupils, who can't grasp the concept of private property. So, although it seemed perfectly natural to be hiding things in this fashion, at the same time, considering the Daley children, it seemed just a bit silly.

Riches can be a burden. Nevertheless my heart does not bleed for millionaires.

June 30th

How I would appreciate it if *no one* were to feel compelled to analyze me, or point out my faults, or suggest improvements in my character. I don't mean Josie—her letters overflow with nonsense, self-inspired jokes, and the lyrics of ballads she is writing, and all this I love to read. Aunt Lydia thinks I'm perfect, so her letters are, of course, a delight. But why—why—*why* does Hobart Gamaliel Carr (*what* a name!) think it is his bounden duty to improve me?

Today's letter expounded on my failings in a gentle, chiding tone which would not have upset the sensibilities of a kindergartener. Not being a kindergartener, I was very wroth, and wrote in reply as follows:

My *dear* Mr. Carr:

I have read yours of the twenty-sixth.

All right—so it isn't the vacant seat I couldn't have that infuriated me—so it was not being thought good enough to sit there—*all right!*

Yours *violently,*
Harriet Brown

Of course nobody likes sermons that hit close to home, and I admit H.G.C.'s are right on target. Just the same, his comments, it seems to me, carry more sting than they should. Now why is this? Because they come from him? I mean, am I hypersensitive to his opinion of me? And is this possibly because he sees through me as clearly as if I were one of those glass walls you have to put colored stickers on, to warn people not to crash into them?

It's all very disquieting.

Tonight we had a cookout, just for larks. I mean, there wasn't any need to, the kitchen was still there in the old house, the floor intact, the stove working. But Maureen poked and prodded Richard (verbally) until he helped her build a fireplace out of some of the rocks they'd been hauling from the vegetable patch, and they gathered wood, dead branches mostly, and hacked them into usable lengths, and got the fire lit by themselves. What could I do but act as if I thought the whole idea was absolutely splendid, and help lug the contents of the kitchen and the dishes and the silverware and salt and pepper and pickles and catsup and the coffee and the salad and the rolls and the hot dogs down the lane and through the stone wall and up the field to where the fireplace was, and I didn't think I ought to grumble because for each of my trips, the children took three.

We hauled the lounge chair over, and Robert stretched out in it. The rest of us sat on the ground. Outdoors all caste systems fall away, and I ate with the family.

Afterwards they threw more wood on the fire, and somebody went looking for marshmallows, which we didn't have, and I got my sweater. Eventually the sun went down but the light lingered for a long time. Then gradually the dusk began to creep towards us from the east.

The children were all looking at the fire and its light glowed and flickered in their eyes.

Mary said, "It looks like fairyland." From her tone I'd have thought she'd been there often.

"I can see dancers," Maureen said. "Look, Harriet, do you see the dancers?"

"I don't like fire," I said, not looking.

"You don't? You mean you're afraid of fire? Are you afraid of getting burnt?"

You can't say anything out of the usual around these children but they'll be at you, pick pick with questions.

"No, I'm not afraid I'll be burnt," I said. "I'm not planning to fall in. I just don't like fire, that's all."

"Why don't you?" Maureen said.

For some reason I found myself about to blurt out that it always reminds me of horrors, of people burning, lynchings, things like that, but I caught myself in time. Maureen would only want to know what a lynching was, and I didn't want to tell her. It wasn't going to be so simple, being a teacher, I thought. There were going to be a number of hideousnesses to be faced, explained somehow, plunged through, and when the children reached the other side, their innocence would be singed a little. I hated to think about it: Hiroshima, suddenly all an incandescent hell, Belsen with smoke climbing like the mark of Cain. Always people, people burning people. History is a kind of furnace, I thought, and the lives of men are the logs, that's what men are, dead logs piled one on top of the other ready for burning. You say the earth moves round the sun? Burn! You say your God pities you, loves you, forgives you? Burn! You say you demand to be free, you demand to be equal? Burn! Burn the Cross! Burn the church! Burn the children!

How can anybody look at fire and see anything beautiful there?

I became aware Mr. Daley was watching my face. "Leave Harriet alone," he said. "People can't always give reasons for everything they feel."

"Animals are afraid of fire," Richard said.

"That's it," I said, and I gave a laugh. "I'm a jungle cat and I'm afraid of fire."

IV

July 2nd

Today, Sunday, there was company here, relatives from the Middle West who were driving through Canada and thought they'd stop in, since they were so near.

I put on a clean white starched apron and a starched expression, and acted like Ye Olde Familie Retainer, and passed the sherry and the cake and hoped I took everybody's mind off the mushroom on the bathroom wall. Something is growing there where the wood is rotting, above the tub where the tiles fell off, and Mr. D. wouldn't let anybody take it away from there until it is mature enough to be identified botanically. We had forgotten all about it, and swoop! just as we had finished dinner, in drove this car absolutely overflowing with kindred.

I am sure everybody must have seen the fungus, though—the visitors were here from one-thirty until six, the bathroom door was wide open, and the mushroom, or whatever it is, now measures four inches by two, and resembles half a pie stuck by the cut side against the wall. It is grey in color and looks most unappetizing.

Mr. and Mrs. Daley took their kinfolk on the four-dollar walking tour—up to the top of the pasture and down to the pond at the edge of the woods, and all around the vegetable garden, identifying every bit of edible flora visible, pointing out the hoof tracks of the deer along the row of beets (now a stubby miniature hedge of stems), into the chicken house and the milking parlor (somebody sometime explain to me the derivation of the word "parlor" in connection with a barn, or any part thereof), and all through the new house. And there was a good deal of mutual snapshot-taking, and urgings of return visits, and then the company drove over the hill and was gone, and so was the day.

So Mr. Daley had to postpone spreading the lime until the Fourth of July, when he has another day off.

July 3rd

This morning being Monday, we were doing the washing, Mrs. Daley and I together, trying to push it so we would either get some paint on the new house or some weeds out of the pea patch or maybe even some dirt out of the upstairs of the old house, an area no one has had a moment for recently, and there we were, neither of us looking like the cover of *Vogue,* when a car came swooping in and there descended from this chic little sports car (dark grey, with pale grey upholstery) Mrs. Daley's Ex-roommate from college, and her latest husband. I inferred this from the explanations of current names which took place.

The Ex-roommate was wearing half a million dollars' worth of simple linen clothing Suitable for the Country, and some white eye-liner, and only one earring, but that was enough because it was large enough to throw her off balance if she hadn't had her husband's arm to lean on. He seemed surprisingly nice, not too chubby and really not too bald. She made a good bargain, I thought: all that money and he's almost presentable.

But there was no way for me to dash to my room for a clean apron, and in they came past the piles of sorted laundry, and brief, correct introductions took place, and then on into the kitchen, past the open door to the bath and the Grey Mystery plainly in sight, and through the kitchen into the dining room, which, this early in the morning, was pleasantly cool in spite of the pinned-shut door, because the window to the west was open, propped with a board.

"I'd ask you into the living room, but it's been raining," said Mrs. Daley. "I'm so sorry Tom isn't home. He'll hate to have missed you."

"Darling," said the Ex in wonder, "how do you do it? You haven't changed at all—you look just the same!"

"Oh, don't say that!" cried Mrs. D. "I'd been so hoping I had!"

She offered them coffee, which I passed with an inscrutable expression. Then she offered them a choice of tours, and they took the quickie, the Brief Circle of the new house. This gave me an opportunity to slick up what children I could lay my hands on, and Mrs. D. presented her offspring as her guests returned to their car.

"Darling Kate!" cried the Ex. "You're breathtaking! So fecund!"

They drove off, and Mrs. Daley stalked into the house and into the bathroom, where she stood before the mirror, and she cried, "*Mille tonnerres!*" and then she held her hands out and stared at their backs, rough and weed-stained, and she cried, "Damnation!" and then she came back and we hung the washing on the line.

"Harriet, seventeen years ago I graduated magna cum laude in French Literature, can you believe it?"

"Certainly I can believe it," I said.

"Yes, but the woman who was here, my Ex-roommate, graduated that same year *summa* cum laude in Geodetic Geology, I believe it was called. Can you believe that?"

"No," I said. "Wait a moment, maybe yes," I said. "Isn't geology the science where you learn to locate various metals?"

To this Mrs. Daley replied that she thought she'd go into town and have her hair done, whenever she could get an appointment. "It's a mistake to overdo this do-it-yourself," she said. I asked her what she thought I ought to do about getting mine cut, where ought I to go? "I'll ask Dora when she can take you," Mrs. Daley said.

And she went into the house and phoned, and agreed to a time this coming Friday for herself, and for me, the following Thursday.

Then lunch, and dishes, and Timmy and John Anthony down for naps, and we were in the pea patch when, at three o'clock, friends of Mrs. Daley's father drove in, to deliver in person the message that He Is Well.

Mrs. Daley's father's friends got the three-dollar tour, which skips the pond at the foot of the hill and the view from the top of the pasture, but covers everything else. I served the rest of the sherry and passed store-bought cookies. Snapshots were taken of the view from the doorstep, and return-visit invitations were extended.

After supper we replanted beets and thinned the carrots, a process at this stage of growth that resembles plucking a fifty-foot eyebrow, but we have to do it now, I am told, otherwise the growing roots will braid and entwine themselves and choke each other to death.

July 5th

Yesterday was, as the whole country knows, the Fourth of July. However it is celebrated elsewhere, here—i.e., on this farm—the occasion is marked by Making Good Use of a Day Off. Mr. and Mrs. Daley went into the fields immediately after breakfast, and she drove the tractor while he heaved around the sacks of lime (eighty pounds each). He had to pile them on the truck, drive to the field, and there drag each one and slit it open and pour its contents into the lime sower, which, simply, is a ten-foot-long wheeled sieve. Timmy and Mary and I went down at ten o'clock bringing coffee and some cinnamon rolls I'd made, and thus we observed what the grownups were up to. They seemed to be enjoying themselves, and I went back up the hill reflecting on the inscrutability of the Facts of Life. In Vermont, work is pleasure, apparently, as long as it is something nobody is making you do and because of which, when all is said and done, you are likely to lose money.

We did not actually have company ourselves, just three sets of tourists during the morning looking for people named Whitehall, and nobody here had heard of anybody named Whitehall. It turned out later that they were all looking for *West* Barnstead; somebody must have made a slight error in issuing summonses. (The Reunion of the Whitehalls was written up in today's paper, and 326 relatives attended. You never realize how well off you are, said Mr. Daley, until something like this makes you stop and count your blessings.)

At noon, I could hear Maureen remind her parents of what day it was. "And sky divers," she was saying, "and Civil War cannons, and an obedience test, and everything! *Please,* Daddy!"

"Honey, I just can't take the time. We've spread only four tons —that's less than half the lime."

"Couldn't Harriet take her?" Mrs. Daley suggested.

"And me!" said Richard.

"And me!" cried Mary.

"We can bring Robert down to keep an eye on the house while the little boys nap," Mrs. D. went on. "I could whiz them in—you could manage without me for half an hour, couldn't you?"

"I could manage without you for the whole afternoon," he said.

"No, you could not!" cried Mrs. Daley, offended.

It was decided that I'd take three children and Mrs. Daley would chauffeur us to West Woodstock, where the Lions or the Elks or some other group were putting on a multifaceted spectacle. Naturally we had to reassure Mary that these were not *real* lions or elks. I changed to town-going clothes, we were each provided with two dollars' spending money (it was a raising-money-for-charity affair, therefore it would be our duty to spend money), and Mrs.

Daley did indeed whiz us in, using the shortest possible route, part of which were roads I thought suitable only for mules. She left us after pointing out the exact spot on which we were to be standing at precisely 5 P.M.

I tell you it was a Glorious Fourth for me. It was like a carnival and circus and church picnic and school field day all rolled into one. The celebration sprawled over the grounds of a new high school which had been built, according to current custom, out in the country. Hundreds of people were milling from one attraction to another, but nothing was crowded. I think I was the only Negro there, but I didn't mind, and nobody seemed to mind me, I was just a shady face in the crowd, and I could look out at the world from inside myself and have a good time, and for one whole afternoon not be a crusader. Oh, it was glorious!

We saw some archers doing incredible things with bows and arrows—shooting not even Robin Hood could better—and we saw various kinds of dogs demonstrate the most uncanny ability to Behave Themselves, trotting and stopping and lying down and staying put and rolling over, all at command. The best were the French poodles, they did everything with such an air of *chic boulevardier*—they didn't actually have a carnation in the button-hole, but that was the impression they gave.

We rode a kind of whirling-cradles machine, and Mary threatened to throw up, but thank God the machine stopped in time. Richard had his weight guessed, and because he looks so skinny he fooled the man, and won a hat with a purple feather. Maureen threw baseballs at a target, which if she hit it dead center would send a boy plunging into a tank of water—it is hard to describe this setup, it was a Rube Goldberg invention of a local genius—but it was a real boy, and a ten-foot tank of water, and Maureen plunged him in again and again until she had money only for two bags of popcorn. "I pitch for the Little Leaguers at batting practice, you know, at recess," she explained casually but in a carrying voice, and basked in the admiring glances shot her way.

And we went into the school building and observed the cake-decorating contest some homemakers' club was putting on, and I bought a chance on the prize-winning cake, but I didn't win it.

And then the cannons were to be shot off, and we went out where we could see as well as hear them, and a number of men in rather tatty dug-out-of-the-attic uniforms (eleven Northerners, one Confederate) were setting up their weapons, and aiming at the wooded slope beyond.

Boom! for nearly an hour. *Boom! Boomboom!* And the smoke drifting smelled of death and glory, and the sound was just like in the movies. I don't know why this surprised me, but it did.

There was too much wind for the sky divers to jump at four o'clock, when they were supposed to, and it was nearly five when the planes—two of them—came overhead, and out leaped tiny dolls, and puff! the scarlet halos spread and down they came and everybody cheering and oh! I could never make myself leap out into air, into *nothing,* just air like that—I'd almost rather crash in the plane! Oh, what terrible choices mankind has set up for itself!

And when Mrs. Daley picked us up, we were all tired and happy and I thought on the way home, *it's as if I had a white skin all afternoon—now I know what it's like.* Not to be white, but rather not to be different, not to be apart—all right, not to be separated, winnowed out, the way you can't help feeling all the time, inside, at any kind of a social affair back home. Because when you see all those Negro faces, you know (even if you don't consciously think about it) that you're there because you're black, too. But this afternoon I was just a particle in a whole, one of many, separate but blending in, and life proceeding smoothly without anything grating. It was a truly lovely sensation, and I thought, *this is what every day is like for white people from the time they are born until they die.*

Mrs. Daley had supper all ready: cold ham and potato salad and pickles and watermelon. And after supper Maureen wanted to know if they couldn't all go back and see the fireworks.

Mr. Daley groaned and Mrs. Daley agreed with him, and the

decision was reached that flesh and blood can stand only so much.

"We can see from the top of the pasture," said Richard.

"Not as well," said Maureen.

"Better than nothing," Richard said.

So we all waited and waited for it to get dark, and finally it did begin to. We left John Anthony and Timmy asleep in their cribs and we helped Robert hobble up the hill, and so we all went up, through the grass now getting damp, and everybody soon sending errand boys (Maureen and me) back after sweaters and even coats (mine), and back up the hill she and I went, to where the family was sitting at the top, and the trees shrank beneath us and the sky was all ours. To the west, where the hills fold into each other, the sky was still light, and the light was apricot where it met the hills, and looked fake, as if it couldn't possibly really be that color. The stars were coming out, first just a few, then suddenly many, and silently. (I know, but I hadn't thought about it before. There they are, and no noise.)

By ten o'clock I thought it was dark enough for fireworks, but nothing happened. At ten-thirty, off toward the east, very far away, some Roman candles silently made little fluorescent scratches on the sky. Then to the south another town sent tiny fountains of gold up and up, with pop! pop! poppoppop! of flashbulbs scattered at the tips, and after nearly a minute the sound of these explosions came, very faint. And at last the celebration in West Woodstock began, over the mountains to the north, and although we couldn't see any but the highest shooting rockets, we could hear the crackles and bangs, and the sky would flicker with light when something below the skyline was going off, and it was interesting. Maureen remarked at least four times that it would be better if we were there, and finally her father advised her to shut up, and she did.

When at last I crawled into bed, it was with the feeling that it had all been a Basic Day. I mean, it was one great big chunk of reality, the kind of day that is *solid* and is going to be right there in the foundation of my life, a day, in other words, on which I can build *me*.

So it was something of a disappointment, this morning, to find myself and everybody else suffering from a natural feeling of letdown compounded by fatigue. Nobody tried to set any records of achievement. Some painting got done, some weeding, a dab of ironing, but mostly we just kept the home fires burning, figuratively speaking.

Only one thing really worth recording: in the afternoon Maureen took Mary and Richard to pick wild strawberries, and they went across the valley and up the slopes to the north of us, slopes which naturally themselves face south, and therefore the strawberries ripen there first and are exceptionally sweet, Maureen says. And there they saw, rooting among the berries, Pig Two, alive and in good health! They were delighted to see him, but he was not delighted to see them, and he fled at their ecstatic approach and disappeared over the brow of the hill.

Mary was brokenhearted but the others displayed their relative maturity by accepting philosophically this particular one of Life's setbacks.

"How do you imagine he ever got way up there?" Maureen said. "It's a good three miles from where we lost him."

"He walked," said Richard.

"No!" said Maureen. "You dumbfound me!"

"What does that mean?" Mary asked me.

"It doesn't mean he found her dumb, God knows," I said.

Maureen fixed the berries and I made shortcake and no wonder Pig Two traveled so far! Yumyumyumyum, if I may quote him.

July 6th

Today was my day off, and you'd have thought I was Mr. Daley, or somebody equally unable to relax, because in the morning, when Mrs. D. went to the corn patch to thin out the suckers, I went along, and not to chat, either; and in the afternoon, when she took Maureen, Richard, and Mary to the dentist to have him count their teeth, as Maureen put it, I got out the power mower and cut the grass. I mean, you can sit around just so long in this latitude and then you get this irresistible urge to get on your feet and fight back.

It was deliciously hot, and since it was, after all, my day off, I put on my shorts and my yellow bandanna halter, and I cut the grass in the orchard and by the big barn and near the chicken house and the triangular patch that points the way to the spring house, and I was still troubled by surplus steam, and had begun to mow a path around the vegetable garden, thinking maybe this evidence of civilization would discourage the deer, when a car purred along the road beyond the hedgerow, and turned and came swooping up the lane. At first my impulse was to crouch out of sight, because I was hardly dressed for company, and then I thought, well, I'm the ranking adult on this place, so I turned off the mower and started around the vegetable garden. The car kept right on going, not slackening its speed at all. I was suddenly alarmed—what if Timmy were to run out of the old house, or Robert come hobbling down from the new—and I began to run, when screech! the car pitched to a sudden stop.

The top was down, and I was treated to an unimpeded view of driver and passenger. He was fat, with a nose the size of a fifteen-watt bulb, and little eyes like pebbles, and he was wearing a short-sleeved sport shirt, so his hairy arm and fancy wrist watch and two-inch stub of stinking cigar were right there for me to admire. She had a fallen face with eyelids and mouth and everything turned down, but I didn't get a chance to study her further because he opened right up.

"Hey!" he said. "Get that damn tricycle out of the way or I'll run over it!"

Not, if you please, "I might," but "I will"—and my adrenalin reacted like Old Faithful.

"This," I said, "is a private road."

And I didn't move.

He was looking me over and I realized I was wearing *short* shorts.

"Yeah?" he said. "I thought this was a farm."

(Explain that. I can't.)

"No doubt you made a mistake back there," I said, and I gestured elegantly towards the mailbox. I did not, however, take my eyes off him. He wasn't the kind of man you do.

He sucked briefly on his cigar. "You live here?" His eyes flicked towards the old house and back to me.

"I am the maid," I said with simple dignity.

"Yeah?" he said. "The maid, eh? How do you like that—the maid! I thought maybe you was a member of the Peace Corps!" For some reason he thought this remark was funny. "What d'ya know, the maid," he went on, and gave me the up and down. "C'mon, gal, what are some of your duties?"

"Archie, for gossakes," said his woman.

"That's all right, ma'am," I said. "Perhaps this gentleman is unfamiliar with a maid." A fat chance, I thought. I looked him in his pebble eyes, and I said coolly, "I don't know where you're from or what it's like there, but up here, the maid—that is, the hired girl—is not expected to perform any of the duties of the lady of the house."

I stalked around in front of the car, and I jerked Timmy's tricycle to safety.

"There's room to turn around there," I said.

And I stood stock still and stared him down. It's easy to stare anybody down if you think of yourself as an arrogant cat, I mean a real cat, one of those sleek cats the Egyptians used to make statues of, to guard the tombs of their kings. It gives you just the right expression.

And I watched him shift the car and back and turn and drive out again, his cigar clenched in his teeth, his negative companion not looking at him, not looking at me, just sort of shrunk into herself.

I finished mowing around the vegetable garden, but all the pleasure in it was gone. And then, for some obscure reason, I went up and checked to see if my ticket home was there under my radio, and it was.

When Mrs. Daley came home, there were the tracks on the dust of the drive. She asked who had been here, and I said just a couple of people who had taken a wrong turn somewhere.

July 7th

After yesterday I really wasn't surprised when Mrs. Daley returned from town, her hair shorter and curlier than when she left, and told me, so stiffly and unsmilingly that I knew she was acutely embarrassed, that Dora was sorry but she's all filled up next Thursday—she'd made a mistake, she'd said.

"She heard I'm colored," I said.

"I feel terrible," said Mrs. Daley. "I don't ever want to go back." She bit her lip. *"I* thought, Harriet, when she gave you that nine-o'clock appointment, that she was—I mean that she knew—"

"You thought she was sneaking me in and out ahead of everybody so nobody would have a fit?" I said.

"Well, I did think perhaps she couldn't trust her customers," she said. "This whole thing is sickening."

"Don't be upset, ma'am," I said. "This is nothing new to me."

"That's what makes me so *sick,"* she said. "That it should happen to you here!"

I felt sorry for her, I honestly did. I didn't have any of that pleasure I'd had before, when I told her about the Southern "ladies" refusing to acknowledge my existence when they passed me on the street. I was beginning to realize, I suppose, that other people, as well as Southerners, have pride in tradition—I recalled Maureen's flare of temper when I questioned the motives of Vermonters fighting in the Civil War—and here was Mrs. Daley being given the first irrefutable evidence she may ever have had to look at, that the Northern tradition is founded on myth, too.

"Never mind, Mrs. Daley," I said. "It's my fault, really. I shouldn't have asked. Everybody told me what to expect in the North—"

"The North, the North!" she exploded. "Damnation, everybody knows the North is pock-marked with prejudice! This is *Vermont!* This is where *I* live!"

Later I heard her phoning, and then she came and I could see she was feeling better even if she wasn't smiling. She said, "Harriet, it's all fixed up. A friend of mine goes to Nan's in Chester, and my friend, Mrs. Perkins, phoned Nan and told her about you and Nan said she'd be glad to cut your hair—you can come any time it's convenient for you, you don't even have to phone ahead if you don't want to."

I said, "Mrs. Daley, please don't bother. I've changed my mind, I don't think I want my hair cut after all."

"What Nan said was, she'd be honored to cut your hair," said Mrs. Daley.

What's this, some kind of nut? I wondered. "No, really, I'll just wait until I get back to South Carolina," I said.

"Harriet, for heaven's sake!" said Mrs. D. "I know people up here who drive three hundred miles to New York to get their glasses fitted, but eight hundred miles—or whatever it is—for a haircut! Now I ask you—that's the limit!"

But I'm not going to have my hair cut up here. It's only seven weeks more, I can manage. I'll wear it in a French twist.

Nobody need sneak me in, and then fumigate the place after I leave. And nobody need use me to polish their halo, either!

July 8th

It's going to be just a bit difficult, this fall, I can see that. There I'll be sitting in Mr. Carr's class, supposed to be coolly taking notes and concentrating on Sociology, et cetera, when all the time in the back of my mind I'll be smoldering over this summer's correspondence.

Today he informs me that I love whites, only I don't know it. I love them *subconsciously,* he says!

I'm not sure which part of this outrageous bit of amateur psychoanalysis I find more insulting: the statement that I love whites, or that I love them on some level of mental activity that isn't even up where I can see it.

Naturally Mr. Carr doesn't stop there. Certainly not—why, he has scarcely shifted out of neutral!

So, I condense his very wordy lecture, and I then shall enjoy myself ripping it to shreds:

The tragedy of Man, says H. Gamaliel, is not that he hates, but that he loves and hasn't the guts to admit he loves. For it takes courage to admit you're not entirely base when it's fashionable to be evil. Furthermore, love is uncomfortable, it makes demands, it complicates our lives, it goads us into doing something, into taking part. Consider the Freedom Riders, how they could have stayed snug and safe at home. . . .

As I read this, I can just see Hobart G. pacing back and forth on the teaching platform as if he were an animal resenting the confines of a cage; and I can hear his voice, the way it gets when he exhorts us to Higher Goals: "Students—don't *spend* your lives, *give* them, *use* them, *dedicate* them—" (Sound of trumpets.)

Now you, Harriet Brown, says he, aren't so much afraid or ashamed as humiliated to admit you, too, have this love-taint. Consider your soliloquy at the cookout, when you were mulling over man's viciousness throughout history: did you confine your thoughts to the sorrows of black men? No. Men with yellow skin came crowding in, and men with white, and it is getting more and more difficult for you, Harriet dear, to keep up this pose of hating those whose color is not the same as yours. You have to keep whirling and snarling and snapping at shadows which you begin to suspect aren't there at all.

Well, thank you very much, Mr. Carr! That's a charming picture, I must say: Harriet Brown, hound dog! Let me tell you about those white Freedom Riders, since you bring up the subject. Okay, I admit they did something for me which I would not do for them. I admit this may prove they are morally superior to me, if that's the point you're trying to make. But I am sick and tired of having them rammed down my throat! I wish they had never come!

The way I see it, the whites have done enough *to* us without now doing anything *for* us, for which we're supposed to be grateful. Gratitude is for dogs. You can leave a dog waiting outside the door until you're good and ready to let him in, and when you do finally get around to opening the door, instead of snarling at you or giving you the good bite in the leg which you deserve, he's all grateful and wags his tail and fawns all over you.

Well, I'm no dog, Mr. Carr, whatever you say. I'll pick the lock or I'll batter the door down, but I'll walk in on my own, and *damned* if I'll slobber thanks!

If white people want to fatten their egos, they needn't expect to fatten them on *me*.

V

❀

Sunday night, July 9th

In a way it would be easier if Life would be consistent, would stay in a pattern of repression and humiliation unrelieved by flashes of humor or decency. Then I could feel as bitter and as rebellious as I liked, and not be troubled by such questions as, am I developing into a professional martyr? or—were I to swallow Dr. Carr's Forgiveness Syrup, that cathartic for sick souls—would I be happier as a righteous saint? But Life, at any rate my life, acts like a plotless seesaw, and I continually find myself emotionally one step behind.

Today—and this is what I'm complaining about—today turned out to be an antidote for the last few days.

To begin with, Robert's leg was much better and he came hobbling down to breakfast, scorning any further bedside service. "I'm going stir crazy," he said. "That's convict slang."

"You mean you want a change of scene?" said Maureen.

"I want some, too!" said Timmy.

"Well, you shall have some!" Mrs. Daley said. "Come along to church with Harriet and me, all of you."

"No, thank you," Maureen said politely. "It would be simpler if I stay and get dinner, and take care of John Anthony. He's really too young—"

"It's okay, we can go, Maureen," said Robert. "It isn't a sin any more."

"Yes, isn't that nice?" said Mrs. Daley, coming into the kitchen at that moment. I caught her expression, and for a moment I couldn't place what it reminded me of, and then I knew. She had that same look of courteous resentment that Reverend Douglass' face had worn when he announced that the rest-room facilities of the town bus station were now open to both races. "Very gracious of them," he had said in just that tone.

"We'll have to get moving, Harriet," she said, "if we're going to turn out these children in churchgoing clothes."

It was quite a scramble, but we made it, with Maureen's help. At one point I heard Mary wailing that she hadn't any pants, and Maureen bellowed at Richard, "Well, lend her some of yours— haven't you any manners?" We were all a bit out of breath by the time we left.

"Catholics do this every Sunday, right down to the littlest," said Mrs. Daley. "It fills you with admiration, doesn't it?"

I thought, so do the Baptists and the Methodists and the Church of Zionists and lots of others, they just don't talk about it so much.

From where I sat in the choir, I could see the family. Timmy was at the end of the pew, in order, I suppose, to be able to see. Mary was next, then Mrs. Daley, separating Mary from Richard, and Robert was next to the wall. Timmy kept leaning out into the aisle and beaming at me, and Mary would hiss at him and his mother would reach across and pluck him back, and this happened several times, but nothing really untoward occurred until the sermon.

Then, when Father Tillington had hardly warmed to his theme, Timmy slipped out of the pew and stood in the aisle. His mother reached to fetch him back. He stepped just beyond her reach. She whispered urgently. Mary started after him, but he was away! Up the aisle he came, his eyes on me and a happy smile on his face. Mary looked to her mother for instructions, then slowly returned to her place. I daresay they felt the less fuss the better. Father

Tillington kept right on with his sermon just as if his entire congregation were under perfect control.

Timmy marched up the steps and into the chancel, his short legs pumping *ca-plip ca-plip,* and he headed straight for me. All my powers were on mental telepathy: child, don't you speak out! I guess my mind wasn't equal to this message, because Timmy said in a cheerful voice, "Hello, Harriet!"

I scooped him into the seat beside me and handed him a hymnal. "You hush," I whispered. "You be still unless we're singing."

So when we stood to sing, Timmy stood, and chirped his birdlike singing. I didn't dare look towards the family for fear of catching Robert's eye, which would be fatal for my self-control, I knew. I kept my eyes on the music, and on Timmy's head, with its interesting pattern of hair growing one way, then another. And it seemed to me that the congregation sang more freely and lustily than ever before.

When the service was over, Timmy walked out with me, his hand firmly in mine. After Father Tillington said the final prayers in that little anteroom, and before he sprinted to the front of the church to congratulate those who had got there, he welcomed Timmy. "Can we count on you every Sunday?" he asked, bending down to shake his hand. "It's such a joy to have anyone join the choir without urging!"

There was general hilarity on the way home.

Robert seemed obsessed with rhyming: "Since when did you aspire to sing in the choir?" he asked Timmy.

Mrs. Daley remarked, "No one can accuse us Daleys of hanging back or dragging our feet."

I couldn't restrain myself from joining in. "Don't be a Waily-Daley," I said, "be a Limber-Larynx, a Tuneful-Timmy!"

I felt a glow of pleasure at the applause which greeted this display of wit. H. Gamaliel would approve, I thought. I admit I like Timmy, and I am acting accordingly.

In the afternoon Mr. Daley could be heard using the tractor on the field above the pond. Mrs. Daley and Maureen were starting the second coat of paint on the north side of the new house, and after I had made a token gesture of taking Sunday afternoon off— I crocheted two more rows on the base of the doily, but I didn't feel like starting the flounces yet—I volunteered to man another paintbrush.

"Help yourself," said Mrs. Daley graciously. "We might as well get the outside painted while the weather holds."

Now and then we could see Mr. Daley as he came around the far side of the field. It looked as if he was plowing.

"What is Mr. Daley going to plant there?" I asked.

"Timothy, probably," said Mrs. Daley. "It's not much good for trefoil, the frost hits it too hard down there."

"It's a shame Mr. Daley can't find somebody to help him," I said before I thought. I paused, at a loss how to continue. "I was just thinking he would probably rather be working on the house," I said lamely.

"He certainly would," she said. "Unfortunately I am no good at plowing."

"Ma'am, I didn't mean you!" I said, and then I saw she was grinning at me.

"Poor Harriet, we baffle you, don't we?" she said. "We honestly prefer to do this work ourselves rather than hire it done, and it isn't just that we know we'll do it better. We want to look at this house and say *we* built it."

"Like your doily, Harriet," said Maureen. "You could buy Mother a doily and she would say, 'This is the doily Harriet gave me,' and all that, but it's not the same thing as saying, 'This is the doily Harriet *made* me.' "

"I can understand that," I said. "It's just—well, Mr. Daley is very talented and where I come from you can find plenty of good help for field work."

"Well, we can't, I'm afraid," Mrs. Daley said. "It's a matter of economics, or job opportunities, or what have you. Up here an able man either owns his own farm, or is in business for himself, or has a job with better pay than a farmer could afford. It's different in the South, isn't it? I mean," she went on, "when we were in Washington we noticed that the restaurants with colored help were more pleasant to eat in, at least for tourists like us, than those with white help. Which really wasn't surprising. In the South, if you have a white skin, any job you're capable of doing is open to you. This isn't true if you're colored, I don't care what the law says. So if you're white and you're working as a waitress, well, that's all you can do. But the colored waiters often seemed too good for their job—they were very neat, very deft and quiet, very courteous. I'm not making this up; any Northerner would notice it. Move over, Harriet, this brush splatters."

I moved over. "You don't think a Southerner would notice?"

"If they did, they'd think it proved just one thing: so Negroes make better waiters and waitresses, fine, that's the kind of job they should stick to. Let me tell you something about Southerners, Harriet—in case you don't know. Before Mr. Daley went to Korea, we lived in the South, and some of my best friends, excuse the cliché, are Southerners. They're charming, friendly, hospitable, cultured—and, on occasion, absolutely maddening. I couldn't *talk* to them. They'd tell me I didn't know what I was talking about. Then they'd tell me I was interfering with something that wasn't my business. You'd think it was a different country! Then they'd point out about Harlem, and declare people in glass houses, et cetera. And at the very same time they simply didn't see what I saw. The buses would be going off the Post into town, and there would be long lines of soldiers waiting to get on, and not one of my Southern friends really *saw* the Negro soldiers stepping back and stepping back and waiting longer than anybody else."

"It isn't always like that now," I said.

"I know; I hear tell the Army has tried to change things." She gave the paint a brisk stir with a flat stick, and went on painting and discussing with equal vigor. "The point I'm making is, Southerners don't react to the same stimuli the way Northerners do—at least this Northerner. Once in Leesville I was in the post office and there was a sign that clearly said 'Open until five o'clock.' Up the steps came a Negro woman, she's tired and it's hot and the steps are steep, and it's ten of five on that post office clock, but when she got in, wham! down went the screen and the post office was closed. I told my friends about it and they just shrugged. The clock was probably slow, they said. Even if they'd been there I know they wouldn't have seen that Negro woman's face, not as I did. And they wouldn't have seen the kind of gloating look, the grins, on the faces of the local yokels lounging on the steps. Damn it, it's *my* country, too!" said Mrs. D. "That was fifteen years ago, and I still get mad!"

Maureen said, "Harriet, you should have seen how mad Mother was one Christmas, when a friend of hers wrote, 'We count among our blessings this year our pride in our governor'—something like that—'defending freedom—' "

" 'Defending what's left of our freedoms,' " said Mrs. Daley. "This was on a Christmas card from Alabama! Hurray for our governor who stood in the doorway and barred the way! Like a cock crowing and all the stupid hens cluck-cluck-clucking their approval!"

Mr. Daley was coming through the pasture gate. "There, there, Kate, simmer down," he said. "I'm out of gas, but I see you aren't. What's your soap box now?"

"If you're black, you stand back! If you're white, you're all right! And peace on earth," Mrs. Daley cried, "not to forget good will to men!" And she slapped the paint on the wall as if she were attacking an opponent.

"Now, Kate," said Mr. Daley, "try to be more tolerant. My stars and bars, all they were trying to do was to convert you to the truth, the holy truth, the gospel according to the Confederacy."

Mrs. Daley said, "Tom, I'm warning you, don't rile me, even in fun. I'm sick of the sacred Southern tradition. It's nothing but a—a damned rock slung about the throat of the nation, that's what it is! Are we supposed to genuflect forever to Southern finer feelings? When I think of how I tiptoed around the sensitivities of our

Southern friends! Hear no evil, see no evil, say nothing, do nothing—what was I afraid of? I'll bet my grandfather was whirling in his grave!"

Maureen said, "Mother's grandfather was at Vicksburg."

"In Grant's army," said Mrs. Daley. "Ha!"

I laughed. "You never mentioned this to your Southern friends?"

"No, it wouldn't have been ladylike," she said with a grin. "That's the trouble: we're all so handicapped because we won. It's such bad manners to win a war. It's coarse. You can't say anything, it wouldn't be sportsmanlike. Look how we don't even criticize the Germans any more, but they criticize us. *Everybody* criticizes us."

Mr. Daley announced he was leaving for the village. "I haven't time to settle all the problems of the world, Kate. I've got to get gas."

"Don't let me keep you," she said.

"Mother always flies into a passion when she paints," Maureen said.

"That's because painting doesn't occupy the mind," Mrs. Daley said. "You have time to think about something else, get to brooding."

"Hitler was a house painter," I said.

"That's precisely what I mean," said Mrs. Daley.

Monday, July 10th

Incredible. Here I was, complaining that Life has no pattern, and in today's mail, following yesterday's conversation by less than twenty-four hours, was a letter from some Southern friends of the Daleys in which they said they'd like to come and spend a week or so, if it was convenient.

Mrs. Daley read the letter aloud at supper.

"Who are these people?" Maureen asked. "Have I ever met them?"

"We knew them before you were born," Mr. Daley said, "when I was in the Army. But I, my dear child, was a civilian-soldier, so when Korea subsided, so to speak, I was out—a free man. Old Bob, however, was Regular Army, a West Pointer, so he, naturally, is now in Vietnam."

"Is that the Army pal you named me after?" Robert said.

"Then they must be very good friends of yours," Maureen said.

"Yes, they are," Mrs. Daley said, "even though we haven't seen them in years. I guess we'd better say come ahead, don't you think so, Tom? After all, she must be terribly lonesome."

"Kate, where on earth will we put four more people? Doesn't Vinnie have three children now?"

"I'll be very frank," Mrs. Daley said. "I'll describe the setup here very honestly, and if she still wants to come, as far as I'm concerned, I'll be delighted."

"Are these people Southerners?" I could hear Maureen ask.

"Virginians," said Mrs. Daley, as if it made any difference.

July 11th

Today was a basic day, Grade B. I mean, it wasn't a day to change the whole course of my life, or anything like that, but it's a day that will stick with me, all right. What happened was this:

In spite of the fact that the lettuce is thriving and the peas are ready for first picking and there are numerous fryers in the freezer, Mrs. Daley declared we had nothing to eat, the larder being empty of staples, and she had to go to town—anybody want to come? Everybody wanted to come, so I should, too, and we went, and what happened, to repeat, was this:

We were just about to leave for home, and I could see Mrs. D. and the older boys heading our way, when Timmy announced he had to go to the bathroom, right now, right *now,* and Mary said there's a bathroom in the snack bar, so I said here comes your mother, you children stay right here, and Timmy and I leaped out and we hustled across the street and into the snack bar and fine, all was well, good, et cetera. When we came out again, we had to wait at the curb for some cars and a yellow bus—some kind of school bus or camp bus—to go by, and just as I was about to step down, Timmy holding my hand, somebody stuck his head out of the bus and hollered:

"Yee-ah-ha! Hey, nigger! Nigger babe! Hey, black baboo-oon! Yee-ah-ha!"

I froze. I simply stood there, like a statue, staring after that bus, more surprised than anything else. That was my first emotion: astonishment.

My next emotion was, of course, rage, but I didn't have time really to enjoy it. A totally strange woman touched my arm.

"I beg your pardon," she said.

"What?" I said, still staring after the bus.

She was kind of shaking. "I beg your *pardon,*" she said again.

I looked at her then. She was a dumpy little woman with grey hair and a pinched look about her mouth. She seemed to be angry. It dawned on me that she *was* angry; indeed, she was furious.

"I apologize," she said, "that such a thing should happen to you here. I live here. I apologize."

We were collecting a small crowd—four or five people, which is a crowd for Vermont.

"Please," I said, "let's forget it." The policeman from the traffic circle was coming towards us.

"Where the hell's that bus from?" one of the men said, not speaking to anybody in particular.

"Dunno," said another man. "Probably one of them rich kids' camps up to the state park. You get all kinds of riffraff around in the summer, looks like."

"Miss," said the policeman, "let me see you across the street."

He stopped traffic for Timmy and me, and we went across. Mrs. Daley was waiting for us on the other side. "What's the matter, Harriet?" she said. "Is Timmy—is everything all right?"

"Hoodlum hollered at her from a bus goin' through," said the policeman. He tipped his cap. "I'm sure sorry, miss. We don't often get that sort of thing up here, and we sure don't like it."

"I wish everybody would just forget it," I said.

We went back to the car and of course Maureen, sharp-eyed as an eagle, knew something had happened and she wanted to know what.

"Somebody hollered rudely at Harriet," Mrs. Daley said.

"You mean whistled at her?" Robert said. "Gee, Harriet, you have to expect that. Men always whistle at pretty girls, and you're so pretty I'm surprised you aren't whistled at all the time."

"Mother did *not* say anything about whistling!" said Maureen. "She said—"

"Forget what I said," Mrs. Daley said, taking the east road and driving faster. "I don't want to hear any more about it, and I'm sure Harriet doesn't."

"He called her a baby," said Timmy.

"Oh, oh," Robert said wisely.

"He called her a nigger baby," said Timmy, proud of himself. Silence.

"How rude!" said Maureen. She lifted her chin and looked out of the window, and the other children acted as if I were suddenly a stranger again. Nobody enjoyed themselves on the way home. I felt dirty, and resentful of the whole incident—that it happened in the first place, and that everybody had been so *very* nice to me afterwards—why I should resent that, I don't know, but I did.

Like a rape case, I guess, which everybody pretends never happened, and everybody is *so* cordial and gracious just to show they *know* she's really pure.

July 12th

Mrs. Daley and I were picking peas and we were by ourselves, the younger children napping and the older children down at the pond fishing, and it was very quiet. What made Mrs. Daley ask what she did, I don't know, but all of a sudden she said, "When did your father die, Harriet?"

I said, "How did you know he is dead?"

"Things you've said. Your aunt raising you, things like that."

I bent over to get some peas that I'd dropped. "He died when I was seven," I said.

I don't know what got into me then. Some kind of a devil got into me. Go on, I thought. Go on and ask me how he died!

"Was it very sudden? Was he ill?"

"It was sudden, but he wasn't sick," I said. "My mother was sick, and I was sick, afterwards, but my father wasn't sick. He was lynched."

She was staring at me in horror. "What do you mean—your mother and you—you mean you and your mother *saw* your father's murder?"

Well, now, I knew of course what I was doing. I was lying, pure and simple, up down and roundabout. I was calmly and coolly lying to Mrs. Daley's face, and I had no regrets, no scruples whatsoever. I'm not sure actually why I did it. Maybe as a game, a childish game to see how far I could stretch a lie and still have a grownup believe me? Or was I an adult now, using a lie as a weapon, to punish and hurt? And if that was it, why did I tell *this* lie, then? Am I obsessed by fire? Fire as a part of Hell? Or is it some kind of tribal memory I have . . . burning crosses . . . the night stabbed with burning crosses and men with sticks burning flaming throwing firelight across faces that you can't see only black holes for eyes. . . . I never saw anything like this, I'm sure I haven't, but it seems to me I've heard talk about it ever since before I can remember, because I keep thinking I have seen someone die because of fire and rope, even when I know that *I* haven't seen it, but my people have. I must have heard talk, that must be it, I heard talk and I couldn't ask anybody about it because the grownups grew angry when I asked and they said, "Now hush, chile—stop that talk, it's wicked sin to talk about such things." But what did they *do* with the fire and the rope?

I said to Mrs. Daley, "Oh, yes, we saw. I don't know why my mother watched—I don't know why she felt she had to—but I wanted to see, I wanted to put inside me, what it was like for my father to be a Negro!" *Black baboon. Nigger.* "Maybe that was why she watched, too," I said thoughtfully.

Mrs. Daley was shaking as if she had a chill. "What did they do, Harriet? Did they hang him?"

"After a while," I said.

Mrs. Daley sucked in her breath. "How you must hate us!" she cried.

"Me?" I said. I looked at her and she was a stranger to me, a strange white woman with a face like all white people's faces, the skin too thin, transparent, colorless. Did she think I'd think she cared what happened to my father? That she could care? And what difference did it make if she did?

"Not just you—all your people! If I were a Negro, I'd hate all whites! I know I would! I'd want to kill them! Don't you feel like that? Harriet Brown—don't you?"

Well, I could see I'd better give Mrs. Daley some kind of an answer.

"I used to think I did," I said, speaking slowly and trying to sort out my thoughts. "But then I came to realize you can't hate somebody unless he's basically like yourself and has the same feelings, the same standards—loyalties, if you will—and he's betrayed these loyalties. Then you can *really* hate him."

"What are you trying to say?" Mrs. Daley demanded. "I'm afraid I don't quite follow."

Oh, well, dive in, I thought. After all, I've got my bus ticket home. I said, "You know how some white man—a politician, usually—will say, real tolerant, to show what a great big heart he has, 'Oh, I'm for the Negro,' he'll say, 'after all, they're human beings, too.' Well, until this summer, *I* didn't think *white* people were human beings. Not really. As you said, they don't see what I see, they don't hear what I hear, why should I think they feel what I feel? And somebody doesn't feel like me, he's not human like me."

For a long time she didn't say anything. We worked down one row and started up another, lifting the vines and looking to see where the pods hung, which ones were full, didn't fool you with just being round and no peas filling them yet. It was hot and quiet, and I thought, I guess I gave her something to think about.

"Harriet," Mrs. Daley said at last, "once I saw a crucifix for a mission in New Mexico, an Indian mission. And Christ on the Cross had the high cheekbones and long braided hair of an Indian. I remember I got a great deal of satisfaction out of looking at that carving. It was beautiful, and it made sense. You know what I thought—what I think? I think Christ was a Jew to the Hebrews because *they* were Jews, but if He should suddenly stand in front of us now, to you He would have a black skin and to me He would have a white, because we are created in His image."

Good lord, I thought, does Mrs. Daley believe in a great-grandfather-like figure gazing down at us from somewhere beyond the clouds?

"That's what Reverend Douglass tried to tell me," I said with a laugh, "one time when I was on one of my I-hate-everybody kicks. I suppose he was trying to save my soul, or something. Anyway, I told him it wasn't true. I said there wasn't a white man living who could believe that God is black."

"Not to them He wouldn't be black," Mrs. Daley persisted, "but to you. Don't you think this is possible?"

All of a sudden I was sick of this discussion. What did I care what she believed, anyway? Her and her benign and tolerant god, catering to her prejudices, flashing on and off his pigmentation like a damned neon sign.

"Mrs. Daley," I said, and I felt savage, "I don't know *what* I think! God is white—God is black—God exists—God is dead: what does anybody know about it, anyway? All I know is, I don't want a white man kindly admitting that I'm a human being same as he is, and I don't want anybody, black or white, graciously allowing God to look like me, or me to look like God, or—or anything!"

Mrs. Daley was watching me the way Aunt Lydia sometimes does her children, as if she'd like to put the world to rights for them if only she could. Did Mrs. Daley feel sorry for me? She'd *better* not feel sorry for me!

"Harriet, I didn't lynch your father," she said, very quiet.

I thought that over, and I had a sudden impulse to laugh. I choked it down. "No," I said generously, "I know that. It was just twenty men," I added, "twenty men from Abbot County, South Carolina."

With a slight assist from me, I have to admit.

VI

July 14th

Hobie called me! Long distance! All the way from South Carolina! Hobart Gamaliel Carr, person to person to *Miss* Harriet Brown!

When Mrs. Daley came running to tell me there was a phone call for me, of course I thought something had happened to Aunt Lydia, and I thought my feet had taken root, I couldn't run fast enough. And when I realized it was Hobie, all I could do was gasp for breath and say, "Who? Who?" like a damned owl. I just couldn't believe it—Hobie calling *me!*

And then I couldn't really talk to him, of course, because the phone is in the old house kitchen and is exceedingly central. Not that I had anything to say that's especially private, or anything. But I was strangely inhibited. I wanted to find out if he had been putting phone calls through to everybody else, but I couldn't ask this outright, much as I wanted to. And all the time my heart was banging away as if I'd been racing up flights of stairs; it was making so much noise I was afraid he'd hear it.

But it was a wonderful phone call just the same, because Hobie was there, right on the other end of that wire.

This is such a strange summer. I feel so peculiar—as if layers of myself are coming off, one after the other, drying up and cracking, and I peel them off and each time I think, well, this is me, Harriet Brown. But no—it's only another layer of me. In the spring, when my life still seemed uncomplicated, I was simply Harriet Brown, Serious Student. Then in June came Harriet the Crusader who was also acutely Harriet the Whites-Hater (Albaphobe?) and now—well, what am I? How will I know when I get to the real me? And what about all these layers—do they persist in any way even after I seem to shed them like a snake skin? I mean, will part of me all my life be the girl who couldn't speak coherently to Hobie over the phone—will this girl still exist when I have become a poised, self-controlled woman whose heartbeat remains steady though riot breaks out in the back row of the classroom and revolution sweeps through the school yard—or am I not, after all, going to be a teacher?

Of course I am!

But this is all so unsettling, to have somebody who was safely in the background of my life suddenly step forward and threaten to dominate center stage. Or isn't that what Hobie is trying to do? Am I a romantic idiot, spinning fancies from a few letters and a phone call?

Yes, but you don't have to take any vows of celibacy to be a teacher.

He *did* call. And he didn't have any news of anybody else, so I don't think he was calling everybody, just me. He simply wanted to calm me down and cheer me up, he said. Of course, he did remind me, very casually, that I do stand out up here, and it behooves me to behave, et cetera. Permeating every layer of me has to be Harriet the Model Representative of Her Race.

Rats!

July 15th

The weather has won. At least I am willing to concede defeat. Summer is upon us, and high time, too, and although we are valiantly fighting back, we are clearly overwhelmed.

The tiny green beans, slender as pencils, are ready for freezing. The early peas have to be picked every day without fail. The deer have decided to leave us alone, and as a result the beets must be thinned and the pullings—tiny beets with their tops—must be frozen. Naturally the weeds are growing faster than the vegetables, and the lawn must be mowed every week, and it would be better to mow it every three or four days. And nothing seems to stem the tide of visitors. Yesterday we received warning, today they came: cousins from Chicago. Very nice and very friendly and really very helpful, in a way, because they shelled peas all afternoon. But they brought as a present a bushel of peaches, which Mrs. Daley was happy to see, the price of peaches up here being unbelievable, and not to be considered seriously, she says, although she is very fond of peaches, and so is the whole family. What I mean is, the balance swung the other way: the visitors didn't shell as many peas as it will take time to spice and can some of those peaches, and fix sugar syrup and freeze more. Richard and Robert said we shouldn't despair, they're willing to eat the whole bushel themselves.

Does Hobie like peaches, I wonder?

This evening I discovered strawberries in the strawberry patch are ripe.

Does Hobie like strawberries?

July 16th, Sunday

Mrs. Daley and I did make it to church, and I think if God fully understood the circumstances, He'd give us triple credit. It wasn't just the strawberries, peaches, peas, beans, beets, hens reaching roasting stage, cow with new calf and therefore needing gentle, sympathetic care (Maureen tells me), but a tree fell over somewhere, or a branch fell off a tree—anyway, something somewhere broke the wires during the night and when we woke up we had no electricity. We couldn't heat water for coffee, and after a while we didn't have water (the pump runs on electricity) and therefore after a while we also didn't have sanitary facilities.

"Let's go to church and pray," said Mrs. Daley, and we set out.

"Are you going to pray for electricity?" I said.

"You pray for something tangible if your beliefs permit it," she said. "I was taught we mustn't pray for things. I am going to pray for a sense of humor for myself and a saint's patience for my husband."

When we got home the electricity was working, but I couldn't see any change in Mr. and Mrs. Daley.

July 17th, Monday

Today the sun shone in the morning, and we hung out an enormous washing. It clouded up by noon, and we raced to bring in what was dry, and it rained on the rest of the washing. Now, of course, the vines were wet, and we couldn't pick peas, nor go near the beans, nor touch the tomatoes, which need staking, nor look for strawberries—we might spread mildew, rust, blight, and rust, in that order.

So we ironed, mended, cleaned house, froze peaches, and made a peach shortcake for supper, thus making good use of this free-of-field-work afternoon.

Mr. Daley came home fit to be tied. He is restoring a house for a woman who wants him, once he gets the foundation firmed up, to repair the walls so they won't leak but *be sure they still lean the way they are leaning now!*

Mrs. Daley has asked me to pray for patience and a sense of humor for everybody, since I was so successful about the electricity.

Would a phone call be considered tangible, I wonder? Or would I be foolish to put my talent to such a test?

July 18th

Today I received my Silky-Strate in the mail, and Maureen and I experimented this evening with hairdos, distinguished, hairdos, chic, hairdos, provocative, et cetera. We agreed the French twist was really the best, and asked Mrs. Daley, and she declared it was *élégant*. So tomorrow when I get in the pea patch, I shall feel very haughty and Above This Sort of Thing. With the head of a lady on my shoulders, I don't know, will I work better or worse? But I do hope I get into the pea patch tomorrow, the situation is crucial! The vines didn't dry today, and the main crop of peas is almost ready, yet the early peas keep coming.

July 19th

Rain. And no letter from Hobie.

July 20th, Thursday already!

Thank heaven! Today the sun shone and a breeze blew and by 10 A.M. we could get back into the vegetable garden, and I utterly ignored the fact it is Thursday and therefore my day off, and I worked all day. We put up 19 quarts of Perfect Green Beans (the labels said), 10 quarts of wax beans, 6 quarts of peas, 7 quarts of beets and greens, and it is so odd to find myself actually thrilled to write out such a mundane list. The fact is, this one day has produced the vegetables for forty-two suppers for this family! *Six weeks* of supper vegetables!

We were trying to figure, Robert and I, the cash value, and we couldn't believe it. About $15, we thought, at 35 cents a quart for frozen vegetables of top-notch quality. My, were we impressed! Then we multiplied the man-hours. From 9 A.M. until 4 P.M., five people (Mrs. Daley, myself, Maureen, Robert, and Richard), 7 times 5 is 35 man-hours; that's a little over 40 cents an hour.

"Why did you have to figure everything out?" Maureen said. "Couldn't you just say the family is richer by fifteen dollars? *I* don't want to know I'm working for peon wages!"

"You don't have to glower over forty cents an hour," said Robert.

Reluctant applause.

I can multiply. I said, "You certainly cannot cheer on a thousand bucks a year."

Maureen demanded I prove it. Okay, 40 cents an hour, a 50-hour week, that's $20, I said. Fifty weeks, that's a thousand dollars.

"I don't care, it's better than the stuff in the stores," Maureen said.

"We are alimentary aristocrats," said Mrs. Daley.

In spite of everything I still made it to choir practice, although I felt a little uneasy about going, as Mrs. Daley did not seem at all cheered by the prospect. However, we went, and I took my doily, as I always do, because there's a lot of time when we are sitting or waiting or talking or something, and I can put on another loop. It's coming along, but not very fast, I'm afraid.

On the way home, I thanked Mrs. Daley for taking me.

"That's all right, Harriet," she said. "I don't mind as much as you might think, hearing me grumble about rush rush all the time. If I really didn't want to take you, I wouldn't. Besides, I love to listen to you sing. Lord, if I could open my mouth and have sounds come out of my throat as come out of yours!" She laughed ruefully. "Last winter we went to hear Odetta, she was singing in Hanover. Have you ever heard her?"

I said only on records. And thought, has Hobie ever heard her? Does he like her voice? And thought, how little I know about him. And thought, it's like a fever, I think about him all the time. . . .

"They don't do her justice," Mrs. Daley was saying. "There's nothing like being right there. We had seats in the front row, and there she was, not twenty feet away, and I could see every slightest bit of expression and hear every softest softest sound and also really be *in* her grand full-throated trumpeting. It was a marvelous audience, all your age—I guess Tom and I were the oldest people there. And the students would be utterly silent and then burst into wild applause—that kind of response just makes everything better, you know. Well, the point is, Odetta has a voice like blackstrap molasses. Rich, raspy, gutsy, smooth as satin—whatever she wants. And she'd been singing and I'd been singing inside, you know what I mean? With her voice. And then she decided on a bit of audience participation, and asked us to sing with her, a chorus of 'When I Wake Up in the Morning' it was. Of course there was practically no sound of anybody else singing, just a kind of mumbling. It was such a—such a *comedown*," said Mrs. Daley, "to have to use our own throats. Nobody could bear to sing out!"

Mrs. Daley never ceases to surprise me. It really hadn't occurred to me that her people are sensitive to the difference.

"Some white people have lovely voices, too," I said. I tried to think of some names, in case she demanded proof.

"So kind of you to mention it," she said. "You almost make me think you're acquiring a little tolerance yourself, Harriet Brown."

From her tone I felt sure she was teasing, and I was emboldened to ask her something I wanted to know, outright, in words.

"Mrs. Daley," I said, "you really think of me as an equal, don't you?"

"Damnation! Of course I do!" She spoke sharply, as if replying to an insult. "Have I said or done anything to make you think I don't?"

"No, ma'am," I said.

"Then why on earth did you ask such a question?"

"*I* think of me as everybody's equal," I explained, "but I don't expect everybody shares my opinion. I just wondered how you felt."

"For the record, I do think of you as my equal, and you may quote me. Because you *are*. Would you like a signed statement?"

I shook my head. "It's really not necessary," I said.

Mrs. Daley is not one to drop a subject quickly. She kept turning this one around, tipping it this way and that, as if it were a glass she was holding against the light. "I don't mean an equal in every way," she said. "I meant that of course you're my equal as a human being, as a citizen—oh, you know what I mean—we're equal as *people,* individuals with rights and duties and taxes to pay and an address where we can be found—that sort of thing. But equal as women—" She paused, and thought. "Well, that's not so simple. You are a complex creature, God knows. Musically, vocally, you're my superior. I'll not argue that. As for keeping a cool head, I think we're about even—you were marvelous when Timmy tasted the oven cleaner, and I flatter myself I did all right when Robert hurt his leg. I suppose we've both shown about as much courage as we've needed, up to now, anyway. But I think I'm ahead of you, Harriet, when it comes to—well, acceptance. I don't mean docility. You're a rebel, but that isn't what I mean, either. I mean you haven't yet learned to say 'So be it' to anything, you keep smashing yourself against things you can't change. And then you're afraid to show your feelings. It seems to me you laugh when you can't possibly feel like laughing—you're trying to hide what you feel, whether it's grief or anger or whatever."

It is a strange thing about cars, and driving at night. Two people inside are so isolated from the rest of the world, there they are, they can really meet, really talk to each other. (No wonder so much courting goes on.)

"Sometimes I feel you are my daughter, Harriet," she went on, "and I see suffering ahead and I wish somehow I could warn you against it, steer you away. You mustn't let your feelings harden. Of course, you have every reason to feel rebellious, and angry, and to scorn meekness, but I wish you would believe me when I tell you the time will come when all you have suffered, everything that has happened to you, will enrich you. You will be so much stronger than if you'd had it easy. You may even be strong enough to be compassionate, even toward my race, which you are not, not yet."

"You want me to be Jesus Christ and say, 'They know not what they do'?" I said harshly.

"Yes," she said.

"Dear God!" I said, and laughed.

"All right, but in twenty years you'll be able to," she said. "In twenty years, Harriet, as a woman you will be magnificent. Remember I told you."

For a moment I couldn't think of a single thing to say. Anyway, I didn't laugh.

Finally I said, "Okay, I'll come visit you in twenty years and we'll see."

"Mind you come in my front door," she said lightly. "I imagine by then we'll have the new house done and there'll be two doors, one in front and one to the kitchen. You just remember, Harriet Brown, that I am *not* Mrs. Ritzbitz Who-Knew-You-When. You march in my front door or I'll *really* be insulted."

"I doubt if I'll be an opera star," I said. "For a Negro, I really haven't a particularly good voice."

"I was thinking more of someone like Eleanor Roosevelt, or Jacqueline Kennedy—women like that."

I felt my face going hot. "Well—I—well," I stammered, feeling very embarrassed, "goodness, I guess if that's what you have in mind, I better be a good Democrat!"

But I still didn't laugh.

You know, Hobie, this place is dangerous. You get to believing all those old fairy tales about You Can Be Anything You Set Your Heart on Being, and all that. I don't know what it is that makes me feel this way, either. It's not the farm, or the Daleys, or the black faces at church, or the surface courtesy in the shops, or anything I can put my finger on. Possibly it's those lunatic stone walls, running all over the countryside, dividing the fields and lining the roads and crisscrossing through the woods. Those walls represent to me such a staggering amount of toil, such a backbreaking exhausting struggle to make a living. Sometimes I get to picturing people like the Daleys—anyway, they have the Daleys' faces—man, wife, and children, all of them dragging those rocks off the land he wants to plow. And then while I am looking at them in my mind they have black faces, because I just naturally associate black faces with this kind of work, and I have consciously to transpose those faces back into white faces.

Maybe that's it. (I feel as if I'm talking to Hobie, writing this, and it's a very comforting feeling.) These people up here don't have to look down on anybody else, for self-respect. Maybe they *do* look down on other people—those who live on a mountain and their road is terrible look down on people whose roads are smooth, and the people who have it colder in winter, or who are older than anybody else and still working, maybe they don't actually sneer at anybody else, but they certainly feel cocky. They have both self-respect and self-esteem.

I think it may be this quality that distinguishes the Northern white from the Southern white—at any rate that's what I would say now. The species Northern white, subspecies Vermonter, doesn't need to look down on anybody in order to bolster his self-respect. It's pretty well shored up by circumstances.

And so he can look out level-eyed at us Negroes.

Sunday night, July 23rd

This is the first chance I've had to draw a steady breath since Thursday. Because Friday morning, very early, I heard Maureen scream. Her room is upstairs and I heard this scream float out, and then I heard strange, groping footsteps, and by now I had grabbed my coat and put it on and I was out in the hall and there, coming down the stairs, was Maureen—I supposed. She had a terrible face like a Dick Tracy cartoon. Her features had disappeared, it was as if she had been blown up from inside. She looked absolutely awful, and if you want to know what I did, I screamed, too.

"Harriet, are you there?" she said in a shaky voice.

I ran to her and took her hand. "I'm here, oh, my God, child, what on *earth!*"

She was wearing her pajamas. "I couldn't find my clothes," she said. "I can't get my eyes open. My face feels funny—I don't think it's *there*."

I guided her into my room, sat her on my bed, leaped into my clothes, and led her by the hand down to the old house.

Nobody was up yet.

I sat her by the kitchen table, by the window. "I'll get your father," I said, and I went and rapped respectfully yet urgently on their bedroom door. I could hear John Anthony commence to bang his crib.

"Mr. Daley!" I said. "Maureen is sick!"

"Coming!" he called, and pretty soon he and Mrs. Daley came out.

"She's in the kitchen," I said, and I was trying to think of some way to warn them, to kind of break the shock, when Mr. Daley caught sight of her, where she was turned towards him, and the ghastly smooth puffed head of her was only too clear in the early sunlight, her mouth a slash, her nose two little holes, her eyes two creases.

"God save us!" he said, and Mrs. Daley screamed.

They got out of her the information that she had, two days before, boasted to Robert of her immunity to poison ivy and she had *rubbed some on her face.*

"And day after tomorrow the Wisters are coming," said Mrs. Daley in a floating kind of voice, as if she was beyond further involvement.

Timmy came downstairs and looked at Maureen and said, "Who's that?"

"It's me," said Maureen, and began to sob. I felt all shook up at this point, because I couldn't imagine Maureen crying.

Mr. Daley used the phone. "Dr. Nord will meet you at nine o'clock at the clinic," he told Mrs. Daley. "He says cortisone and I don't know what else, anyway, he says don't despair."

So we flung breakfast together and Mrs. Daley and Maureen drove off, and Mr. Daley left, and the rest of us thought, what ho, in forty-eight hours we will have four more people here, the question is where? But this wasn't a question I had the rank to answer.

"It's too cold for them to sleep in the barn with only a ladder over them," I said, and Richard thought this was very funny.

"It certainly is a pity if you think that is witty," said Robert.

"Sour grapes," I said absently.

"You make a poem, Harriet," said Mary wistfully.

"I say, 'Sour Grapes!' for goodness' zapes!" I said.

I got the razzberry from Robert, which I deserved.

But we did clean Robert and Richard's room thoroughly, completely and unmistakably. You had only to walk in and your eyeballs ached. The woodwork was scrubbed. The floor was scrubbed and waxed. The windows gleamed. The junk was picked up and hidden.

"It won't last," said Richard, "but it sure looks impressive now."

"Mother will come home and she will say, 'Oh, what good children!' " said Mary.

"All you have to do is keep it this way for ten days," I said. "Just ten days. You start littering up the place before the company leaves, and I *personally* will hold you responsible."

"God!" said Robert.

Mrs. Daley returned with Maureen just before lunch.

"I had a shot in my seat," Maureen announced.

"Oh, is that swollen, too?" said Richard.

"Unfair. She can't see to clobber you," I said.

"No, it isn't, you *rat fink,*" said Maureen.

"She'll live," said Robert. "If she has enough zip to keep a flip lip—uh—we'll not worry if her face poison ivy doth erase! How's that?"

"Mighty callous," I said.

In the afternoon we went up to the new house and cleaned Maureen and Mary's room. Then we swept all the debris—pieces of board and bits of sheet rock and so on—out of the living room and carted boxes of the stuff to the cellar. And we did the same for the dining and kitchen areas.

After supper Mr. Daley, Richard, Mary, Timmy, and I went to a neighbors', whom I had never met before, nor even seen, but they were living there in a red-painted house with big barns, and I had never seen them because they are raising many cows and milking them and had never had time ever since I came to stop and see how the Daleys are, and the Daleys had certainly never had time to stop in and see how they are, and Mr. Daley said we must get together sometime, and they said we certainly must. We loaded two cots and a daybed into the truck and came home and installed them in the living room of the new house.

"This is the South Guest Room," said Mrs. Daley. "Here we shall put Mrs. Wister and her daughters, age thirteen and nine."

"What are you going to do about walls, Mother?" Richard wanted to know.

"Details, details—I'll think of something," she said. She added in a worried voice, "We mustn't forget to rig up a good light in the cellar. It's the only easy way in and out."

I was thinking, but didn't say, that it might not be a bad idea to tack warning signs on the inside of the kitchen door and the front door. There aren't any steps outside yet, and anyone rushing out without previous briefing is likely to find himself sailing into space like a sky diver.

Mrs. Daley had done the shopping that morning, Friday, when she took Maureen to the doctor. So the next morning, yesterday— is that possible? only yesterday?—which was Saturday, we did a washing of clothes. And we straightened and vacuumed Mr. and Mrs. Daley's room, which is also John Anthony's. And we cleaned, really cleaned, Timmy's, upstairs in the old house. And we shut and fixed a lock on the storeroom beyond, but before we did lock it we dragged boxes of unmended mending and a half-made braided rug and some furniture that needed fixing—Mrs. Daley claimed they were Priceless Antiques and I would agree, they certainly were nothing you'd put a price to—and all this we hid in the storeroom.

Then we went into the living room—I mean the one in the old house—and I looked around curiously because I really hadn't looked at it before, it was just a place I went in and out of, chasing John Anthony. The wallpaper was hanging loose in some places, and the sofa was Priceless, all right, and there was a TV, which nobody ever turned on, as far as I knew, and there were more boxes of books stacked against the inner wall, where they would be safe from rain.

"I wonder if it would look better if I pulled off the wallpaper," Mrs. Daley said.

I didn't offer an opinion.

"Somehow I don't think so," Mrs. Daley said.

"They aren't coming to see your living room," said Mr. Daley. "They are coming to see you."

"That's what you think," said Mrs. Daley.

"Do you want me to pick peas?" Richard asked through the window.

"No!" said Mrs. Daley. "Yes! Oh, heavens!"

"Daddy, what should I do?" Richard said.

"Pick peas, son, pick peas," said Mr. Daley. Mrs. Daley was yanking the paper off the wall, starting with the part that was coming off by itself. "My God, Kate, that is not going to improve *anything*."

"All is illusion," said Mrs. Daley, ripping away.

What we did before bedtime is really literally a kind of blur in my mind, as if I was in some kind of delirium at the time. It seemed to me that Mrs. Daley believed (though if you had asked her point-blank she'd have denied it) that the honor of the family and the reputation of her husband as a provider and herself as a homemaker *demanded* that no matter what the circumstances of the season/weather/work, both houses must be as immaculate as if she had a full-time cleaning woman, the meals set before her guests must be as varied and delicious as if she had a full-time cook, and the lawns and flower beds must appear as if she had a full-time gardener. I knew she must feel this way, she must be driven by some such ideas, because of the incredible amounts she forced herself to do, of cleaning, straightening, moving of furniture, polishing, and painting—yes, painting: she painted the walls where she had peeled off the wallpaper, because she found a half-full can of the latex-based paint with which she had painted the wallpaper seven years earlier, and the paint was still good.

About 10:30 P.M., we were in the new house tacking up sheets on the two-by-fours which indicated the position of the wall between the South Guest Room and the hall. These sheets were new ones, in deep colors according to the latest fashion, and although she didn't have enough of one color—two were deep green, two deep blue—the effect was really very good.

Mr. Daley came marching in, a tall glass in each hand. "Harriet, go to bed," he said. "In this sovereign state, as they say in your native habitat, you're too young for any of this firewater, it's illegal to drink if you can't vote, and anyway, it's only Kate here who needs sobering down. Kate, for the love of God, what has got into you? Why this orgy of preparation?"

I could hear them very plainly because they were just across the hall from my room, with no walls to speak of between.

"Now why should I have to justify making a few simple gestures when we're going to have company?"

"Few simple gestures, hell," he said. "Drink your whiskey and see if you can clear your head. Who is coming? The President? General Eisenhower? A former beau? No, just old pal Vinnie and her three kids. I bet they all put their feet on the furniture and eat with their fingers. There's no need for you to kill yourself this way."

"Vinnie has been to Japan since we saw her," Mrs. Daley said, "and she's been to Germany, and in both places she lived *very* decently, with at least three servants, and I'm sure she was leading a very cosmopolitan life. Her husband is now a lieutenant colonel—"

"What is this, some kind of feud with the Army?" he demanded. "Are you trying to prove us crummy civilians ain't such slobs, that sort of thing?"

"Tom, haven't you any pride? Don't you care how the place where we live *looks?*"

"Now I get it," he said. "The nesting instinct, running amok. Poor Kate. She can't help it. Freshen it up with a twig here, a bit of string there."

"Just once, just this once, Tom Daley," said Mrs. D. in a voice which I recognized, because it sounds the same, coming from black or white—it was the voice of exhaustion blown up into rage, from which all reason has flown—"your charm has lost its magic. Your humor leaves me cold. In fact, *you* are absolutely the last *straw!* I am *not* playing a game, Tom Daley! I am trying not to look quite like the shoemaker's children, do you understand me?"

"Loud and clear," he said. "The way you live just isn't good enough for you—do I read you right?"

"There you go—twist everything around and make it *my* fault!" she cried. "And all over Vermont, on practically every mountain, there is some outrageously charming house, perfect in every detail, utterly livable, every single part of it absolutely *right,* a house which you have built for some woman who already *has* a house in Connecticut or Long Island or somewhere—"

"My God, I do it for money!" Mr. Daley roared. "Those women are not some kind of harem of mine! I am trying to earn money—M-O-N-E-Y—so you can *eat!*"

"I already have so much to eat I'm getting *fat!*" Mrs. Daley said.

There was a short silence, and then, "Always complaining!" said Mr. Daley, and I held my breath and then she started to laugh and kind of cry at the same time, and then there were some snuffling noises and some low murmurs, and I thought, oh well, they won't get a divorce this week, anyway, thank God, with all that company coming.

And instantly it was morning. *This* morning, Sunday. I made my groggy way down to the old house. The birds were yawping their fool heads off in the orchard and everywhere I looked, the sun, leering at the world from well above the horizon to the northeast, was splintering into a million stabbing bits of light from dew on every leaf, twig, and blade of grass.

The early bird, I thought, is welcome to the worm. Serves them both right.

I found breakfast ready, and coffee hot. I drank, and looked about me. A number of people had already eaten. What time was it? And whence came those bucketfuls of ferns and daisies and wild roses? I drank a second cup of coffee. Beyond my window the birds began to modify their notes from shrill to trill, and the sunlight softened its focus. Maybe I would survive the day after all.

I could see an expedition returning down the hill. Mrs. Daley, Richard, and Mary, bringing armfuls of flowers, branches of some tree that has fragrant white blossoms, and long graceful strands of honeysuckle, filled pitchers and vases and jars with their treasures, and put them all over in both houses.

"The hand is quicker than the eye," said Mrs. Daley.

And she was right. Both houses looked charming, *élégant* in a strange way, individual, chic—proving that all is illusion, indeed.

We went to church in a kind of trance. We drove home.

"I have to decide," said Mrs. Daley in a faraway voice, "where to put Marion. Would a fourteen-year-old rather have a blanket roll in the kitchen area of the new house—we could borrow Richard's mattress, Richard could sleep on the box spring—or would he rather use the sofa in the old house? I mean, the bathroom down there does have its drawbacks, and you know how teenagers are about bathrooms. They go in there to worship. It's a kind of cult."

"Mr. Daley uses that bathroom," I said.

"So he does. We'll put Marion in the new house," she said.

I wondered if it had occurred to Mrs. Daley that she was putting four guests from Virginia in a situation where they'd have to share toilet-room facilities with me. Since she obviously took this hospitality bit very seriously, ought I to mention this point? I decided, for a number of rather subtle reasons, that I should not.

We had dinner at noon. Mrs. Daley said she didn't know just when they were coming, this afternoon or this evening, and we would adhere to our regular schedule.

"Ha!" barked Mr. Daley. "Back to normal, eh? I wish I could believe it!"

Immediately after dinner Robert and I deprived Richard of his mattress. Maureen trailed in to see what Richard was supposed to sleep on. She had been moping in her room (except for meals) ever since she was stricken, and this was the first good look I'd had of her in two days. It seemed to me the swelling was down a fraction; if you looked sharp, you could detect the color of her eyes between the swollen lids.

"All this sweat and strain for nothing!" she wailed. "Those children are all the wrong age. A *nine*-year-old girl! What a *bore!* A thirteen-year-old girl—I bet she uses *lipstick!* And a boy fourteen!" She didn't elaborate on this last disaster. I gathered she considered the bare statement enough.

"They are probably saying the same thing about this family," I said. "A girl eleven! What a bore! A *nine*-year-old boy! What an impossibility!"

"How could anybody object to me?" Robert said. "Dr. Spock says I'm cheerful and cooperative."

"There's no percintage in complaining of vintage," I told Maureen. Robert whooped. "I need two clean sheets for the boy's bed," I went on. "Who has two sheets?"

No one had any more sheets. Sheets not in use were tacked to the living-room walls.

"I hear a car!" Richard shrieked. "They've come! They're here!"

Maureen fled to her room and the boys and I clattered down the cellar stairs.

They were indeed here. A good deal of cheek-kissing among adults was going on as Robert and Richard and I reached the front lawn. Mrs. Wister was pretty and plump. Her elder daughter, Alma, was slender and pretty and was smiling politely. The younger girl looked sullen, as if she had been compelled to come along against her wish, or possibly better judgment. The boy had a bad case of acne but a friendly expression. Somebody ought to tell him to hold his shoulders straighter.

I had a feeling it was going to be a long week.

Everybody began to move toward the house. The girl Alma turned and acknowledged my existence by saying coolly, "Bring my footlocker. It's the one with the initials A.W."

Mrs. Daley stopped dead in her tracks and gave the child a measuring look. Then she recovered her manners, and said pleasantly, "We're putting you all in the new house, and I think it would be easier to drive up closer. Don't worry about your luggage, Alma, with all these *manly* muscles available."

I took John Anthony and went to romp with him on the lawn while the tour of the old house took place. I could hear Mrs. Wister exclaiming, "Oh, now isn't this dahlin'! Isn't this quai-aint!" (I can't keep putting in the Southern accent. Everybody knows what a Southern accent sounds like, and Mrs. Wister sure has one.) "But you've fixed everything so *sweet*, Kate! You mean you're movin' out of heah? My, but it's just so *sweet!*"

The tour emerged and headed for the new house, the Wister children trailing the group. After a few paces, the boy Marion skillfully siphoned himself off from the rest and eased his way back to the old house.

Probably shy, and glad to see a bathroom, I thought. I was wrong. A few minutes later, when John Anthony had me down and was crowing in triumph above me, the boy emerged from the house and headed my way.

"Hey," he said, "better call a repairman."

I sat up. "What?" I said.

"The TV," he explained. "It doesn't work."

"It doesn't?"

"No, it doesn't," he said. He stared at me. "I didn't know people up North had colored help."

"Oh, just everybody does," I assured him.

"Well, it's broke," he said. "Did it work this morning?"

"How should I know?" I said.

"Didn't you turn it on?"

"On *Sunday* morning?"

"Yeah, that's right, today's Sunday," he said. "How many channels can you get?"

"How should I know?" I said. I stood up. "It's not *my* TV." It wasn't his, either, I was thinking.

"Don't they let you look at it?"

Mr. Daley came around the corner of the lane by the garage. Timmy was riding his shoulders. "Harriet, pop this fellow down for his nap, please."

Young Master Wister approached his host. "Say," he said, "the TV doesn't work."

"I know," Mr. Daley said with admirable calmness. "It hasn't worked since last February."

"What's the matter with it? Wouldn't anybody come out here? Or couldn't they fix it?"

Mr. Daley grinned. His face had a devilish look. "That's what I was afraid of," he said. "That they could. So I took the precaution of not calling anybody."

Oh, oh, I thought as I transferred Timmy onto my own shoulders. Mr. Daley is getting his dander up. This is going to be a *very* long week.

The afternoon passed, and it was for me a very strange afternoon. I prudently kept in the kitchen, although I knew that just beyond my sight the peas were swelling, the beans were lengthening, the summer squash was proliferating, and the strawberries were possibly fermenting. Now and then I would see Master Wister cruise past the window, as anchorless as any visitor to a strange land where he can't speak the language. He was plainly and frankly miserable.

Finally he wandered into the kitchen, and opened the refrigerator.

"Just a minute," I said, and slammed it shut. "You want something, you *ask*."

He looked surprised. "Golly, I was just going to see if there's any cold Coke."

"There isn't," I said.

"Well, gee, where is it kept? I'll put some in."

"We don't drink that slop here," I said. "Soft drinks rot your teeth, don't you know that?"

He was staring at me, not mad, not embarrassed, just as if I weren't quite reaching him, as if we were on different wave lengths.

"Hey, this place is kind of crazy, isn't it?" he said. "I mean, is everybody here some kind of nut, or something? Hey, no TV since *February*—I can't get that straight, know what I mean? I mean, are they too poor to have it fixed? Gimme the straight dope."

"You," I said, "are the nut, boy. Only *rich* people don't have TV, don't you know anything?" I could hear somebody coming, so I switched tracks. "If you're thirsty, I'll fix lemonade, or iced tea—which would you like?"

"Hey, iced tea—yeah, that'd be great!"

It was Mrs. Daley.

"Master Marion would like some iced tea, ma'am," I said primly, and enjoyed her startled look. "Shall I prepare enough for everyone, ma'am?"

"Why, thank you, Harriet, that would be nice." She looked exhausted, and I wondered if Mr. Daley had any gin I could use to spike her glass. She needed some high-octane gas, in my opinion, or she'd fizzle out before night. "I thought I'd give you a hand with getting supper started."

I was just saying I thought I could manage, when Master M. cut in, having obviously never been briefed on who gets priority in conversations.

"Say," he said, addressing Mrs. Daley, as anybody could tell who observed which way he was looking, "have you ever watched Ed Sullivan? He's on every Sunday night."

"Who?" she said. "Oh, yes—yes, I have, now and then."

"It's a rerun tonight," he said, "but it's going to be good. He'll have that little mouse."

"I'm so sorry," said Mrs. Daley. "The TV hasn't worked for months."

"I'll bet you could get somebody to fix it if you called."

After a moment, she said, "Does this program really mean that much to you?"

"Yeah, well, after all, I'm going to be here a *week*," he said, making his point, God knows.

"Yes, so you are," said Mrs. Daley faintly. "I'll discuss it with my husband."

Master Marion was leaning against the peach tree on the front lawn and eating cake and drinking iced tea when Mr. Daley stalked past him without a word.

He went directly to the phone and began dialing furiously. "Will you kindly tell me why the *hell* I didn't lay in a damned good supply of whiskey?" he demanded. "Here's to Hospitality, may we all survive it. I need a week's mint juleps on hand. Were you advising me? No. Off somewhere scrubbing latrines, that's Harriet Brown. Never opening her mouth with good advice. Yes? Hello? Is Joe there? Oh, he is? Yeah, I guess I want to talk to him." He covered the phone with his hand. "How's that for being unreliable—right at home on Sunday afternoon, by God! Hello— say, Joe, this is Tom Daley. Yeah. Oh, fine, never better. Say, Joe, that TV you sold us—yeah, the one we bought in '55—that's the one. Well, it hasn't worked since last winter and as it happens we have house guests and I was wondering, you don't repair them on Sunday—oh, you do?" He listened, frowning. "Well, that's damned decent of you. Thanks. Thanks a lot." He hung up. "How do you like *that*? He'll be right over. You can't depend on any-body, Harriet. Makes you bitter, doesn't it?"

I was fixing a tray with glasses, pitcher, cake, and all. "Mr. Daley, sir," I said, "Mrs. Daley, the poor lady, is all tuckered out, seems like. I was wondering if maybe you, sir, would care to slip a little gin in her tea?"

"My God, Harriet, watch out, your background is showing," he said, grinning. 'That's what I'm complaining about, my lass. We finished the whiskey last night, and in all this orgy of preparation, nobody thought to lay in what restores the red cells. The ladies are calming down the little girls. Calming them down and cheering them up. I was afraid I would strangle them, so I left." He drained a glass of iced tea. " 'But where do we hang our dresses?' 'But, Mama, this room doesn't have any floor!' And does Mama pound daughter to a pulp? No, nothing so satisfying. 'But they're building a new house, darling, isn't that marvelous? It just isn't quite finished, dear!' Hell's fire! Are they typical?"

"Sir?" I said cautiously.

"You know what I mean. Are these typical samples of the finest flower of the South?"

"I thought they were your friends," I said, genuinely puzzled.

"Okay, I deserved that," he said.

"No, I mean I thought you used to know them pretty well."

"I never met the next generation, Harriet, they didn't exist. And I dunno—it's been fifteen years. I guess people change in fifteen years. I'm sure I have, Lord knows."

But as for his question, I didn't have to answer it, which is just as well. Because I swear I never in my life saw anything like it. I told Maureen as much. Maureen refused to leave her room, refused to come down and meet the company, refused to emerge for supper, and kept her door locked.

"Nobody comes in here except Mary," she hissed through the panels. "I'm not coming out until I'm well."

"You are counting on a chamber pot?" I hissed right back.

"I can crawl through the storage room under the eaves," she said in a stage whisper. "That gets me into the closet right next to the bathroom. Then I just dodge out."

"You are being ridiculous!" I hissed. "You're handsomer right now than Master Marion, believe me! You should see his skin! He lives on Coke and potato chips and hot dogs! He told me so himself!"

She unlocked the door and opened it a crack. "Hurry!" she said, and I slipped in. "When did he say this?"

"After he found the supper nearly inedible," I said. "We had corn chowder and a big tossed salad and homemade rolls. Unfortunately they were whole wheat."

Maureen swallowed miserably. "I love corn chowder," she said. "I could eat a quart of it. And homemade rolls—"

"If you will open the door more than six inches," I said, "I will bring in your tray."

She ate with an eagerness that did my heart good. I had fixed a very fine salad, with little snippets of all kinds of fresh greens, only to see it spurned by three of the pickiest eaters I never hope to see. Mrs. Daley's rolls were very fresh and anyway she had taken the trouble to make them. Did she deserve the comment, "Gee, I never saw rolls like these"? The treatment of the corn chowder was not so outspoken, merely the toyed-with spoon, the disgusted look.

"Didn't they like anything?"

"They loved the watermelon," I said. "I'm sorry, you don't get any. I had a piece saved for you but it disappeared."

Maureen was buttering her third roll. "Which is the one that whines?" she said. "I could hear her, she whines all the time. 'Mama, she's got my hair rollers! Mama, do I have to go see the cows? I don't wanna see the cows!' Like that."

"That's Gail," I said.

"She kicks, too. I heard her give somebody a good one. The mother had gone out."

"Listen, Maureen," I said, "I need you. Cut out this drama and join the living, will you? You look lots better than you did, and anyway, there's no beauty contest running. The fact of the matter is, no mere recital will do these people justice. I may crack under the strain. I need your moral support, Maureen. Honest."

"You move me to tears," she said. "Okay, Harriet, I'll come to breakfast. You can count on me."

I took her tray, and then I gathered my crocheting and retreated to my room, and first I wrote to Hobie, and then I started this report. That was hours and hours ago. I see by the unearthly bluish light glowing in the window of the old living room that somebody is still watching TV. I'll bet they'll be cheerful and cooperative tomorrow.

VII

Monday, July 24th

Maureen came down for breakfast, and it was sensational. Mrs. Daley had briefed her guests, but not one iota of suspense or shock was destroyed. When Maureen walked in, I thought she looked much improved—her nose was reappearing and there was more of her mouth than yesterday—but Gail dropped her cup of cocoa on the floor. Just let go of it, open the fingers and let gravity do the rest. And, of course, gasp in horror, and stare.

"I have the Poison Ivy Plague," said Maureen, "but relax, it's not contagious."

"It's my sister, the cortisone kid," Robert said.

Alma asked her if she was in pain, and Maureen said, "Only in my pride."

Master Marion didn't say anything—well, he did say "Hi"— and then, having eaten (fortunately we had some cornflakes he could substitute for our cooked cereal, which he never eats, he told us), he returned to his incubator, the TV. He came out for lunch and for supper, which is now dinner, I suppose in deference to our guests, but otherwise he needed no entertaining.

After breakfast, Mrs. Daley asked her friend Mrs. Wister if she wouldn't like to have the lounge chair over by the vegetable garden, so she could rest and relax and chat while she, Mrs. D., got after the garden. "Kate, honey, I *suhtinly* am not goin' to sit aroun' while you *wuhk!*" she said, and the two disappeared towards the garden, both in shorts and halters, Mrs. Wister's tan nice and even, I noticed.

Maureen asked the girls if anybody had showed them around.

"What is there to see?" Gail said.

"There's the barns and the milk house and the chicken house—" Maureen began, when Gail said, "What's in there?"

"In where?"

"In the chicken house."

Maureen said, "*Chickens* are in the chicken house."

Gail said, "Who wants to see chickens?"

"I do," said Alma.

"You would," said Gail with a sneer.

Alma glared at her sister. "What did you come for if you don't want to see chickens? What did you think there *is* on a farm, anyway? You're only going to be here a week. You certainly can look at chickens *once*."

It was quite a conversational style.

Maureen kept Timmy and John Anthony from under foot, and I got the washing out. Mrs. Daley picked peas, and brought them in baskets to be shelled for freezing, and her friend trailed her, apologizing for not being much help. "I declare I don't see how you can keep it up!" she kept saying. "I just cain't help but *mahvel* at your energy!"

In the afternoon, while Mrs. Wister was resting, Maureen came to help with the freezing.

"Where are your guests?" her mother asked her pleasantly.

"Improving their suntans," Maureen said. She made a contortion of her features that resembled a smile. "That's what they said. 'We have to work on our suntans,' they said, 'because Mama promised us she'd take us to the shore at Cape Cod if we came here.' "

"Poor Vinnie," said Mrs. Daley.

About half an hour before supper Master Marion emerged from the living room to check on the menu. He informed me amiably that he could eat the pork chops but that Swiss chard gave him gas.

"No!" I said. "And you so young!"

"What's this thing?" he said, picking up my crocheting where I had left it on my table.

"Put that down!" I said sharply. "You'll unravel it!"

"But what the heck is it?"

"It's a doily I'm making."

"A what?"

"A *doily*," I said, raising my voice as if he were deaf. "Don't you know what a doily is?"

"No," he said.

I stared at him. "It's something you put on a little table and then put a vase on it with flowers," I said. "You know what a vase is?"

"Sure," he said. And he wasn't mad or annoyed or anything. It was like poking putty. "But we put our vases with nothing under them."

"Other times, other customs," I said.

"I have to be through eating by six-thirty," he said. "There's a spectacular on then." He opened the refrigerator door, then hastily closed it. "Didn't anybody go to town today? Get any Coke?"

"Out," I said, picking up a knife. "Out of my kitchen. *Out.*"

He went.

Mr. Daley was delayed, and when he came there were mint juleps in the orchard, and dinner wasn't even served until quarter to seven. When I came to announce it was ready, I heard Mrs. Wister saying in a warm, happy voice, "It's just wonderful of you to have us! Oh, it's so good for the children! I wrote Bob that I did so want the children to see their own country—see how other people right heah in America live! Army children never really see very much of the way civilians live and wuhk and all. Oh, this is such a grand opportunity for them!"

Over the serving of the pork chops, casserole of potatoes with onions and sour cream, and Swiss chard, Mr. Daley cordially inquired of the young guests if anybody had given them the ten-dollar tour. "That includes a swim in the pond," he said.

Alma said, "Maureen did ask if we'd like to, but I tol' her I prefer salt water."

"Sorry, no ocean," said Mr. Daley. "But you did see the animals?"

Gail shuddered. "Boy, I'll say we did," she said. "Boy, does everything *smell*."

There was a pause.

"Well, damn it to hell, *all* farms smell!" said Maureen clearly. "Sorry, Dad. I was just making up a poem—"

"You may leave the table," said Mr. Daley. "Eat in the kitchen."

"Yes, sir," said Maureen.

She brought her plate out and set it on my table.

"—less than *othuh* farms, deah," Mrs. Wister was saying.

Maureen looked at me with burning eyes, and I was pleased to see her features were identifiable as her own. By tomorrow she should look like herself entirely.

"Welcome, outcast," I said very softly. "This table is integrated."

"I hate her," Maureen said just as softly. "She has four bathing suits and each one cost more than fifteen dollars. She told me so. And her sister was wearing a bathing suit this afternoon that cost twenty dollars. Her sister didn't bring her *good* one, she said—she's saving it for a date with her *boy* friend."

"Don't get ulcers," I said very very softly. "Women like that age early. You'll see."

What worries me about all this is that I find myself caring. It's all very well for Hobie to write me that he doesn't think I have a shriveled-up soul—that's a comforting thought, and I'm glad he thought it—but I really never believed I would ever give a damn about any white's problems, not even if somebody got crippled or lost his job or was doomed to an early death from some lingering disease, or anything. Tough, I would say (so I thought) from inside my well-armored immunity. And here is this utterly asinine situation, so silly and really so crashingly unimportant when viewed against almost any place you care to name: Little Rock, Oxford, Birmingham—Watts, even, just to look at it from another angle—and yet I find *I* am involved, my nerves tingle with genuine resentment. Why should I care that we have work to do, and here are these leeches, sucking the summertime away?

And that's another thing. I am continually using the word "we." Lord, do you suppose emotionally I'm a Negro only skin deep? I *despise* Negroes who wish they were white! If you aren't proud of what you are, you're *nothing*. I'm scared to peel off another layer of me—I'm afraid that from here on in, I'm hollow.

Harriet Brown, White Sympathizer!

Tuesday, the 25th July

Today I was ironing and the girl Alma brought her soiled clothing and said to me, "When you wash these, be careful of that sweater, hot water will ruin it."

I said, "Did Mrs. Daley tell you to bring those to me?"

She looked at me and said loftily, "I wouldn't think of bothering my hostess about my laundry."

I said, "Don't you know how to wash your own things?"

She said, "Are you refusing to wash my laundry?"

I said, "That's right, I am."

She said angrily, "What are you, one of those uppity Northern niggers?"

I said, "Educated people in this country say 'Negro.' I'm from South Carolina, and we always heard Virginians took pride in their manners. Where did you get yours, off the scrap pile in Germany or Japan?"

She glared. "Are you *darin'* to criticize my manners?"

I said, "I would if you had any to criticize. You've been here two days and you haven't said 'please' or 'thank you' yet."

She bit her lip. "You are one of the rudest people I've ever known! Aren't you the maid here? Why shouldn't you do my washing?"

"No reason," I said, "except that you're fully able to do it yourself. I'm hired to help Mrs. Daley with *her* work, and doing your washing is none of her duty, God knows."

She went to the laundry tub and began to fiddle with the water. "I'll ruin my manicure!" she said angrily.

"What of it?" I said. "You don't tell a lady by the polish on her nails."

She swished and swirled her few things around in some suds, and rinsed them, and then she said, "Where do I put these to dry?"

I said, "Try the clothesline."

She said, "But that's in the sun! This is my twenty-dollar bathing suit and I always dry it in the shade!"

"Hush," I said. "Don't talk like that here."

"What?"

"Don't talk about twenty-dollar bathing suits in this house," I said, "where the first room they are finishing is the library. We do not hold aquatic aristocrats in high esteem."

She said, "You sho' have a strange way of talkin'." She went out. She came back. "I need some clothespins."

"Please," I said.

"What?"

I went on ironing.

"I said I need some clothespins!"

I looked at her.

"Please," she said.

I handed her the clothespin bag. She turned to go.

"Just a minute," I said. She looked back. "You forgot something. You forgot 'thank you.' "

She looked at me for a long moment, her chin up, her eyes very pale, her hair so pale it was colorless. Then she smiled. *"Thank you,"* she said sweetly. "You can tell a lady by her manners to her inferiors, that's what they teach us in Virginia."

"I'll file that," I said, and she flounced out.

Later on, Master Marion came out of the living room to see if there was something he could munch on. I told him I was fixing lunch in three-quarters of an hour.

"Gee, I dunno," he said. "That's a long time. Don't you have any crackers or potato chips or anything?"

The way he was leaning against the wall, I thought maybe the boy actually is hungry. It's possible. He can't seem to bring himself to eat at meals.

"Have an apple," I said, "if they don't give you gas."

"An apple?"

"Or a hunk of cheese. Just don't make a habit of it. I'm not running a short-order café."

"Why are you so mad all the time?" he said amiably. "Hey, here's some of that cake—*hey!*" He drew back his hand. "Say, what did you say this is?" he said, pointing to my crocheting.

"A *doily,*" I said.

He said, "It sure doesn't look like much."

"It's nowhere near done," I said. "You keep adding to it and it gets fuller and fuller. Then you starch it very stiff and iron it and it makes a frill like a ruff, you know, like one of those collars Henry the Eighth wears—" I had lost him. He was staring out the door.

"Hey, how about that!" he said. "I'll take one, yeah, man!"

It was the mailman in his four-wheel-drive powerhorse, a vehicle a little bigger than a jeep, and painted a brilliant yellow with two lights on top, flashing golden lights.

There was a C.O.D. package for Richard Daley, $1.00 plus 30 cents C.O.D. fee, 20 cents some other fee, and 10 cents postage.

Marion thrust his hand into his pocket. "I think I've got that much," he said. "Somebody can pay me back."

I thanked him kindly, and hefted the package. It felt like a book.

"Where is everybody?" Marion said. "There's nobody around. You aren't going to wait lunch or anything, are you? There's a bowling match—"

"They've gone on a pig hunt," I said.

"You kidding?"

"There is a pig loose in these hyar hills," I said. "Our pig. Every now and then, when there's nothing urgent scheduled, somebody goes and looks for it. It's a motif running through our days."

"What will they do if they find it?"

"That's a very good question," I said. "Move over, I have to get to the stove. No, don't lean on the refrigerator. Look—outside, okay?"

When the safari returned, empty-handed, I presented Richard with his mail. "You owe Marion a dollar and sixty cents," I said.

"U.S. coins," Richard said, in that worshipful tone older males use for "Baby, you're beautiful." He and Robert vanished out the door.

When I went out to scoop John Anthony from his playpen, I found Richard and Robert sprawled under the peach tree, prisoners of dejection and gloom.

"I tried to tell you," Robert was saying. "God, Richard, you should have used your *head*."

Richard wasn't saying anything. His face had that sucked-in look that means he's scared he's going to disgrace himself crying.

"Of course you feel terrible," said Robert. "A dollar and sixty cents for bad news!"

"What's the trouble?" I said.

"Richard had some coins—"

"Shut up!" said Richard savagely.

"—that he thought were worth a lot of money, only they aren't," said Robert.

"It *said* six thousand dollars for a nickel!" Richard said. "It didn't say a certain, special, very very scarce one."

"Yeah, but you should have *realized*."

: 151 :

"Oh, shut up!" said Richard.

"You aren't really six thousand dollars poorer," I said. "It isn't as if you lost some money you had. Come on and eat, that always helps."

"That's the way to take it, Harriet," said Robert. "Chin up. You'll manage somehow."

"Shut *up,* you nitwit!" Richard said. "She doesn't know anything about it!"

Well, I was going to, after that.

"He was going to give you—" Robert began.

"It was *my* idea," said Richard.

"Who says it wasn't? He was going to give you the money, or as much as you need. For college."

Damnation, as Mrs. Daley would say. Unfair.

"You're not obliged to help me through college," I said. I had to restrain an impulse to give Richard a hug. "You find any buried treasure, hang onto it. You have to help pay for your own college education, don't forget."

"Yes, but it's specially tough when your father's dead," Robert said.

"Who told you that?" I said sharply.

"Mother did," Richard said. "She said, 'Harriet's father is dead so don't make any stupid remarks around her about orphans or fatherless children or anything.' "

"Come and eat," I said helplessly, "or everything will be spoiled."

Thursday morning, July 27th

Yesterday was an astonishment from start to finish.

The first thing was: Alma came down as I was getting breakfast and asked if she could help.

"You feeling all right?" I asked.

"My mother said I should offer," she said.

"You may set the table," I said.

Second surprise: the poor child did not know how to set the table. Age thirteen. How underprivileged can you get? I showed her how, and I was so sorry for her I did not lord it over her at all. With all those bathing suits, she'll probably be married at sixteen, and then what?

Gail came in and whined that *she* wanted to set the table, how come *Alma* gets to do everything? So I had her put John Anthony in his high chair and feed him, and it interested me to see that John Anthony put up no fight at all, but ate as if mesmerized.

The morning was hot and dry, and a steady wind blew from the west and kept little flurries of dustdevils dancing down the lane. We picked peas earlier than usual, because the vines were dry, and besides, everything hinted we were going to get a storm. The birds were discussing it back and forth in the orchard, and the leaves on the poplars kept flipping over to show their silvery undersides, a sure sign of rain, Maureen said.

It began to rain about noon, first a splatter across the windows and then a steady drumming. I raced to the new house to close the windows, and then I raced back, and the sky was black overhead and light along the horizon, and I thought, oh, oh, we are going to get it. And we did!

It was a deluge. The rain streamed so thick we couldn't see the hills. They were hidden behind a blurred curtain of grey water. The drive turned into a river, puddles appeared on the lawn, and Mrs. Daley, Maureen, and I ran with pots and pans and put them where plop! plop!plop! plop!plop! the water was coming through the ceiling in the living room, through the ceiling in the storeroom upstairs, through the ceiling in Timmy's room. Then we ran with towels and stuffed them along the windowsills where the rain was pouring in along the cracked glass and where the putty was gone. Then we ran with old mattress pads, rolled them into dams, and rammed them as barriers against the water pouring in under the dining-room door, and under the workroom door.

Then we ran to empty the pots and pans, and to put washcloths or small towels in the bottom of the pots and pans so the water would not splash out as it hit. Then we ran to move Timmy's bed, because a new leak had developed right over it.

And all the time the rain came down, and the driveway began to wash away in ruts, and the only consolation was that the *new* house, thank God, does not leak, Mrs. Daley kept saying as a kind of litany.

And the company watched the rain, and watched our efforts to keep the house from being flooded, as if they were caught in a dilemma of courtesy: our performance frankly fascinated them, yet wouldn't it be more polite to pretend that nothing was amiss? Alma was inspired to pass a compliment. "Harriet knows just what to do," she observed. And she smiled sweetly.

And the wind grew stronger, and the rain more horizontal, and the old house shuddered and a branch blew against the wall and we could see a piece of shingle flip away down the driveway, and the bushes and trees danced wildly, helplessly, in the wind. I didn't like it at all. It was as if the storm had drawn back a fist and was striking and striking at us.

Then, as suddenly as it sprang up, it was over. We went out about four o'clock to view a sodden world, drenched, soaked, littered with torn leaves, the orchard scattered with half-grown apples shaken from the trees, the flower beds enough to make a gardener weep, iris blossoms in tatters, spikes of blue flowers—larkspur, I think—broken, hollyhock on the ground.

Mrs. Daley didn't stop to lament her flowers. She hurried to the vegetable patch, and I hurried right after her.

The corn was the worst. It wasn't so much broken as uprooted. The rain had soaked the soil until it was soupy, and then the wind had flattened the top-heavy stalks. They were lying like toppled toy soldiers, neatly collapsed in one direction.

Beyond this devastation we could see that some of the tomato vines had been blown from their stakes, and the tallest peas, the last of the main crop, were tilted into the next row, stakes, wires, and all. Nothing else was really hurt, although the leafy vegetables, lettuce and chard and so on, were mud-spattered, and the beans wouldn't be so clean and quick to pick, either. But such problems could be dealt with. It was the corn that made us heartsick.

We had been joined by everyone except John Anthony, who was still asleep. Even Marion was on his feet. He sloshed over to tell us the electricity was off, and he took note of the state of the corn. "Gee," he said, "can't you kind of make 'em stand up?"

Mrs. Daley straightened one stalk, and she stamped around its roots to firm the soil, and then she let go. The stalk remained erect for a moment, then swayed slowly, weakly, and fell across its comrades.

Gail said, "I bet *I* can make it stay up!" She scrunched down in all that muck and scooped at the sloppy soil with her hands, pyramiding the soil around the base of the corn stalk.

"Gail is always playing in the sand at the beach," Alma said.

"I'm not playing now!" Gail said, her eyes flashing and her lips drawn back like an animal. "I'm not standing around like a movie star, either! Why don't you *do* something, you lazy dope?"

Gail's corn was standing—the first one . . . and the next . . . and the next.

We sprang to help. After a moment, Alma came forward, too. And then her brother. Mrs. Wister stepped delicately into the row, and lifted stalks and held them while Mrs. Daley shoved soil about the roots. We worked as teams, and it was really work. The stalks were heavy, and soaking wet, and cold to the hands. Trowels and spades were of little help. The soil was wet, lumpy with small stones, cutting with large stones, and harsh with half-rotted humus. It had to be packed about the roots, and for this one's own hands were the best tools.

We worked desperately. I got the feeling I was rescuing prisoners, and the faster I worked the more would be saved, and at any moment some unspecified horror might stop my rescue operation, and so I worked without stopping for breath, Maureen and I together, alternating tasks in order to ease our backs. Richard and

Robert were working like heroes, shouting encouragement to each other and announcing at the top of their lungs their score: eighty-*four,* eighty-*five!* The two ladies worked together, and Alma and her brother. Mary was watching Timmy, and bringing little handfuls of soil to whoever was near her. Gail worked by herself, holding the stalk with one hand, scooping the soil with the other, snarling at anyone who approached to get out of the way and keep their big feet off her corn and stop swiping her soil, and this refrain stepped up in volume and acidity when the one venturing near was the girl Alma.

"What would happen to those two, I wonder," Robert remarked, "if you put them in a bare room and locked the door?"

"What kind of a room?" Mary asked.

"A bare room."

"The bear would eat them up!" Mary said, and burst into tears.

We were all getting exhausted. We were soaked and muddy and hungry, and I could hear John Anthony wailing because no one had got him up, and I was debating whether I ought to ask leave to get him, and get supper, or would this be interpreted as a form of chickening out, when the sound of a car toiling up the hill distracted us. We stopped work and stretched our aching backs and listened.

It was Mr. Daley's jeep. As it ground its way into the lane, performing a kind of discothèque dance over the ruts, the children converged in that direction, shouting news of our disaster.

"I thought I might have to get out and hike," he said. "Washouts all over the place. Hailstones smashed a couple of greenhouses near Bridgewater, and the wind took out a picture window in Pomfret." He was staring at the slaughtered corn while he delivered this news bulletin. "My God! You mean just the wind did that?"

"We've been propping it up," Mrs. Daley said wearily.

"It was *my* idea!" said Gail. *"She* was just standing around but *I* thought up what to do."

There were two one-hundred-foot rows still to be rescued. We had done (roughly) seven such rows. This adds up to a lot of corn for a family of eight, but the children sell the surplus (if there is any) to summer people, and are allowed to pocket the money. Understandably, no one wanted to abandon the last two rows.

"Come on, men," said Mr. Daley. "We'll finish while the women fix supper."

Gail whined, "What about me? It was *my* idea—why can't *I* help?"

"Quit griping," said Mr. Daley. "You are top sergeant, so don't set a bad example for the troops."

It was the first time I saw that child smile. It startled me. She was almost pretty—I'd never have thought it possible.

The electricity was still off, so we were very sparing with the water, but there was enough for us to clean up—what luxury, a clean skin!—and dry clothes felt so good. With the stove not working, supper threatened to be difficult, but we fixed sandwiches of peanut butter and cream cheese and so forth, and put on dishes of pickles and raw onions and other seasoners, and there was ice cream for dessert, and naturally *this* meal brought forth praise from our guests.

"Gee," said Gail, in case any of us were too dense to get the point, "this is what I call food!"

The electricity came on about eight o'clock, saving Marion's evening, and I was able to wash the dishes, saving mine, and Mr. Daley could have his coffee, saving everybody else's.

As soon as I had finished, I went to my room and went to bed. No radio. No reading. No letter to anybody, not even Hobie. Sleep! In thy sweet oblivion all men are equal. (I made that up.)

This morning I thought I'd better just forget it's Thursday and I put on my one remaining clean uniform and I went down to help with breakfast. Mrs. Daley sent me right back.

"A day off is a day off," she said.

So I changed into my white blouse and black cotton skirt and I felt conspicuous, believe me, strolling back to my room after breakfast, and Mrs. Daley and Maureen doing dishes, but I'm paid to do as I'm told and not argue, so I didn't make a scene, just left the kitchen gracefully, stepping aside to let Alma enter (she'd overslept) and ignoring her stare.

I loafed about, wrote up the above account of yesterday's happenings, added several yards of loops to the doily, and felt useless, vaguely lonesome, and strange. I would have preferred to sit in the lounge chair, but the whole world was still dripping wet. I could have gone to the old house and caught up on my own ironing, or even romped with John Anthony, but I knew I'd feel even more strange, loafing in plain sight, although I was fully entitled to be doing nothing.

It occurred to me that perhaps I was being used for propaganda purposes: we in the North do not exploit our Negro help, but honor the verbal contract of a Day Off no matter what the circumstances, et cetera. In which case I ought to be seen relaxing—I could cooperate that much, couldn't I? So I strolled down to check on the corn.

I was really cheered by the sight of it, proudly perpendicular. The only sign of yesterday's battle for survival was a certain devil-may-care look, like veterans of combat who scorn parade-ground perfection in dress and affect an air of tattered dishabille.

After lunch I put on an apron and stood at the sink, and as Maureen brought out the plates, I said to Mrs. Daley, "Ma'am, you said I could spend my day off as I please. Right now it pleases me to do up these dishes."

Maureen lent me a hand, and when we had finished, she suggested a game of Canfield. Mrs. Daley was sorting freezer boxes in the kitchen, so we took our cards and sat at one end of the dining-room table. At the other end the Wisters, mother and daughters, were writing letters—I suppose they were letters, at any rate they were writing something—the world outside being still too wet for sunbathing. Mrs. Daley's insistence that I take my usual day off was having one odd result: the Wisters and myself in the same room, and all of us seated. It was a social landmark.

After Maureen tired of playing and drifted away, I laid out a hand of solitaire. As I studied my cards, it came to me suddenly what it is that makes the Wisters seem so different from the Daleys. It isn't so much their accent, or their attitudes; it's the fact that they never seem to read anything. They've been here five days, I thought, and this letter-writing is the first hint I've seen that they are literate.

I became aware that Mrs. Wister was looking at me. Perhaps I ought to gather up my cards and depart? No, it appeared that wasn't what was on her mind.

"Harriet, tell me," she said, "did you have any difficulty in getting admitted to the college of your choice?"

It wasn't so much her words that surprised me, although they did have a certain familiar ring, calling to mind the titles of those magazine articles that blossom every spring as regularly as the trees leaf out. It was her tone of voice. Mrs. Wister spoke to me casually, agreeably, without the slightest hint of the imperative mood. You'd have thought she considered me in the same category as her daughters' friends, that is, persons on the same social plane but suffering from youth and inexperience, to whom, therefore, an adult should address a friendly remark as a matter of courtesy, to put them at their ease.

I said no, I had been accepted without any trouble.

"Well," she said, "I'm surprised to hear you say that." (I still can't be bothered with the phonetics of her accent: "Ah'm suhtinly su'prised to heah yo' say thet.") "Everybody keeps saying that the Negroes in the South just don't get a decent education." She curled up the tail of this remark to show she considered it a question.

I said, "It isn't as if I tried to get into Swarthmore or Oberlin or some place like that. Jacob's Ladder is a Negro college, strictly segregated, you might say, so I was competing for admission only with students whose opportunities have been no better than mine. Of course," I added, "I did go to an integrated high school for two years."

"We have three Negroes in my class," Alma said, as if she deserved a medal or something.

Mrs. Wister said, "Wouldn't you rather have gone to a school

: 159 :

with all your own race? I mean, isn't it more comfortable for you now, in a Negro college?"

"I admit I didn't enjoy being a guinea pig," I said. "I was very much aware that I was being watched like a mouse in the lab, to see if I could do the same work as the white students, if my brain would work the same as theirs. But I put up with it, because there were some college-prep courses I wanted."

"Where we live," Gail said, "all the *new* schools are for the Negroes. Boy, are they terrific! They have fancy tables that fold up into the wall in the hot-lunch room, and some even have *showers!*"

"They really are much nicer than our own," said Mrs. Wister. "Wouldn't you rather go to a lovely new school, Harriet, and no strain on you, be among your own people?"

God knows what she was hoping I'd say. Something quotable, no doubt, to prove her point, whatever *that* is.

"Mrs. Wister," I said, "I don't want any special treatment just because I'm black. Don't you see, those brand-new buildings with all their extra-special fancy touches are nothing but a bribe, a bribe to make me forget you don't think I'm good enough to sit in the same classroom with your children. They're an insult, actually. The same kind of insult as the buses, only with a thicker sugar coating. Maybe you were overseas and you didn't hear about that—" for she was looking at me blankly. "But we were paying the same fare as white people, our dime was good enough to get us on the bus, but not good enough to get us a seat anywhere we saw one vacant. We had to go to the back of the bus, and if there wasn't a seat back there, we had to stand. Now, if we were going to get second-class treatment, should we have had to pay the same fare as the whites?"

Mrs. Wister said, "But, Harriet, that would have been special treatment, wouldn't it? A cheaper rate for colored?"

"And I would have resented it very much," I said. "A nickel for Negroes, and let them stand, a dime for whites, a seat on demand." Not bad, I thought; I must remember that for Robert. "No," I went on, "that would be un-Christian, and I couldn't accept it."

"Un-Christian?"

I said, "I just don't believe God made any mistakes when He made the world. I don't think He tried and tried and tried and tried, four times, to make Man in His own image—black and brown and red and yellow, getting the job better and better as He went along, until at last—hey, man, looky! White like Me!" I shook my head. "I think He did it on purpose. I think He likes variety."

"My, you certainly are . . . unexpected," Mrs. Wister said. I couldn't tell whether she meant it as a compliment or not.

I said politely, "I imagine you think so only because maybe I'm the first of my race you've ever talked to."

She laughed. "For goodness' sake, how can you say that? Why, I was born and raised in Virginia, I've talked to colored people practically every day of my life."

"And what did they say to you?" I said. "They said, 'Yes'm, it sho'ly is a fine day,' or, 'Ma'am, this chile is tuckered out,' or, 'Ma'am, I can't come tomorrow'—words that weren't anything but window shades pulled down tight. What they were thinking you had no idea."

Gail said sharply, "What were they thinking?"

I shrugged. "How do I know? It all depends. But you can count on one thing, they weren't saying what they were thinking."

"Prove it!" said Gail. *"Prove* that Negroes don't say what they think. What are you thinking right now that's different from what you are saying?"

Oh, no, you don't, I thought. I can't be got at on demand. I'm not going to tell you what I think because I don't like you well enough. I'm not giving a chunk of my insides away to just anybody.

I laughed. "If I told you," I said, "I'd be *dis*proving what I said, don't you see?"

And I gathered up my cards, and went into the kitchen, feeling pleased with myself. I'd kept up my end of the conversation quite creditably, if it was a conversation we'd been having. On the other hand, if it had been a debate of some sort, darned if I didn't think the honors went to me. Harriet Brown, Argumentarian.

Mr. Daley phoned he would be delayed, the storm had washed out some foundation forms, he said, we'd better go ahead with supper without him. So Mrs. Daley fried a quartet of chickens, Mary said grace, and I put the platter of golden toasty savory deliciousness in front of Mrs. Daley.

Gail said, "Ugh! Fried chicken!"

I froze in my tracks. Mrs. Daley simply sat there, not moving, her arm with the serving fork poised over the chicken, and her face went red, then drained pale again.

"My God," she said, and I got the distinct impression she was praying.

Verbal window shades, apparently, are not expected to be pulled in the Wister household. Whatever comes into the mind may go out the mouth.

"Why, Gail, I thought you like fried chicken," her mother said mildly.

"I do, usually," said Gail. "It's just that I have seen where these chickens came from. Boy, oh boy!"

Maureen rose, turned to her mother, and said between clenched teeth, "May I be excused, Mother, before you send me away?" and she marched into the kitchen.

"I must ask you to overlook Maureen's temper, Vinnie," Mrs. Daley said sweetly. "She isn't used to children raised by the permissive method. Tom has very old-fashioned ideas, you know; he says he can't subscribe to the steam-valve theory, it's much too hard on the parents."

"Steam valve?"

"That's what he calls it, the theory that if children repress any of their feelings, they're likely to build up pressure and eventually blow up. Of course, considering Tom's temperament, I must say I agree with him, it would never do for our family."

She stabbed at the chicken and I passed plates.

"And this is Maureen's," she said to me, "and this is yours,

Harriet. We'll stack the dishes and do them when we get home. I'm taking Harriet to choir practice," I heard her say as I retreated. "One of the other churches, I forget which one, is having a festival on the green tonight. Most of it is 'swapping attics' but there are some delightful things to do, like riding in a 1914 car, that sort of thing." I could hear them debating who cared to go.

Maureen sank her teeth into a leg of chicken, not bothering with knife and fork. "What delicious flavor!" she said, not lowering her voice, either. "It must be the chicken manure, don't you think? Boy, what a yummy cobwebby taste, yum yum, or is it seasoning of spider? Imagine passing this up—some people don't know good country cooking—"

"You be quiet," I muttered. "We've got to get your mother through Friday and Saturday yet. I thought for a minute she was going to lose control."

"And Sunday, too," Maureen said. "They're not leaving until Monday. Sunday traffic, you know."

"They bucked it coming," I said.

"That's different," Maureen said with a wicked smile.

As it turned out, only Mrs. Wister came with us to choir practice. The Daley children had been to church fairs, and weren't tempted, apparently, by antique cars; besides, Maureen wanted to serve her father's supper, whenever he should get home. The Wister children could not bring themselves to neglect the TV. So Mrs. Daley and Mrs. Wister investigated the booths on the village green while I practiced modifying my decibels.

When I came out again into the warmth of the evening, the air moist and still under the maples, there were paper boxes of home-baked goodies stacked on half the middle seat of the car, and on the floor some slatted wooden boxes held chunks of soil which bulged with some sort of fleshy roots. I waited by the car, propping myself against the hard metal of the fender, and listening to the children's voices echo under the canopied branches of the trees. There were ropes of colored lights glimmering through the heavy

: 163 :

leaves, and the scene should have appeared festive, but the heavy air and the dusk and the voices and the laughter all blurred into a mood that made me strangely sad. I had come out of choir practice with the music still warm in my throat, and now here was this strange aching emptiness, washing over me suddenly like a wave you don't see coming.

Mrs. Daley and Mrs. Wister emerged from the crowd. "Look at these treasures!" Mrs. Daley said gloatingly, beaming at the limp plants she was carrying. "Heuchera! I never have any luck with heuchera—and they're supposed to be so easy to grow. Maybe these won't die on me—they're from the Methodist parsonage garden and surely they had a proper start. Keep your feet out of the day lilies, Harriet. Do you suppose firm discipline is the answer, Vinnie? For heuchera, I mean."

The ladies got in front and I sat in what was left of the middle seat and we set out for home.

You would think on an evening like this, we could just go on home and never mind the archeology. But no. Mrs. Wister's attention had been called to the layered personality in the middle seat—me—and she commenced to pry. Maybe she thought this was the chance of a lifetime to excavate that enigma, the Other Race. Maybe she was simply curious, as women are curious about people. Maybe, God help her, she thought she was being courteous, steering the conversation to include me. In any case, whatever the reason, she certainly tried to take a peek at what was beneath the opaque surface.

"What do you think of the North, Harriet?" she said.

"It's all right, Mrs. Wister," I said.

"You mean you're happy here?"

"I'm happy wherever I am," I said.

"Well, supposin' you had to go on livin' here—do you think you'd be just as happy livin' up here as back home?"

For one split second Mrs. Wister had me scared. Stay up North—for the rest of my *life?* Always and forever everything strange, lacking something, like that gathering on the village green this evening, with me always and forever on the outside, standing on the edge, listening and looking and seeking something . . . but what? For birdsong in the dark, splashing like a fountain—was that it? Or was it the voices, they were all wrong, they didn't have the right flow, they didn't come in little ripples, slanting up, kind of lilting, or in spurts, or with sudden explosions of laughter—or anger—or whatever it is that makes voices sound as if they come from black throats. And the evening air didn't have the right smell, either, no scent of honeysuckle, heavy, walling the country lanes, no feel of dust, warm and thick beneath one's feet, no warmth, no enfolding warmth anywhere. . . .

I said primly, "There are things I'd miss, but I make it a point to be happy wherever I am."

Mrs. Wister said doubtfully, "I wish I knew what you're really thinking right now, Harriet."

"I'm thinking it's a lovely evening," I said, which was God's honest truth. That's what I *was* thinking. Or had been.

Mrs. Daley gave me a sharp look in the rear-view mirror. "You know, Harriet," she said briskly, "you have to learn to meet people half-way. Okay, so for three hundred years nobody let you open your mouth. Can't you see that's all past and done with? Nothing is ever going to be right between us until you Negroes will tell us whites what it is you're really thinking, and we listen. An awful lot depends on you responding as soon as we *can* listen, you know, Harriet. Slam the door in our face and God knows when we'll try again, before we say once more, 'Come on, we want to know how it really is with you.' "

I said, "Mrs. Daley, I think that's what we're doing right now. I think we're hollering at the top of our lungs what we really think, how we really feel."

" 'Freedom Now,' " said Mrs. Wister. " 'We Shall Overcome.' " She nodded to show she was really hip, boy, she was plugged right in to the twentieth century.

"Well, we don't believe that's all you're thinking," Mrs. Daley went on. "Naturally I don't mean *you*, Harriet Brown, I mean your people. We believe you Negroes are thinking, 'Just wait, just you wait, you whites—as soon as we can we'll give you just what you gave us, only worse!' That's what we think they're thinking, Harriet, because that's the way we white people would think if we were Negroes!"

"Well, ma'am," I said carefully, "I'm sure there are lots of Negroes who do think exactly that. I'm not saying they will *act* that way, but I don't deny they think they'd like to."

"What about the Negroes you know—don't they feel that way?"

I stared out at the watery green light, fading from the hills now, draining into the sky. It looked so peaceful, what a shame we couldn't just look at it, just ride along and never mind getting all churned up inside.

My father . . . would he want a white man to die the way he did? And I didn't think he would, no, not any man, coughing and coughing his life away all that long, sweet spring, that long, slow summer. And grieving all the while for my mother, and she wouldn't wish on any white woman her death, nor her life either, I knew she wouldn't. Okay, take Aunt Lydia, waiting on the porch for her pupils, her arms wide and loving, waiting to embrace them in the warmth of her love. "Why here comes Amanda Jackson— good mawnin' Miss Amanda! I been waitin' for Amanda this mawnin'! Now heah she is and I'm so happy now!" Vengeance? Retribution? Aunt Lydia? I could imagine what she'd say if I suggested such a thing. "Mind yore tongue, chile!" she'd say. "The Lawd isn't asking me to step into His shoes!" Well, what about Josie—Josie McNair who meekly and lovingly went tripping off to jail that time she was arrested for doing her Virgil translations where white folks were being served coffee—the evidence all pointed to Josie really and truly believing in "turn the other cheek." Who else but Josie would write me all lighthearted and serene that she's "working for a couple of kooks, all right—they insist I eat at the same table with them—" and never a hint that she resented being Exhibit One, Look How Tolerant We Are. Or maybe she honestly didn't feel that way. With Josie you never knew. All right, that leaves Hobart Gamaliel Carr . . . Hobart Gamaliel Carr, on whom can be poured catsup in a public café and he does not so much as raise his voice let alone his fist. . . .

"No, Mrs. Daley," I said at last, "the Negroes I know, I guess they all really believe the non-violent bit, the love-thy-enemy stuff."

"But *you* don't—is that it?"

Now why did she think she could probe as much as she pleased? Just because she pays my wages?

"It works, doesn't it?" I said cautiously. "So I have to believe in it, don't I?"

Mrs. Wister smiled. "Yes'm, it sho'ly is a fine day."

I shook my head. "No, ma'am, I'm not giving you that. I just don't know what I do believe, exactly. Sometimes I suspect I put on non-violence the way some people do Christianity—you know, just to be thought respectable, put it on and wear it like a decent dress." I laughed. "I have a teacher who believes that someday there won't even be a color problem any more. He believes the time will come when we won't think about the color of people's skin, not the way we do now."

"How do you mean?" Mrs. Daley said. "Maureen has red hair, Mary is a blonde, Harriet has a brown skin—you mean like that? A detail that helps to describe you, but that's all?"

"That's what he says," I said, and laughed again.

"You think it's impossible?"

"I *know* it's impossible," I said. Mrs. Wister was looking at me as if she had dug up some fragments she didn't know if they were fake or real. I said to her, "Could you ever forget, I mean *really* forget, I'm a Negro?"

"No, I couldn't," she said, and she didn't have to take any time to think it over, either. She had the answer right there ready.

"And I could never forget you are white," I said.

Ever, I thought. Forever and ever, as long as I live, I could never forget.

And that's what's going to defeat this love-thy-enemy stuff, Hobie. We neither of us, white nor black, will ever forget. No matter how long we think it over, no matter how much singing and praying we do together, no matter how much crisscross holding of hands and bearing witness and all that. It isn't going to change what we see: we're black and they're white and that's what we'll see until the earth we're standing on freezes for good or burns up like a match flaring, or whatever actually puts an end to the whole mess, of which I am getting just a little sick and tired, to tell the truth.

VIII

Friday, July 28th

I am such a fool. Dolt. Blockhead. Will I *never* learn? Know thyself, saith the sage. I do, I know me well by now: Harriet the Haranguer, who gets carried away by my own oratory until I'm seduced into saying something I really don't mean. Or I mean only at the moment of high emotion. Yes, but this is a human weakness, a forgivable flaw. The stupidity for which I cannot forgive myself is that I not only make such overwrought statements but I *write* them—write them and mail them! Oh, what a lunkhead! Nitwit! Oxbrain!

Naturally, being a really first-class fool, I sent my letter airmail, and now it is impossible for my apology to precede it, or even to arrive at the same time. Hobie has a full day at least to behold, without antidote, the brilliant flashing of my forkèd tongue: "Oh, how noble is the Negro race, which can wear a bloody crown of catsup in regal majesty . . ." and so on and so on and so on. I *hate* myself.

It isn't as if I really believed what I said. Actually I admire anybody who has the courage to be non-violent. Just because I don't have the strength of spirit to turn the other cheek in loving forgiveness, must I sneer at those who do? Maybe I'm jealous because I know I don't measure up. Maybe I'm proud of this weakness, maybe I exploit it, the way some men who are useless when there's hard work to be done will make self-satisfied little speeches about their tricky knee or ailing back, or women who can't have children will boast about their narrow pelvis. That's probably it: I have a soul-sickness in which I take pride.

Today was the kind of day in which there's lots of time for thinking. The sun shone, I did a washing, Mrs. Daley and Mrs. Wister picked peas and beans with the children's help, and all afternoon we "rammed 'em in the freezer," as Maureen puts it. The child Gail demanded her own personal pile of beans, over which she snarled, not permitting anyone to help snip. But no one talked about race problems or anything similarly intrusive, and while my hands were busy, my mind was free to explore a problem of my own.

Which is: the importance H. G. Carr has assumed in my life. I think about him constantly. Either I am trying to see everything with his eyes, or else I am trying consciously not to see with his eyes but somehow to keep my own viewpoint intact. It's all very disquieting. It's also too soon. Hobie is a complication I'm not yet ready to accept, but I'm not so stupid as to expect I can quick-freeze him until I'm ready, and then thaw him out, good as ever.

Funny, it was only yesterday I was so confident one is in control of one's life. Today I can't imagine whatever made me think anything so naïve. Now I clearly see that the big things, the enormously important things, start small, and quietly, and they sneak up on you until suddenly there they are, so entwined and interlaced with the fabric of your life you can't possibly prune them out any longer without serious damage to yourself. I had no intention of falling in love, certainly not until I would be all through with my education. Now here's Hobie. Supposing I can remove him—supposing I do—what would be left? An abyss. A great, gaping, torn empty space without bottom.

When the supper dishes were done, I went out and sat under the peach tree and first I wrote a short, poignant cry of apology, and then I tried to focus my mind on my crocheting, which unfortunately is not the ideal activity to help one forget what a fool one is, as it leaves nearly as many loopholes for the mind to escape as there are loops of thread. I mean, why catsup? Are moments of high emotion in my life doomed always to be laced with low comedy?

I could hear Mrs. Daley at the telephone, inviting the neighbors to the picnic planned for tomorrow night. "We never see you," she would say, "it's just dreadful the way the weeks pass and we never see our friends! Of course you're busy . . . well, come after milking . . . you do have to take time to eat, you know, even if it is summer!" She sounded very social and clackety-clackety like a lady worried about filling the vast void of her leisure.

I began to enjoy the sensation of the rough bark at the back of my neck and the warm earth beneath me and the air all around very soft and still very warm. The sun, no longer sinking down in the utter northwest but now more conservatively toward the west northwest, seemed to be in no particular hurry to set. The light was golden and the sky beginning to glow with apricot, and I could almost imagine I was home, the branches of the peach tree overhead looking correct for a tree, and familiar, though there weren't any peaches ripening. Here and there dangled some withered black baglets, which proved it was too far north, after all, for peach trees. I wondered if the tree had been planted on purpose by some optimist, or had just happened, the result of a peach pit tossed away. I wondered if the peach tree was symbolical, showing what would happen to a Southerner transplanted North, he would survive but that's all, not bear fruit, I mean. In other words, I was enjoying a pleasant sadness when my reveries were scattered by the boy Marion.

"Hey," he said, "guess what. The tube just went black."

"Tragic," I said.

"You can get only two channels on their set, how about that?"

"I don't see how you've stood it," I said.

"They could get lots more if they put up a bigger aerial," he said. "Naturally I didn't feel like suggesting it."

"I think you showed commendable restraint," I said.

He propped himself on one elbow and peered at my work. "What did you say that is?"

"A doily!" I said, borrowing Gail's voice.

"No, come on, what is it?"

I sighed. "Okay," I said, "I can see there's no use trying to kid you. It's a floor mop."

After a moment he said, "You can buy mops like that in the five-and-dime, didn't you know that?"

I said sharply, "Listen, boy, those store-bought mops are for poor folks. Only *rich* folks have mops like this."

He said, "Okay, so don't get mad."

Nearly midnight, Saturday, the 29th July

This morning, Mrs. Daley was baking pies and jelling one kind of salad and boiling some chickens she planned to serve sliced cold and Mrs. Wister was in charge of baking the ham and I was fixing several gallons of potato salad, with Maureen, Gail, and Alma chopping the celery and onions and green pepper and dill pickle, when the day reached—for me—its apex, its acme, its summit, its peak, its zenith! The mailman brought three letters from Hobie! One! Two! *Three!*

One had been sent to Canada, I can't imagine why. The second was stamped NOT IN VA, and someone had penciled, *"Try Vermont."* The third came straight here. Very odd, the U.S. mails. Deus ex machina.

Gail brought in the mail, trumpeting, "Three letters for Harriet! And they're all in the same handwriting!"

Alma said, "From a man?"

And Gail said, "Is H. G. Carr a man, Harriet?"

And I said, "I'll thank you for my letters."

Gail said, "Ha! I bet H. G. Carr's a man, all right!"

Alma said, "He must be Harriet's boy friend!"

Maureen said, "Why don't you shut up?"

Gail said, "Harriet sits up all night writing him letters!"

Maureen said, "Why don't you keep your nose out of other people's business?"

Alma said, "Well, a woman suhtinly isn't goin' to sit up neahly all night writin' to a *guhl* friend!"

"Scratch scratch scratch till two A.M.," said Gail, hooting.

The boy Marion said, "I bet she's a spy, she's writing a report to her chief. She's a spy for the Black Muslims."

I said, "Oh, sure, I'm a spy. Harriet Brown, color-schemer."

"She has to look over the lay of the land," said Marion, "so when the Black Muslims move in, they can take Vermont without losing a man!" And he doubled up laughing at his own wit.

I was surprised. I hadn't realized he could have an original idea.

Mrs. Daley said, "Harriet, go read your mail."

So I did.

This was the high point of my day. From here everything drained downhill with depressing speed. In fact, except for Hobie's letters, I would hardly describe today as a *succès fou*.

At noon we had watermelon for dessert, and there was a piece left, waiting for Mr. Daley, who had reluctantly consented to spend part of his Saturday diagnosing the condition of an architectural treasure tarnished by time (actually it was suffering from sinking sills), and I was in the kitchen cleaning up when the child Gail came galloping through, pausing only long enough to scoop out a chunk of watermelon from the center of the slice—using her hand, not a fork or spoon or anything formal like that—and then she trotted on her way, her snout burrowed into the melon.

I said, "Hey, wait a minute!" and I was right after her. Mrs. Daley and Mrs. Wister were arranging platters on the dining-room table but neither Gail nor I stopped to pass the time of day. I caught up with her in the living room and I grabbed her by the scruff of her neck and I steered her right around back through the dining room and into the kitchen.

"Put that back!" I said, and helped her to do so, shaking her hand by the wrist. "Now you listen to me!" I said, not troubling to lower my voice. "You want something, you ask for it, you don't snatch it like a wild dog, understand? I've been trying to teach you some manners ever since you came. You don't seem to have learned anything. Now you keep out of my kitchen until you know how to behave!"

I went to the door of the dining room and I said, and my voice was shaking I was still so mad, "I'm sorry, Mrs. Daley, I know it's not my place to teach the children of your guest any manners, but *somebody* has to."

For a moment this remark hung quivering in midair, while we all contemplated it. Then Mrs. Wister laughed pleasantly and said, "My gracious, Harriet, don't apologize! I wish we'd had you with us overseas, instead of those kindermädchen and all—of course we couldn't let *them* discipline American children! I told Bob all along that what we needed was a good old-fashioned black mammy!"

I looked at her pretty face, calm, sweet, good-natured. No, I thought, she isn't hitting back; she means it, she means just what she says. She has just patted me approvingly on the head, as if I were a domestic animal. Does she think my air of emancipation nothing but a pose, that underneath I really am a frustrated mammy? Ignorant, humble, loyal, happy to serve her, pleased to be noticed, satisfied to be taken care of? Dinah in the kitchen and an ol' banjo, halleluiah.

Oh, yes, Mrs. Wister certainly understands "her" Negroes, yes, she is sure she does.

It would be a comfort if I could think her unique, an isolated, one-of-a-kind anachronism. Lord, no, there she stands, the New South (White), dry and snug under her glass dome like a bouquet of dried flowers, and the sounds and smells of the world outside herself—my world—never reach her. That's what she is, that's what her whole class is: an artificially preserved bit of quaint uselessness, composed of a sprig of Southern Chivalry, a spray of Benevolence, a cluster of Pure White Females, a clump of Southern Honor, all intertwined with the vine of White Supremacy, which is a parasite, like mistletoe. . . . As I went on with my work in the kitchen, I took a good deal of pleasure in elaborating this simile, especially its logical denouement: what happens when the glass dome gets taken off, or is tipped over and smashed? What happens to the charming bouquet then?

As the afternoon wore on, the children seemed possessed to get in the way. I snapped at Robert and shooed Richard out and I was icing a cake when the child Gail entered the kitchen, all memory of our earlier encounter apparently having fled her mind. "Harriet," she said, dripping graciousness, "did you know there's a snake that is thirty-seven feet long?"

"Really?"

"Also there's a snake that can eat an ox."

"Indeed," I said.

"There are five hundred kinds of snakes in the world, of which two hundred are poisonous to man."

I put down my spatula. "Would it be possible for us to continue this conversation some other time?"

"I was just trying to cheer you up," Gail said, huffily, and left. Alma entered.

"I don't need any more cheering," I said.

Alma said, "I wasn't plannin' to cheer. I've simply come for some advice."

I went on swirling the frosting.

"Harriet, do you know very much about men?"

"I have some knowledge of the subject," I admitted, "but I do not claim to know everything."

"Well, do you think a girl should let herself be pinned?"

"Just exactly what does that mean?" I said, on guard.

"*Pinned*—you know, accept a boy's fraternity pin."

"So what's involved?" I said. "You wear the pin—then what?"

"Then you can't date anybody else," Alma said. "And I have this boy friend, he wants to pin me—"

"You are dating a college man?" I said sharply.

"Lawd, no—he's a junior in high school!"

"You have fraternities in high school?"

"Why, of co'se! Doesn't everybody?"

I told her no, everybody does not. "And to answer your question," I said, "the thing to do when you're thirteen is to *be* thirteen."

"What kind of advice is *that?*" she said.

"Good advice," I said. "Leave going steady for old women of sixteen and seventeen. Live while you can, free and footloose. Be a butterfly."

Alma smiled. "That sounds chahmin'—gather honey heah and theah—Harriet, that's a truly beautiful cake!"

"It is, isn't it?" I said, annoyed to find I was being sweet-talked into a better mood.

Mr. Daley lent us two pairs of sawhorses and two plank doors, and these we set up for serving tables—naturally the picnic was to be buffet-style—and covered their surface with red-and-white-checked oilcoth, a vital precaution, said Mrs. Daley, if she ever hoped to have his doors on loan again. And we brought out our potato salad and jellied fruit salad and the ham and sliced chicken, with all necessary things to eat these with. Mrs. Daley warned me not to be startled when the guests came bringing food; she said in Vermont this is the custom, it is no reflection on the generosity of the host, but a sensible way of easing the burden on the hostess and at the same time helping the guests avoid feeling too beholden to anybody. It also ensures a feast, I thought, as I helped arrange a turkey-roasting pan full of home-baked beans, a wooden salad bowl big enough for a birdbath filled with cabbage and pepper slaw, a salmon mold, a dish of cucumbers and onions in sour cream, four kinds of pie, three kinds of cake, and a crusty blueberry dish you spooned thick cream onto. Maureen's teacher, Mrs. Platt, came bringing one of the pies. The children built a fire in their fireplace and some summer people cooked little balls of ground meat which they called "meeteetay"—I don't know how to spell it—with strange spices and everything is rolled in a cabbage leaf. The Drakes were there, they brought homemade rolls and pickles so strong if you needed your tonsils out the job was done. There was also lemonade, and milk, and iced tea, and hot coffee, and gallon jugs of white wine and of red wine.

And everybody ate as if it was the last of the seven fat years and starting tomorrow would be the lean. I took a spoonful of every single kind of food there was, and I ate until I felt like a turkey looking for a branch to roost on.

Mrs. Daley said she hoped I would enjoy meeting the neighbors and friends who were coming, they were interesting to talk to, she said, and some of them had remarked they were looking forward to meeting me. So I was there as a guest to enjoy myself, as a member of the family to help see that everybody else enjoyed themselves or at least didn't go away hungry, and as hired help to keep an eye on the whereabouts and behavior of Mary, Timmy, and John Anthony.

I never did get an accurate count of how many people came. For one thing, some arrived at five-thirty, some at six, when expected, and some at eight-thirty, when chores were done. And a few left at nine, others at ten or so, and still others are still here, and it must be past midnight. But I would guess that about thirty-five people were here, in addition to the Daleys and Wisters, I mean. And everybody knew everybody else, except me.

I chatted with the neighbors, though. I spoke when I was spoken to, and I said at least ten times that yes, I certainly do like it here, no, I really would rather not live here always, after all, my home, that I'm used to, is very different. How different? Well, not so cold, for one thing.

Someone said, "You mean summer doesn't come on the second Friday in July?" and they laughed.

I was listening to some talk about the mysterious disappearance of a certain fund, left to the town for one purpose, not spent on that, but gone—gone where? no man sayeth, no man knoweth—when an old woman turned to me and said, "You are Harriet, of course. I'm Maud Perkins, my dear, and I think you are a proud and foolish child." After a moment, I placed her: the friend, the arranger of entrée to the beauty shop of Nan, liberal of Chester, Vermont. Mrs. Perkins had eyes with little hoods for lids, and old, mottled hands with many rings, and a voice crackly with age. "Your hair looks stunning, I must say—I like it this way. It sets off your neck and ears."

It is the prerogative of old age to say what it thinks. Nevertheless, I was embarrassed.

"—yes, and after waiting *two hours* for the fellow to return," a woman with long silver earrings was saying to Mr. Daley, "it turned out he hadn't fixed it after all! And when I said, 'Oh, dear!' or words to that effect, he said, 'Say, would you like to see my wife's gallstone?' He had it in a jar at the back of his shop, on a shelf right over his workbench."

Mr. Daley said, "Some men are incurably romantic."

"It was as big as an egg," said the woman, and held out her glass to be refilled with wine.

"Tania," Mrs. Perkins said to her, "bring Harriet for tea whenever she has any free time. I want to persuade her to let me sculpt her head. It's the way you hold it," she said, turning to me. "Your spirit shines through. I think I'll call it 'Freedom Now.' "

Mrs. Silver Earrings said, "Mrs. Perkins is a very famous sculptor, Miss Brown. You should feel flattered."

"Rot," said Mrs. Perkins. "Why should she feel flattered? It's her head and if she lets me do it I'll be the lucky one. Besides, sitting for me is hard work."

Mrs. Silver Earrings called nearly everyone by the last name, and Mrs. Perkins called everyone without exception by the first name. Another prerogative of age? An assumption of social equality? Whatever the reason, although I preferred the formality of Mrs. Earrings, I did not object to the familiarity of Mrs. Perkins.

About now the ten-o'clockers left, remarking that they hated to go, but after all, it wasn't all that long until milking time.

"Milking!" said Gail. "But tomorrow's Sunday! You mean you have to milk on Sunday too?"

And everybody turned and stared at her, pleased to have another "city visitor" story for the community *répertoire*.

I had put our little ones to bed, John Anthony who had fallen asleep in his father's lap, and Timmy who had fallen asleep in mine, and Mary on a cushion by the fire. The moon rose, lopsided, and it was getting cooler, and I was glad of the fire and sat closer, although I did not look at it. And now the mood of the picnic was changing. After food, birds and humans are inclined to be talkative, and so were these Vermonters, whether summer migrant or year-round resident. But instead of bouncing lightly from one frivolous subject to another, the conversation appeared to have lost its momentum and commenced to whack away, recklessly, at one topic.

"From Virginia?" Mrs. Earrings was saying to Mrs. Wister. "I'm afraid I don't know Virginia at all well."

"Charlottesville," Mrs. Wister said. "Or, rather, my parents live there. In the Army you really don't have a home."

"Is that anywhere near Prince Edward County?"

"No," said Mrs. Wister rather coldly.

"We're having school problems, too," Mrs. Earrings remarked, following a chain of thought that was perfectly clear to me, at least. "Vance and I adore the city, but we may have to move farther out, though he dreads commuting, such a bore. You see, they're talking of closing our school and transporting the children across the city—something to do with evening up the races—imagine!"

I admit I felt a shiver of apprehension. The topic was so explosive it probably ought to be banned from social occasions—and no doubt is, back home. But I was also pleased: I hadn't had to say a word, or do any prompting; I simply had to listen, and I'd get Hobie's thesis handed to me, chapter and verse.

Everybody was terribly sympathetic, of course, to the tragic plight of the Negroes—that was their phrase, "tragic plight," and I bet they were proud of it. Of course something had to be done. Oh, of course. But whatever that something was, it certainly could not be anything which might involve a sacrifice on the part of their own children.

Mrs. Earrings said, "The school board talks about 'equalizing the educational climate'—something like that. Well, if you're bringing it up for the Negroes, you must be lowering it for the white children, aren't you—if it's being equalized?"

Mrs. Wister said gently, "It's not as simple, is it, as you would have us think?" She had a little smile on her face, as if she was enjoying herself in a way they didn't quite understand.

And then I was yanked from my safe perch as onlooker.

Mrs. Perkins said, "Harriet, I have the feeling you're an expert in this field. Would you care to comment?"

Mr. Daley said, "Now, Maud, leave Harriet alone. She's supposed to be enjoying herself."

"Nonsense," said Mrs. Perkins vigorously. "I bet she's aching to say something. Hush up and listen to her."

"I don't mind, Mr. Daley," I said, although I certainly did mind. Why should I have to be a spokesman for my whole race all the time? And why do they think twenty million of us all think alike? I said, "But I really don't know anything about the race problems of the North, only what I've read."

Mrs. Earrings said, "What I want to know is, what good is it going to do the Negro children—how is it going to help them—to drag my children miles across town to a school that is nowhere near as good as the one a block away?"

I couldn't help laughing. "I don't expect anybody thinks those little white children are going to give off some kind of magic rays and improve the schools by their mere presence. And the Negro parents can't be all that anxious to have their children mixing with whites. Not very many Negroes I know feel that their children have simply got to play with white children or they won't be normal."

"Hear, hear!" said Mrs. Perkins. The wine bottle was going around and she held up her glass.

"I would guess it's politics, a slick trick by the Negro leaders," I went on. "You know—'If you won't fix up these schools for us, so send some of your children here, maybe you'll do something then'—like that." I had to lower my eyes (modestly) to my hands folded so ladylike in my lap, so no one would see the sudden gleam of fierce pride I was feeling: a sweet taste of triumph, that my people could outwit and outmaneuver Whitey—and in the North! in the North! where we're isolated in pockets, surrounded, outnumbered!

"Miss Brown, are you implying"—I turned to see who was speaking; it was Mrs. Platt, Maureen's teacher—"that there's nothing wrong with segregated schools per se, it's just that the Negro schools tend to be neglected—is that your point?"

"No, ma'am, that's not what I mean at all," I said. "But as a Southern Negro I certainly can't approve of sending white children across the city," I added, "when after all that was one of our chief objections to segregation: so many Negro children had to go miles and miles past a white school to get to theirs. It wasn't only the insult, my goodness!" And then I said, feeling very clever, "But I thought we were supposed to stop making such a fuss about race. Well, if you're going out of your way to mix the children, isn't this just another kind of race consciousness?"

Mrs. Daley said, "You mean you don't think it's important that the schools reflect our heterogeneous population?"

Mr. Daley whistled. "Anybody who can say that can have another glass of wine," he declared. "Stand back, Harriet. I want to swing at that one. Let's say it is, let's say it's right and proper that every school be blended one-tenth Negro. What about the other races, huh? How about them? The Indians, the Japanese, the Chinese, and don't forget the Eskimo, by God. And don't forget national origins either, while you're about it. Every school must have a soupçon of Spanish, a pinch of Italian, if we have to jet the children from coast to coast."

Mrs. Daley said, "Tom, please be serious."

"I am being serious. I say the whole thing is damned idiotic."

"Because it's artificial," said Mrs. Perkins. "Sooner or later the artificial always strikes you as absurd."

"Are we all agreed, then," said Mrs. Platt, "that small children have too long a day as it is, and all children of every race ought to go to the school nearest home?"

I expected someone might move the meeting adjourn. But no. *"Provided,"* Mrs. Perkins declared, jabbing the air for emphasis and setting her bracelets jangling, "you make that school good enough! Who's to see to that, eh? Go on leaving it to the local school boards and we'll go right on having slum schools in Harlem, tumbledown termite-ridden shacks in the South, firetraps in Chicago—"

Mrs. Wister leaned forward. "Ah'm afraid," she said, "yo' have been misinfo'med. Our schools in the South are *subtinly* not shacks—"

"My dear," said Mrs. Perkins, "I was born in Georgia, raised in Boston, and a Vermonter by marriage. There's nothing you can tell me that will make me cast my vote for local control of the schools."

"What makes you think it'll be any better if it's all in the hands of some country-bumpkin-once-removed down in Washington?" Mr. Daley asked. "Although I grant you, Maud, the idea has its attractions—distance can lend a certain illusion of functioning intelligence. Take Congress—"

Mrs. Daley said, "Now, Tom—"

I thought she was going to say, that will be enough, but she didn't. For the moment, the discussion flowed around me and left me alone, and I felt no urge to thrust myself back into the mainstream of conversation. However, I listened, and in a way it was amusing to hear them, some of them, whose names were strange-sounding, whose speech had the overprecision of the foreign-born, happily discussing "our" schools to which they might be liberal enough to admit "them"—Americans to the fifth, sixth, seventh generation, but with dark skin.

"The trouble with you Southerners," Mrs. Perkins was saying with more spirit than tact, "is that you want the rest of the country to keep hands off unless it's a handout. Our money you will take, but our standards—you'll thank us to keep them at home, please. Am I being unfair? Isn't that what you want?"

"But it's ouah money, too," Mrs. Wister said, matching spirit for spirit, "and Ah do think it's a shame yo' No'theners are so sure your standards are higher than ours, you just won't listen to what we believe. We just *know* mixin' the races at school is bound to bring more trouble. Next you'll be mixin' everywhere else—I don't mean the law will make you, I mean nobody will see anything wrong with it—at the theater, at dances, in people's homes—and then you'll be havin' *intermarriage.*"

From the way she spoke you could see this was worse than death and damnation.

"Harriet," said Mrs. Perkins, her eyes dancing with mischief beneath those hooded lids, "do you think this is a danger? You attended an integrated high school, I understand. What happened socially?"

In an instant I was angry, and in no fit condition to take part in this press conference, or inquisition, or whatever it was. I am always infuriated by the attitude of whites toward intermarriage: that it is a disaster—for the white, socially and genetically a dragging down—of the white, an unnatural aberration which ought to be anathema to all pure-minded Caucasians. Never, never once do they consider the reverse, what intermarriage means for the Negro.

Mrs. Platt was observing me as if I were a fractious pupil in the front row. She now remarked, "I have never ceased to marvel at the Vermonters' reputation for taciturnity. Miss Brown, I'm sure you'll agree with me that it's completely undeserved."

"That's because we're all rough edges," Mrs. Daley said. "Rub two Vermonters together and the sparks of conversation at once commence to fly!"

Add the fumes of alcohol, I thought, and the situation is Pow! But I had had a moment to compose myself, and I said, "Why, nothing happened of a social nature at all, Mrs. Perkins. Most everybody acted as if we didn't exist. Those who condescended to notice us were hardly social in their approach. I wouldn't say that a whisper, 'Git out, nigger gal, take your nigger-stink back to the pigsty you come from,' is exactly *social.*"

Mrs. Silver Earrings ignored this verbatim report. She leaned forward. "But supposing integration starts much earlier—supposing it starts in the first grade. It's likely to be really accepted then, isn't it? Children will think it's only natural to mix the races. They'll grow up that way. Won't intermarriage really be a problem then?"

"Look," I said, "I didn't ever play with white children—that only happens if your mother works for whites and takes you along, and my mother did not work for whites, so I didn't 'integrate,' if that's the word, until my third year of high school. So I really don't know how a Negro might feel if she's associated with white children ever since she can remember, grown up with them. All I know is how *I* feel, and I know I would never marry a white man."

"You see?" said Mrs. Wister in a kind of triumph. "We've always said the Negroes prefer their own people!"

"You can't have it both ways, Vinnie," Mr. Daley said. "On the one hand, intermarriage spreading like a plague because of school integration, and on the other, the Negroes wanting to keep to themselves. Make up your mind—which will it be?"

But nobody is mentioning the *whites* wanting to keep to themselves, I thought savagely. How does it happen, my fine white Americans, that practically no Southern Negro has pure African blood? Three hundred years of black baboons outraging God's purest creatures, the Southern white female? No, that wouldn't exactly explain it, would it?

But this is a social occasion, I reminded myself. It sho'ly is a fine day.

Mrs. Perkins waved her hand to silence Mr. Daley. "Your point of view interests me very much, Harriet," she said. "Why wouldn't you consider it? What would hold you back? The possible repercussions against your husband—his white friends dropping him socially, his employer not recommending him for promotion—that sort of thing? Or would your Negro friends resent your marriage, perhaps feel you are trying to climb above them?"

: 184 :

I looked at her and I hated her, too, I hated them all, every one. Climb above the blacks—there it was, there it always was: the whites a higher order, the Negroes a lower. You'd think mankind is ranked by the weight of pigmentation, the whites floating on top, the Negroes sinking to the bottom.

I said, "A woman ought to be in love with a man before she thinks of marrying him. And I can't imagine being in love with a white man. I can't imagine marrying one. I don't see how some Negro women bring themselves to do it. The whole idea is repulsive." To hell with it's a fine day. I said, "I don't think I could stand it, to have a white man put his arm around me, put his mouth on mine and kiss me. As for bearing him children—" I paused. There are limits to what I can say right out loud. "The whole idea makes my flesh crawl," I said lamely.

They were staring at me as if I were a mouse biting a cat.

Someone said, "Well . . . really!"

Mr. Daley said, "You asked her, now listen to her."

"No, that's very odd, don't you think so?" I had turned to look at the fire and I didn't see who was talking. "Very . . . unconventional," the someone said.

I was staring at the fire and it was my father I saw in there, my father, and my mother was there, too; her body was swollen and she was bending over my father where he sat at the table; she was trying to coax him to eat, but he didn't even look at her, he just sat there, hunched over, his big hands on the table, big rough hands that looked so strong, the little finger on his left hand nothing but a stump where the saw bit it off. He sat there holding himself up with his hands flat on the table, and he wouldn't look at her. You could say my father begun to die that day, because that was the day they told him to pick up his tools, pick up his tools and not come back, since he couldn't do a day's work no more. . . .

I said, "I mean what I say. I could never let a white man court me. I have too much self-respect."

Yee-ah-ha to you, Whitey Gawd-Almighty.

Someone reeled the conversation in onto safe ground, but I took

: 185 :

no part. You aren't going to get another crumb from me, I thought. How stupid could I get, to think I'd been in any way "accepted"—I'd been tolerated, that's all, that damnable phrase of superiority. I'd been permitted to be there, very gracious of them, when it served their purpose of self-flattery, or I was useful, to hand them their plate. I'd been an object of idle curiosity, an exhibit in a living museum of the calibre that caters to tourists, punch the button and see it move, *gee Ma lookit that funny-lookin' critter, you suppose it has any feelin's? thinks like us? knows it's alive? wants the same things out of life? knows it'll die someday?*

My bitter thoughts were interrupted by a crash. There was a spilling of metal objects onto the rocky ground, and there, snuffling among the scattered bowls and serving dishes, could dimly be seen a pig.

Mrs. Daley cried, "The pig's loose! That's our last pig!"

Mrs. Perkins ordered, "Grab him! Head him off!"

Mr. Daley shouted, "Drive him into the barnyard!"

The feast which had turned into an inquisition now became a rout. The night was filled with shouting. There was another crash as the second table went over. Men raced about, children squealed, women let out yips of warning. Over this swirling mêlée the fire-light flickered and danced, and the shrilling of the pig was heard above all.

I did not bestir myself. Not even the news, reported with high emotion by the child Maureen, that Pig One was safe in his pen, it must be Pig Two on rampage, not even this news moved me. I sat where I was, the onlooker from Outer Space. I gave a passing thought to the money value of Pig Two—he'd looked, in the glimpse I'd had of him, as if he was thriving—but I didn't give a hoot. If asked, I'd have said I considered Pig Two a community pig, that is, he belonged to the white community. Let them catch their own pigs without any help from me.

Mrs. Platt sat down beside me. "I am indeed sorry, Miss Brown," she said.

I had nothing to say to her. I got up and shook myself—I was stiff from sitting so long—and I made my way back to my room, and wrapped a blanket around my shoulders because I was cold, and I turned to my journal and my own thoughts for companionship.

Let them catch their own pigs and solve their own problems and learn to live with themselves, and leave me alone.

Sunday, July 30th

This morning the picnic area was a mess. Mrs. Daley went up early to clean it up, and some vestigial sense of duty dragged me up after her.

"I don't see why this family can't have a peaceful party, like other people," she said.

I didn't say anything. I was collecting the tableware, and wondering what to do with two spoons and a fork which had been stepped on and bent.

"All this damage and still Pig Two got away," Mrs. Daley said.

I didn't say anything.

"I'm sorry you're upset," she said.

"I'm not upset," I said.

"Yes, you are, and you have a right to be. The discussion got inexcusably out of control. I suppose it's because we see so little of each other that we Vermonters are such a plain-spoken people. Our conversational style resembles a man clearing a hedgerow with a hatchet."

I shrugged. "It's not important," I said. "But I was surprised at Mrs. Perkins, the way she led the pack."

"Her frankness, you mean? When she's so liberal?"

"I hate that word," I said.

"But she really means it, Harriet, she's not just paying lip service to the idea. She freely and unquestioningly accepts you as her equal in every way—which is amazing, when you remember she was born in the South—and if you're really her equal, why should she treat you differently from the way she treats everyone else? She's that frank with everyone—everyone she likes, that is. With her it's actually a sign of affection, and I've always considered it a compliment to have Maud Perkins meet me on equal terms mentally, even if she does sometimes leave me gasping."

"She didn't believe me any more than anybody else did," I said. "They asked me what I think and how I feel, and when I told them, they didn't believe me, because it didn't suit them to believe me, it didn't suit the pretty picture they have of themselves. But they'll all go right on believing they 'understand' me." I laughed. "Why, that child Alma came down to breakfast this morning and she said, 'Poor Harriet! Ah just hope you were never crossed in love!'"

"Alma is just a child," Mrs. Daley said.

"She gets her ideas from grownups," I said.

Mrs. Daley didn't say anything more, and I didn't, either. It was like one of the first mornings when I came.

The Wisters, it turned out, were going to church. The boy Marion offered to stay home, in case the car might be crowded, but his mother said this would not be necessary, they could always take the two cars. Mrs. Daley said that she and I usually went by ourselves, there was plenty of room and we'd be glad to have them come with us.

I wondered if the Wisters would prefer I get out and walk the last block or two, so they need not be seen driving up in an integrated car. I had no intention of suggesting anything; I just wondered.

When the Negro crucifer came in, and the four little Negro acolytes followed him, and the young men and their charges from

: 189 :

the camp rose, in their usual pews, I thought of the Wisters again, briefly, distantly. I noticed there were new dark faces scattered throughout the congregation, little children, in ones and twos like raisins in a pudding. Now what? I wondered. Somebody playing Gracious Lady and teasing the children from the slums with a taste of decent living?

For the first time, I was sorry I came to church. Nothing seemed right. The responses, all new this week, over which the choir had worked so hard at rehearsal, were new to the worshipers, too, and they stumbled unhappily half a beat behind us. I had a hard time keeping my voice reined in. It didn't seem fair that I had to sing with half-voice just because the rest of the choir lacked the proper physical equipment. I wanted to sing, I wanted to let it all out, my loneliness, far away from home, from my own kind, I wanted to laugh and cry with my own kind, I wanted to sit and talk and crack jokes and argue and make plans and just *be,* be with my own kind, not these pale cool people with their colorless hands and their transparent voices and their thin pale cool souls. I wanted to sing out, *It's me, it's me, it's me oh Lord!* with all my breath, with all my body, with all my being.

And I sang, "With shining face and bright array," in a cool voice, and finally we walked out, and I sang, "Above the noise of selfish strife," and I was careful of my volume, and I didn't feel sorry for anybody that this was all they knew of "making a joyful noise," I just felt sorry for me.

And I didn't feel that I'd been to church.

On the way home I stared at the dark trees, pines and hemlocks, blackened green shadows, and at the rocky land heaved up restlessly, and I thought, four weeks more of exile, how can I bear it?

Mrs. Wister was overflowing with questions. Who were all those Negroes? Did they live up here? How long had the church been integrated? Had anybody made any trouble for the minister?

Mrs. Daley shrugged. "Honestly, I don't know, Vinnie. There's a camp nearby, and of course this is the time for the fresh-air children—"

Those children. Where were they from? Harlem? Did they stay right in people's *homes?*

Of course. Where else would they stay?

The man carrying the Cross—who was he? Wasn't that an honor of some kind?

"He lives here," said Mrs. Daley, as if that should be enough.

"But what do you do about Communion?" Mrs. Wister said. "Do you let them take Communion?"

"I don't understand," Mrs. Daley said, although I thought from the two spots on her cheeks that she understood only too well. "You don't have to be confirmed in this particular church, I mean right here in St. Michael's—"

Mrs. Wister said, "But I thought you used a common cup."

"They have two cups," I said. "A gold one for the white folks, and a tin cup for the niggers."

"Harriet!" said Mrs. Daley sharply.

I didn't say anything. I wasn't going to apologize. I'd walk to Windsor and take the bus home first.

And Mrs. Wister didn't say anything more.

I didn't see much more of the guests. I reminded myself that after all it was Sunday, I needn't thrust myself forward looking for chores to do, they'd be right there waiting on Monday morning. While the little boys were napping, I found a spot within hearing of the house, and I wrote a letter to Josie, a mopey sort of letter in which I sang the blues, it's been so long so long since I've been dancing, that sort of lament. I was honing this keening to a fine edge when the girl Alma drifted up, sat down without being invited, and said, "Just think! Tomorrow at this time Ah'll be swimmin' in the ocean!"

"It must have been rough, this week," I said.

"Oh, Mama's friends are all right, Ah suppose," she said, trying hard to be generous, "if only they weren't so horribly old-fashioned!"

I looked at her, my pen poised above my paper, my expression intended to convey that I wasn't obliged to entertain her, she wasn't *my* guest, and after a few moments she read my message,

: 191 :

rose, and drifted off. And then I found my pen was out of ink, and I went to my room for another cartridge.

When I went into my room, I had the oddest feeling that somebody had just left. I stood still, sifting over this feeling, weighing it, wondering if I was one jump from the jungle, or what. I couldn't hear anybody else in the house. But my room didn't look right. It didn't look exactly as I'd left it. I was sure this, at least, wasn't my imagination. My books were kind of chucked into a pile, instead of being neatly stacked on the floor next to the radio, and my cot was rumpled.

The first thing I did, I checked my pillow. Hobie's letters were there all right, but surely I hadn't left them just rammed inside the pillowcase. I always put them inside the zippered ticking. Had somebody been reading them? There wasn't a damn thing in them to give anybody else any kicks, but they were *my* letters, and the idea that anybody else might look them over made me feel sick, as if somebody had been spying on me naked.

I counted them to make sure they were all there, then I restored them to my pillow. Idiotic place to put them, I thought. It's the first place a snoop would look.

What about my pay? Maybe the little sneaks had been looking for more than just vicarious thrills! I slid my hand behind the insulation and was relieved to find my baking-powder can right where it belonged. My money was all there, too, I found, when I counted it. I put the can back and stuck the insulation in place. Then I bent to straighten my books, and without thinking why, I picked up the radio and checked for my bus ticket.

It wasn't there. My bus ticket wasn't there. Not the ticket, nor the envelope I'd put it in . . . nothing was there but some dangling pieces of tape.

My God, I thought, they've taken my bus ticket, my ticket home!

I really couldn't believe it. I kept picking up the radio and looking, as if the ticket would reappear by magic before my eyes. I looked behind the box and on the floor and under my bed, and I picked up my books and shook them, and I turned back my blankets and sheets and searched my bed, all the time telling my-self it was just a prank, somebody had found the ticket and wanted to frighten me and had hidden it in my room. And all the time I knew I wouldn't find it, and panic punched me in the belly.

No one would believe me. I knew that. If I told them my ticket is lost, they'd never believe that I had taken good care of it. They'd think I was just making it up, all that business about hiding it so carefully. No one would believe me if I said my room has been searched and my letters disturbed, and my ticket stolen. They simply would never believe me, and what was I to do?

In a turmoil of mind I went down to help with the supper. And then I could hardly wait to get through the dishes. I rushed back to the new house and I searched the luggage of the guests. I was swift, but I was very thorough, and as far as I could tell I left no trace of having touched anything, even though I practically turned the belongings of the two girls inside out. I was so sure they were the ones who'd been reading my letters, I couldn't believe it when I found nothing whatsoever of mine among their things.

It did cross my mind to look in the rooms of the Daley children, but I dismissed this idea at once. My ticket wouldn't be there, I ought to know that. If it was— But it wouldn't be *there*, for heaven's sake!

I suppose I can buy another. Perhaps somehow I can get into town and buy another without Mrs. Daley knowing. How much will it cost? Thirty, forty, maybe even fifty dollars? But he'd tell Mrs. Daley anyway, the travel agent would. And she'd know I lost it, and they'd think me just a stupid, careless nigger gal, that's what they'll think. "They are just like children"—that's what the Mrs. Wisters are always saying, and the Daleys would have to agree. Nobody would believe it was stolen. "They lie like children, they don't know right from wrong"—that's what the Mrs. Wisters always went on to say, and the Daleys would reluctantly agree.

What the hell do I care what the Daleys think? I've lost my ticket, I can't spare the money to get another, and what am I thinking of, worrying about what they'll think?

But that's the awful part of it. I *do* care what they think. I care terribly, for some reason which isn't quite clear to me. I suppose all along I've been trying to prove something, and now this has happened, and everything will be ruined.

At least I made sure I wasn't caught searching. I was back in my room before Maureen brought Mary up to bed.

I wish I could talk to Hobie. It makes me so *furious* to be a *slave* to the whereabouts of a dozen square inches of paper!

What *am* I to do?

Monday, July 31

When I awoke this morning, I could hardly wait to have a head-on collision with the Wister girls. Right after breakfast I went up to the new house all helpfulness to see what I could do about their last-minute packing, and I waited for my chance to get those girls alone.

When Mrs. Wister went to see if Marion could get his suitcase shut, I leaned near to the girl Alma and I said grimly, "Give it to me, you hear? Give me my ticket."

She turned and stared at me. "Whatever are yo' talkin' about?"

"My bus ticket home," I said. "Come on, where is it?"

"Bus ticket?" she said. "Yo' lost a bus ticket? Wheah to?"

"Abbot's Level South Carolina that's where to," I said. "I know you have it, or you know where it is. Come on, let's have it," and I thrust out my hand.

"Are yo' accusin' me of stealin'?" she said haughtily. "Why on earth would Ah want a bus ticket to Abbot's Level South Ca'-lina?"

"How the hell do I know?" I hissed. "But you took it—you or your sister, when you were snooping and prying in my things yesterday."

Alma looked at her sister. "Were we snoopin' and pryin' in Harriet's things yesterday, Gail?"

Gail drew back her lips in a smile. "Us? That's crazy, that is. I never do anything with *her,* not even snoopin'."

I was furious because I was helpless, but I wasn't going to beg. "One of you did," I said, looking from one to the other.

They stared back at me, and Alma said, smiling sweetly, "Ah'm afraid yo' ovuhestimate yo' fascination."

Mr. Daley was coming in to get the footlockers, and I turned on my heel and left the room. God, I thought, how I hate a Southern accent.

I was washing the dishes as good-byes were being said on the front lawn. I could see the farewells from my position at the sink. Mrs. Daley and Mrs. Wister hugged each other and kissed each other on the cheek, and Mrs. Wister kissed Mr. Daley on the cheek but without any hugging. There was a kind of crisscross good-bye–good-bye between Mrs. Daley and the Wister children, and Mrs. Wister and the Daley children, but of good-byes children to children there were none.

"Give old Bob my best," Mr. Daley said, "and don't rub it in what a soft life we civilians are having."

I thought he concealed his grief at this parting very well.

When they had gone, Mr. Daley got in his jeep and left, too. Mrs. Daley said we'd leave until tomorrow the restoring to proper place of bedding and mattresses and all, that if Maureen would look after the children and I would tackle the washing, she would zoom into town to refurbish the larder. And so the morning passed, and the lines were full of clean clothes billowing in the wind, a sight which always makes me feel better no matter what's wrong, when Mrs. Daley came back, accompanied by boxes and sacks of just about everything edible the farm doesn't produce. And we fixed sandwiches and had lunch out in the orchard, and it was peaceful sprawled on the grass, nobody here but ourselves. Mary licked her fingers and nobody corrected her, and Timmy had a white mustache of milk, and it was all like taking off a tight shoe.

I was glad it was today and not yesterday, although nothing was really any better, of course, it was just that I could put a little distance between me and my troubles.

After lunch the children paired off, John Anthony and Timmy to take naps, Mary and Maureen to make doll clothes, and Richard and Robert to dig worms for fishing. Mrs. Daley and I took a couple of bushel baskets down to the vegetable patch to pick beans.

In the few days we'd neglected them, the yellow beans had grown long, wide, thick and tough, and were fit only for Pig One. The green beans still were starting new ones, and Mrs. Daley said we'd pick these young and tender ones and ignore those that were too old. There is a limit, she said, to the horizons of human achievement.

The sun lay across my back and it felt so good, hot and reassuring. The earth smelled elemental, full of life, decaying and coming again and decaying—I can't describe it, but it was a kind of smell that made me think this old planet was going to keep on spinning through space, that it would be here tomorrow and tomorrow, and I'd live to see my children and my children's children. This isn't a thought that's very common to my generation, and it was comforting to be thinking it, and I was further thinking if you could bottle this smell and sell it, it would be better than tranquilizers, when Mrs. Daley spoke to me.

"Harriet," she said, "you never mention your mother. Is she still living?"

"No, ma'am," I said.

"Oh," she said. "I'm sorry I asked."

"She died when I was seven years old," I said. "She was going to have another baby, but something went wrong. She tried for two days but the baby wouldn't come. Then the baby did come, but it was dead, and my mother died right after."

Mrs. Daley was standing stock still and staring at me. I straightened my back and looked at her. I don't know why, I don't know what got into me, but I was talking just as if I was passing the time of day.

"And couldn't the doctor do anything?" she said, horrified, as if her horror now, a dozen years later and a thousand miles away, could fix everything fine.

I said, "She didn't have a doctor. There wasn't any Negro doctor near, not in those days. Granny McNair came to stay with my mother, but she couldn't help."

"But there must have been a doctor, Harriet! Wasn't there even a white doctor near?"

"He wouldn't come," I said.

We were staring at each other like strangers.

"Why wouldn't he?" she said.

I found I wanted to tell her, I wanted her to hear. Did I still want to punish her for being white? I don't know. But I wanted her to hear what happened to my mother.

"Granny McNair was there with my mother," I said, "and I was supposed to stay out of the house, and I did, except when I was hungry, but I stayed close to the house, and I could hear my mother crying. This went on for a long time—two days that I remember, but maybe it was longer—and all that time my father, sick as he was, stayed there with her, and I'd hear my mother cry out, 'Oh, Jesse! Jesse!' That was my father's name," I said carefully. "Jesse Brown, he was. And finally the baby came, but it was dead, and my mother was bleeding, and Granny McNair couldn't get the bleeding to stop. My father come out of the house looking for me, he said to me, 'You go get the doctor—you bring him, you hear? You bring that doctor because your mother is dyin'.' I ran as fast as I could, but he wouldn't come, and when I got back my mother was dead."

I felt so cold, remembering, and I wrapped my arms across my chest to stop the shivering.

Mrs. Daley was picking beans again. "I don't understand," she said, "why the doctor wouldn't come."

I was back there, living that night over again, running through the piney woods and cutting across the schoolyard and then down the alley to the board fence that was along the doctor's back yard, and the gate creaked, and then I was up on the back porch and knocking at the kitchen door, and somebody opened it and called him and he came, the doctor came, and stood there, peering down at me, and he said he didn't treat niggers.

"I said my mother is dying," I explained to Mrs. Daley, "and he said he didn't treat niggers."

Mrs. Daley straightened and she said sharply, "That's what he said? You're sure now—you're not making this up? The doctor said that?"

"That's right," I said, "and when I said once more that my mother is dying, he said to get the midwife, and I said she's there but she can't help, and he said his patients wouldn't stand for it if he was to treat niggers, and he shut the door."

"I simply can't bring myself to believe this, Harriet!" Mrs. Daley cried.

"I know," I said. "That's how I felt, too. Of course I knew white doctors didn't treat Negroes but I always thought if somebody was dying it would make a difference. I thought that man must be the Devil, he was so wicked, that's what I thought then, but now I know he wasn't really evil, he was just weak—he was nothing but a poor weak old white man."

Mrs. Daley said, "What did your father do? Did he do anything to the doctor?"

I said, "What could he do?"

"Punish him somehow," cried Mrs. Daley. "Report him to the medical society—have him arrested! I'm sure there must be *some* law—"

I felt suddenly very tired. I felt like somebody trying to explain war to a child. There is nothing in their lives to relate it to.

"The idea wouldn't enter his mind," I said. "He wouldn't dream of doing such a thing. He'd know, sure as he was born, we'd all find ourselves in some terrible trouble. That was something we all learned very early: just keep your mouth shut, no matter what happens, just act like it didn't happen, not to you it didn't." No, I thought, you weren't even there, you had nothing to do with it, it wasn't up to you to protest, there wasn't any cowardice in your silence, your soft erasing yourself away from whatever it was. . . . How could I make Mrs. Daley see this? That to do nothing was a way of surviving, that's what it was, a way of *winning,* actually. "The hardest thing for a man to do," I said, "is to do nothing. To say to himself, 'You can't do nothing, Jesse Brown.' It can just about eat your insides out, Mrs. Daley. It can just about kill you—"

And all of a sudden, to my great surprise, I was crying.

Mrs. Daley picked up her basket. "Come on," she said. "We've got enough to keep us busy all evening." And I picked up my basket and followed her. We sat under an apple tree and I wiped my face with my hands and we started snipping the beans. I could feel Mrs. Daley looking at me.

Then she said, "Harriet, you were telling me the truth just now, weren't you?"

I blew my nose. "Oh, yes," I said. "That was the truth."

"But when you told me about your father's death, I clearly got the impression that your mother saw—I mean that she was alive at that time—"

"No, ma'am," I said. "My father didn't live very much longer; it was like my mother's death just finished him and he didn't want to live, but it was a couple of months later, anyway."

"You told me your father was lynched," she said evenly.

Oh, Lord! How could I forget what I had already told her? No wonder she thought I must be making it all up!

"That was somebody else," I said. "I don't know who. My father died of his lungs—of tuberculosis." She was looking at me steadily, her hands fixing the beans, her eyes on me. "That's the truth, Mrs. Daley," I said, my face hot. "My father just—just died, for nothing, he just got sick and died and left me without anybody and I went to live with Aunt Lydia and—well, people talk about things like that—lynchings—I heard talk about it, the grownups talking —it seemed to me people thought they were heroes, those who got lynched. So I—I kind of borrow that sort of death for my father, because—I don't know—it makes more sense—"

"Makes more sense!" cried Mrs. Daley.

"To me it does," I said stubbornly. How could I explain to her—to anyone—how I had felt betrayed when my father died, as if he'd done it on purpose, just given up and died, had left me, as if he hadn't loved me enough to go on living? Once he had told my mother he was living for the baby coming—couldn't he have lived for me? And his death was such a quitting kind of death, and I had loved my father until I couldn't bear to think how he had died, turned his face to the wall and died. And this terrible barren feeling swept over me again, as if I were all alone on a great sandy stretch of nothingness, just me, and nobody to call me in to supper, or to comfort me, or to look for me.

A man can live and not matter to anybody but his own family, but if he dies by lynching, by God he matters then.

The damned tears were rolling down my face again, and I was so ashamed of them, like a great badge of cowardice they were, and I pretended they weren't there. I turned a little bit away from her so she wouldn't see, and I said, "The truth is, I guess I'm kind of upset this morning. I—I've lost my ticket."

What the hell, let's get it over, I thought. Harriet can't tell a story straight about her own father's death; naturally she's going to lose her bus ticket.

Mrs. Daley was bewildered by this switch from the tragic to the trivial. What on earth did I mean? Had I lost my *bus* ticket? Well, where had I kept it? When had I missed it? Where had I looked? Was I absolutely sure I hadn't mislaid it?

She was trying to be kind, but I knew she was irritated, I knew she thought I was half-witted, because she spoke to me the way she speaks to Robert when he mislays his shoes. When precisely was the last time I knew for certain my ticket was there? Exactly why did I suspect the Wister girls had been in my room?

"I just have this feeling," I said. "I can't prove anything."

Finally she said, "There's no point in working ourselves into a froth before we find out whether or not it can be replaced. I'll go call the travel agency."

She went to the house, and I finished snipping the beans, and gathered the baskets, and went down to the old house to fix supper.

"They can't replace it, Harriet," Mrs. Daley said in an undertone. "We won't mention this to Mr. Daley until after he's had supper."

So Mr. Daley ate heartily and I sat at my window in the kitchen and poked at my food. After I had brought in the dessert, I heard Mr. Daley say, "What is this, Black Monday? I've never seen Harriet so overcast." And Mrs. Daley said, "Why don't you finish eating?" and Mr. Daley said, "I have finished. I am simply drinking coffee. So out with it—what's wrong?"

Mrs. Daley told him, and Mr. Daley whistled. "Maybe we can get a refund," he said.

"Not a chance," Mrs. Daley said. "I phoned and asked. The trouble is, anybody can use that ticket; they're not numbered, like plane tickets."

"I can't see why anybody would want to take Harriet's ticket," Maureen said. "Wouldn't they have to ride to Abbot's Level to get any use out of it?"

"They could cash it," her mother said. "They could get the money."

"But then the travel agent would tell you, or have them arrested, or something!" Richard said.

"They don't have to cash it here," Mrs. Daley said. "The agent said she—anybody—could mail it to the main office in New York."

So that's what they thought I would do! Steal it and then lie about it being stolen!

"Yeah, and the money would probably buy her at least one, maybe two swimsuits!" Maureen said angrily.

"That will be enough, Maureen!" said her mother sharply. "We have no idea, no idea *at all*, that the Wister girls were in Harriet's room! Don't you suggest such things!"

I could have bawled. I went to the dining-room doorway and I said, "Mr. Daley, how much did it cost? I'll make it up to you. I'll work Thursdays—"

"My God, Harriet, you're working Thursdays now," he said. "I wish you'd told me before they left. I don't know exactly what I could have done and remained the perfect host, but if this is anybody's idea of a joke—"

"Tom, I cannot *believe* that Vinnie's children would do such a thing!"

"Oh, come now, Kate," he said. "Children can be pretty amoral without being eternally damned, you know." He turned to me. "You're sure it wasn't in their luggage? And you searched the new house thoroughly?"

"I searched my room," I said.

"What about the children's rooms? You didn't search there?"

"You mean *my* room!" cried Maureen, outraged. "Daddy, you don't think *I* would swipe anything of Harriet's, do you?"

"It could be planted," said Mr. Daley.

Chairs scraped and Maureen, Robert, and Richard dashed from the room.

"Harriet, sit down," said Mr. Daley. "You make me nervous, standing there." I went and sat on the front two inches of a chair. "What about your pay?" he went on. "What safe place have you got that?"

"In the wall, in a—a baking-powder can," I stammered, "so the mice wouldn't chew it." (They're just like children, you have to think for them.)

"You must have quite a wad by now," he said. "Hundred twenty-five, hundred fifty or so."

"One hundred seventy-five," I said, "less what I've spent."

"Yes, well, unless you've money to burn, that's a ridiculous sum to keep in the house, and I suggest to you that the next time Mrs. Daley drives to town, you accompany her and open an old-fashioned savings account. I would hate to be faced with a moral obligation to replace your pay."

"I should never have given her the ticket," said Mrs. Daley. "It wasn't fair to put the responsibility on her."

I wished they would make up their minds whether they considered me a fool or a thief. I rose to my feet and I said, "Mrs. Daley, I honestly thought it would be safe where I hid it. Mr. Daley, I swear to God I did not take that ticket, I am not just pretending it is lost—"

Mr. Daley thundered, "Is that what you think we think?"

I said, "Why not?"

"You really think we think you are planning to cash that ticket and then tell us you lost it? You think we think you're capable of some such lowdown, sneaky, conniving maneuver?"

"I—I wouldn't be surprised if you thought so," I said defensively.

"Aren't you accustomed to having people take your word for anything?"

"No, sir," I said. "Not white people."

"Oh, God," he groaned, "here we go again. Can't you keep race out of anything? Do you honestly believe, although you've been a member of this household if not of this family for nearly two months now, that neither Mrs. Daley nor I have any idea what kind of a person you are? Do you think because you have a black skin and we have a white skin, we immediately lose all judgment of people?" He stood up. "You listen to me, Harriet Brown," he said. "I don't have any idea where the hell that ticket is, but I know one thing for sure—neither do you."

Mrs. Daley was smiling at me the way those mothers had looked at their children graduating, proud but with their eyes wet. "That goes for me, too," she said.

"Well," I said, "thank you very much." I searched around for words. "I didn't expect it," I said. "After all, I lied to you, Mrs. Daley."

"About your father? For goodness' sake, all children do that, change facts around to suit them; that's not what I think of as lying. It's just a child's way of making the world bearable. Adults do it, too. But any time you tell me straight out that something is the truth, I will believe you, Harriet."

"I wish I knew why," I burst out, as if driven. "Do you trust everybody? Do you believe everybody?"

"No, we are very picky and choosy," said Mr. Daley with a grin. "We believe only honest people. We believe you because you are you."

I gathered up some dishes and carried them to the sink, and I felt curiously light, as if I was floating.

Because I am me, Harriet Brown. I am *me,* that's why. Because I am what I am, myself. That's enough to be. Me.

The children came dashing in to say they couldn't find the ticket anywhere. And Maureen helped with the dishes and then Richard and Robert wanted to go fishing before dark, they'd be biting now, they said, did I want to come along? I said I was planning to freeze beans, but I could manage by myself if Maureen wanted to go. I felt as if I could take on the world single-handed.

The younger children were in bed and Mrs. Daley and I were still freezing beans when Richard, Robert, and Maureen came up the lane in the fading light. Richard had a little fish dangling from a stick.

They came in the kitchen and announced that they were hungry.

"Have some bread and peanut butter," his mother said. "Is that all you caught?"

We stared at the fish.

"They weren't biting," Robert said.

"This one bit twice!" Richard said. "It was a friendly little fish. The second time it bit, I kept it!"

"It doesn't look like six inches," his mother said.

Richard said, "It shrank on the way home."

I dumped a colander of blanched beans into cold water and I said, "Now here's a fishy tale: it shrank when out of water. It was a full six inches, but now it's one inch shorter."

Robert let out a crow of approval.

"Hi, Harriet," he said. As if I'd been away, or something.

What a way to begin a new month!

Mr. Daley came in to eat breakfast and the first thing he said was, "Harriet, did you look in your letters?"

"Oh, yes," I said, "they're all there."

"I'm not asking if any got swiped for a souvenir. I asked if you looked *in* the letters. How do you keep them?"

I felt silly. "I told you, Mr. Daley—inside my inside pillowcase."

He said with exaggerated patience, "Listen to me, Harriet. There are many ways of keeping such letters. Some women"—he shot a glance at Mrs. Daley—"keep them in their original envelopes, in bundles tied with ribbon. These women are the sentimentalists. They never look at them again, they just want to know the letters are there. Others chuck away the envelopes, smooth the letters out and keep them in a box, handy for rereading. These women are sentimentalists, too, but brooders. Then there are others who send them to their lawyer or even have them published, but we aren't discussing women like that. Now you—"

"I keep them in their envelopes!" I said.

"Yes. Now imagine yourself surprised when reading somebody else's mail," said Mr. Daley. "Imagine you have found what appears at first glance to be another letter, but no, it's only a bus ticket. However, you haven't time to put anything back properly—"

"Tom, for heaven's sake, *let* the child go and *look!*" said Mrs. Daley.

I ran.

The bus ticket was in the sixth letter I looked in.

!!*!* That's how I felt—like skyrockets going off, like stars bursting inside me. My relief was so enormous I thought I couldn't contain it, I might explode. I shot down to the old house and I was laughing like crazy and I said, "Here it is! Oh, here it is! Mr. Daley, you are a genius!" And Mr. Daley said, "That's prob-

ably a minority opinion but I thank you just the same." And I was so happy I had to hug somebody so I picked Timmy up and gave him a big squeeze.

"Is it somebody's birthday?" said Mary.

"The sneaks," Robert said. "Snooping and prying among your letters—"

"That will be *enough*," Mrs. Daley said. "We do not *know* how that bus ticket got misplaced, and we are not going to blame *anybody*."

And she would not let anyone say any more about it.

In the afternoon Mrs. Daley and I had another go at the beans. We had our baskets and we were picking, and I felt that some kind of statement was called for, some formal declaration of gratitude or appreciation or something of the sort, and I cast about in my mind how to express what I was feeling. I began by saying, "Mr. Daley is a very fine man."

"Yes, he is," said Mrs. Daley with a little smile.

"He reminds me in many ways of my friend and teacher, Hobie Carr," I said, "although they are very different in temperament."

"If they have traits in common you're lucky," she said.

I said, "I'll never forget how you both took my word."

"Harriet, that will be *enough*," she said lightly. "We don't deserve any medals, goodness knows." Then she hesitated, and she looked at me as if she was making up her mind about something, as if she was deciding something about me. "There's something I've been meaning to tell you, Harriet, ever since you spoke to me about your mother's death." She was speaking seriously now, and quietly, as if this wasn't anything she cared to shout. "You see, Maureen isn't the first child we had. Our first child was a boy. I found him dead in his crib one afternoon. He was four months and five days old."

She looked at me and her eyes were burning dry and I thought, okay, so a white skin doesn't keep you safe. And right away I knew I had thought that only from habit, and I was ashamed.

"The doctor said it happens quite often, no one knows why,

maybe a sudden fever, maybe some swift kind of pneumonia, but it wasn't anything I had done or had not done. That's what he said. But for months, years, even, I went over and over in my mind everything about that day, what he had to eat, how I put him down, how I fixed the shade at the window, everything. And then I would imagine that I had gone in sooner, you know, maybe half an hour sooner and found him choking or something—whatever it was—and picked him up, and saved him. I even imagine this sometimes now."

She looked at me with her eyes dry and burning, and I thought, can't white folks even grieve like other people? Why don't the saving tears come? They came for me. And then I thought, she is all cried out about this, years and years ago.

"But not once, Harriet, not by word or look or anything, after I found him dead and before the doctor said what he said, never for an instant did my husband make me feel he blamed me. All my life I shall love him, for many reasons, but this would be enough." She stopped, as if to sort her words, then she went on. "I'm trying to tell you that the time to trust anybody is before you have all the proof. It's always worked pretty well for us."

She was smiling at me.

"After all," she said, "when you told me about your mother, you were trusting me, at least I thought so, you were taking down the 'private, keep out' signs, you were trusting me with your grief. How could I respond by not trusting you?"

I felt a clap of astonishment. She was right. I realized it as she spoke. That was why I had told her: I had let down the bars, I had opened myself up, I had invited her in.

I suppose there is simply no use denying it. Mrs. Daley is now my friend. It seems strange to say it: I have a friend who is white.

This evening—just a little while ago—Maureen came into my room on her way to her own, and she said, "I'm glad you found your ticket, Harriet."

"Thanks, so am I," I said.

"It's funny about that ticket," she went on. "I know for a fact it was right where you left it Sunday morning—you know, when you were in church." I stared at her. "Well, anyway, I'm awfully glad you never thought any of *us* took it."

Jolted, I sat up straight. "Hey!" I said. "How do you know I didn't?"

She grinned her impish grin. "Oh, just a feeling I have," she said, and started out.

"*Wait* a minute!" Maureen had been going down the trail ahead of me, I remembered, down Boulder Hill, and she'd been offended—what was that she'd said? "The way you feel about white people —you never give them any credit—" and I'd wondered about it then, I'd thought she must have a private crystal ball. . . . "Maureen!" I couldn't believe it. "Were *you* in my letters?"

"Of *course* not!" Her eyes flashed. "Don't you know *anything?* It's dishonorable to read other people's mail!"

"But you did read my journal, is that it? And *that's* okay, I suppose!"

"Well, maybe not exactly okay, Harriet," Maureen said, "but it's different—I mean, it's more like spying. Checking up on you." She spoke as if this were all perfectly acceptable practice nowadays.

"You were reading my journal, then? You admit it?"

"Was that so awful, Harriet? I mean, was it really very wrong? I just wanted to know what you're like. Inside, I mean. Everybody says you aren't any different from me, it's just the color of your skin. I wanted to see if this is true."

"Well, is it?" I said acidly.

"Boy, *I'll* say!" She grinned, mimicking Gail's voice. "No, honestly, Harriet, we might be twins. You keep wishing you were different—you know, better—but just the same you know you aren't going to turn into an angel, or anything, and you're relieved. It's the same way with me. My father, for instance, would be very disappointed in me—in fact, he'd have a fit if he ever knew I'd been reading your journal. Just the same, I'm glad I did."

"It would give me great satisfaction to wallop you good," I said.

She said, "I bet your palm is itching."

"You mean you're going to keep right on spying on me? Sneaking into my room? Prying into my journal?"

"Of course not! I don't need to any more—don't you see? I found out what I wanted to know. I'm sorry you're upset, Harriet. But I warned you. I told you people fascinate me."

She was right, of course. We are alike, Maureen and I. The same devious honesty, the same curious traits of self-appraisal, and self-approval, actually, which is what it amounts to when you admit your faults and find you're fond of them and don't intend to change them.

Maureen came over and curled herself on my bathmat-rug, as she had done that first evening I came. "You think just because I've got brains I'll know things," she said. "But you can't learn everything with your brains, Harriet. Some things you have to know in your bones." She groped for words. "Well, now I know in my bones you're no better than I am."

I didn't know whether to laugh or be mad. "I'm not?"

"No, you're not," she said. "For a while I was scared you were some kind of saint, or something—you know, all meek and loving—and that would have spoiled everything. I'm so glad you're you." She wrapped her skinny arms around her skinny legs and grinned shyly. "In fact, I'm awfully glad you came, Harriet," she said. "Don't ever *really* go—know what I mean?"

I said I did, and I promised I wouldn't. It's a safe promise, because I know one thing in my bones: I can't ever really go. This summer threatens to be basic—know what I mean?

Wednesday, August 2nd

Well, Hobie, you were right. I admit it, I admit it! In fact, I'm eating crow. Celestial crow, but crow nonetheless.

It all began with the arrival of the mail. Your letter came, and as a direct consequence I have had great difficulty all day in remaining in contact with the ground. I've been feeling like a dirigible tugging at those ropes that restrain it from sailing off into the sky. I'm so wildly incredibly lucky that you are you.

It's hard to tell about today, because I'm not sure how much of what happened was because of how I was feeling, how your letter affected me, I mean. Question: is life subjective or objective? Answer: both. But I really don't think, Hobie, I was looking at the world with your eyes. I think I now look at things with my own eyes, but you have made me see more clearly.

So: the mail. There was your letter, and also a great stack of bills over which Mrs. Daley became slightly hysterical. She opened the first one, which was from the electrical company, and she cried, "Damnation! They want fifty-five dollars!"

I said, "Oh, there must be some mistake."

"It's for two months," she said. "I just wish they'd skip the whimsy." She handed it to me. "Look at that, Harriet. Pop art on bills, yet!"

There was a little cartoon of a character labeled Reddy Kilowatt, and an arrow pointing to the sum due him.

"Those are his wages," Mrs. Daley said bitterly. "I'm paying his wages, isn't that sweet?"

Robert said, "Remember when we got bills from Lanky Planky? The builders'-supply company?"

Maureen said, "I thought Daddy made that up. You can do it to lots of things. Like Niftie Giftie—you know, the gift shop."

Well, we were off and away.

"Flakey Bakey," I said, "the bakery shop!"

"Weedy Seedy, the garden-supply center!" cried Mrs. Daley.

Richard: "Dirty Shirty, the laundry!"

Robert: "Munchie Crunchie, the grain store!"

Maureen: "Hunky Dory, the Granite Quarry!"

"What's the point to that?" Robert said.

"There isn't any, but it sounds good."

Me: "Fancy Dancey, the dancing teacher!"

Mrs. Daley: "Oily Poil, the Fuel Oil Goil!"

"Nippy Sippy!" cried Maureen in triumph. "The state liquor store!"

We were all wiping our eyes at our own wit, when the phone rang. Great news! Pig Two is in custody! Gawdawful news! He was apprehended breaking and entering a fruit-storage shed on a farm about three miles away, and it was clearly implied that further charges of malicious mischief would be appropriate. In fact, the damages incurred while capturing him may amount to more than he is worth.

Mrs. Daley promised that Mr. Daley would go and stand his bail, and then she hung up. "Damnation!" she cried.

The Daleys' muse was dancing on my tongue. I said,

"There's a lamentable lack of rejoicing
    At the return of our prodigal pig,
        For he spilled twenty bushels of apples
            And squashed them by dancing a jig!"

"You, too, Harriet!" Mrs. Daley cried. "Please—I'm *averse* to any more." She waved aside our applause and continued, "Let's celebrate the capture of Pig Two—let's take the rest of the day off!"

And so it was decided. Immediately after an early lunch, Timmy and John Anthony would take condensed naps, and then, as soon as they woke up, we'd drive around to the other side of Boulder Hill and go up as far as we could by car, and then we'd get out and hike the rest of the way. And from the top of Boulder Hill we would look out at the world. And when we had seen enough of it, we would come home again.

And that is what we did.

I don't know how it happened, actually. I can't look back and say: this, and then this, added up, and then it happened. I don't think it was anything that anybody said or did. It just happened, and I guess I had better accept it like that, a moment in time, handed to me. A moment given.

We drove past the cemetery where the stones are falling over and a dark-green vine is covering everything, and we turned just beyond and went past a number of white gates suddenly appearing where there are turnoffs from the woods road. And then we went past a beaver pond edged with purple iris growing wild. And then we started to climb and the car complained and the road grew narrower and more rutted and once we had to stop while Richard and Robert dragged a fallen tree out of the way. We were getting higher, the hedgerows on either side were thinning, and we could see meadows being invaded by pines. Then we turned into a dooryard, and there was the house where somebody had once been living but no one was there now, nor had been for fifty years or more. It was a clapboard house that might never have been painted, the roof sagging and half its shingles gone, one shutter still clinging to the wall, the rest fallen off, rotting among the trunks of the towering lilacs. Leaves blew in and out of the doorway. And against one wall a thick row of orange lilies stared at us, like a crowd of people watching an invader.

"The Boulders lived here," said Mrs. Daley, "or some of them did. There were four sons."

We set out on foot. Up a path across a high meadow, and then the path was gone, and we walked through thin grass and our feet sank in the mat of wild strawberry plants beneath. Through a tangle of birches and hemlock and fallen stones slippery with ferns and treacherous with hidden lengths of rusty barbed-wire fence. Then up and up across the rock of the mountain, skirting blackberry patches, wading through green spreading juniper bushes, higher and higher, and right to the very top and over and down a little ways on the other side, to a place Mrs. Daley knew, where a rocky shelf had caught the soil and there was enough grass to sit on. And Mrs. Daley put down John Anthony, and I set Timmy on the grass, and we all sat down.

And we ate the fruit we had brought, and we rested, and we marveled at the world.

Below us the hillside fell away, past rocks and ripened grass and blueberry bushes, and then it dropped from sight, and far below it came into view again, a line of trees marking the road, and the roofs of farm buildings like toys, and the fields a design like an abstract painting, and then there were more woods and roads winding. Beyond all this was the irregular gleam of the river, and beyond that the hills of New Hampshire rising to become mountains, grey-purple. And everywhere there was more space than seemed necessary.

We perched there on the thin grass with rocks scraping our stretched-out legs, and the sun was warm, and we could have been birds resting, we were so high. And, Hobie, it was so strange. For the first time in my life I was conscious of the way the earth curves away from us, around and around out of sight and it just keeps on going, on and on and curving, and all around on it, all the way around, little tiny specks are stuck on, hundreds and thousands and millions of people, smaller and smaller the higher you get, like the man I could barely see on a tractor, so small and so far away I couldn't tell where he left off and the tractor began. And I felt small, as if a gust of wind could blow me up into the sky like a brown leaf, blowing helplessly, and then I felt *good,* I don't know, as if I could stroke the earth with my hand, and all those trees would feel soft, like velvet, as if my hand were enormous without measure.

And it happened then. I looked at the children and I didn't see their white skin. That's all they were, just children I knew. And Mrs. Daley, holding her baby, was only another woman, her hair blowing, her face with bones underneath and skin stretched over, but I didn't see the color of her skin. *I didn't see it.*

It's hard to describe the moment, because it came and it went and after it had gone I realized what had happened to me. I had looked at white children and they were children, not embryo enemies, and I had looked at a white woman and I had seen nothing but another woman, just another human creature like myself.

It may never happen to me again as long as I live, but it happened once.

And that's what I want to tell you, Hobie: that you are right. It is possible.

Because if it can happen to me, it can happen to anybody, anybody at all.

ABOUT THE AUTHOR

MELISSA MATHER was born in Chicago and lived in New Jersey, Ohio, Maryland, Louisiana, Kentucky, Kansas, and Virginia before settling in Vermont. She writes: "I've lived nearly half a century, have raised or am in the process of raising nine children, like to cook, eat, and garden, hate billboards, neon signs, junk cars and signs of too many people generally. Wish the country had only one hundred million people—that would leave the trees standing. Maybe I ought not to mention the nine children—it makes me sound so inconsistent."